WARPAINT

WARPAINT

Stephanie A. Smith

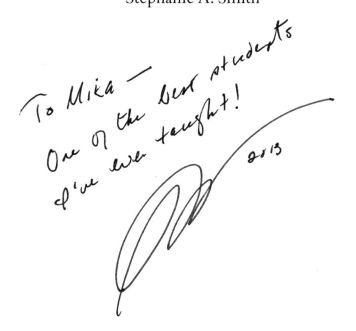

To Mika —
One of the best students
I've ever taught!
2013

THAMES RIVER PRESS

Warpaint

THAMES RIVER PRESS
An imprint of Wimbledon Publishing Company Limited (WPC)
Another imprint of WPC is Anthem Press (www.anthempress.com)

First published in the United Kingdom in 2012 by

THAMES RIVER PRESS
75-76 Blackfriars Road
London SE1 8HA

www.thamesriverpress.com

A CIP record for this book is available from the British Library.

ISBN 978-0-85728-200-2

Cover design by Laura Carless

This title is also available as an eBook.

CONTENTS

Contents

PART IV   SWAN SONG

PART I

RETROSPECTIVE

1. THREE LIVES

A famous anthropologist and a very old friend of the Davis family once called the artist Liz Moore a witch. "I mean a real one," he said on an August night in 1947 out on Montauk Point. Once the War had ended, the Davises took pains to reconnect with old friends, like Al Kroenen, who'd himself made it back from hell. That evening the weather, so miserably hot and close for a week, lifted a bit. The setting low-angled sun caught in frosted martini glasses and flared.

"One of yours, Tom?" asked the anthropologist, gesturing with his sweating birdbath at a large painting hung over the granite hearth, a canvas of floating amoebic shapes, crimson with ruby centers fading outward to a shimmer of rose-ochre on a background of textured gold-leaf.

"That? Oh no," replied his host. "I only paint sea. That's —" he broke off, having glimpsed a stride across the rise of his lawn. "Here's your artist, Al." Tom put down his drink to greet the woman who stepped in from the screened porch of the converted farmhouse. Oddly dressed in a man's cotton shirt and denim pants, she was lithe and switchblade thin and wore her straight black hair in a bob.

"Liz," said Tom to the new guest. "Glad you could make it! I'd like you to meet Al Kroenen – Al, Liz Moore. Al was asking after your painting, my dear."

"Oh? Which one?" she asked, having given the Davises three: a small self-portrait for the sitting room, two abstracts for the formal living room.

"That," said Al, gesturing again with his martini at the vivid amoeboid shapes that seemed as if they might, at any moment, untether themselves from the canvas and levitate, to mingle on the warm air amongst the guests.

"*Wirkorgan,*" said Tom. "It's called *Wirkorgan.*"

"Oh that," said the painter, glancing up at Al with large, slanted, olive green eyes. "A commission from the good doctor. Do you like it?"

"Impressive," he paused, at a loss. "Different."

"It's just a painting," she said flippantly, turning to Tom. "Where's Nancy?"

But before Tom could locate his wife, a child with thick-curled, fuzzy blond hair flew over the threshold. "Dad!" she cried. "Dad, Ted won't let me –" and that was as far as she got because Liz, in farmer's denims without shoes, left the girl dumbstruck. She knew their neighbor-lady-artist was weird, but blue jeans and bare feet at a dinner party?

Mrs. Davis appeared, a small, sturdy brunette in a proper summer dress, pearls and perfume. She carried a tray of hors d'oeuvres. Al's wife, Patricia, large, blonde and mild, followed with a basket of crackers.

"Charlotte Clio," said Nancy Davis sharply to her daughter. "How impolite. Close your mouth and say hello to your Aunt Liz."

"Hello Aunt Liz."

Tom laughed. "That's better. Now, Charlie, tell me: what won't your brother 'let you do' *this* time?"

C.C. sidled up to her father, bent him down by his elbow so she could whisper, and kept her eye on the gangly, bare-foot guest to whom Nancy handed a glowing birdbath. Liz took a sip and then, quick as a wren, zeroed in on C.C.

"Honey," she said, her eyes alight. "You've seen my bare toes before. I didn't grow an extra."

"Yes, my goodness, C.C!" said Nancy. "But here, now, you two haven't been properly introduced – Liz Moore, Pat Kronen. I take it you've met Al?"

"He's been admiring my work," said Liz, gazing at Pat, who smiled wanly and asked, "What work?"

"That painting over the fireplace. Nance, where's Tuck?"

"Upstairs, asleep," she said, setting various painted china plates of delicacies on the coffee table. "Try a deviled egg, Liz? Caviar?"

"Tuck's asleep already?"

"Yes, and thank goodness." Nancy patted a permanent wave back in place. "He's getting to be such a handful. Al, Pat – did Tom tell you what sort of mischief Tucker was up to last month while we were down in Florida?"

"No," said Pat, her eyes still fixed on Liz, who had quit the adults and was folded onto the oval braided rug with C.C. Just then, Ted Davis, curly as his sister but dark like his mother, ran in, looked around, hitched up his pants and said:

"Dinnertime!"

"Not yet, young man," said Dr. Davis. "Come here. We need to have a little talk."

"So what happened?" Al asked Nancy.

"Tuck gave his father quite a scare," she said.

"And you, Mother," Tom shot back.

"Oh, yes, of course, but it all happened so fast, the alligator was back in the lake before I even knew it had been out."

"'Gator?" said Al, taking a pipe from his pocket. "Mind if I smoke, Tom?"

"No, go ahead. Matches are in that metal sconce near the fireplace – see them? Now Ted, your sister tells me…" at which point he lowered his voice.

"This is a match?" said Al, examining one he'd taken from the sconce. "I could burn down Rome with this thing. So? What 'gator?"

"My younger son," Tom said, turning away from Ted, "decided to tease one. 'Bout this long," he held his hands as wide apart as he could, "and fast. I had no idea those things could run."

"Tuck was faster," said Liz, "but only a snack, for a 'gator. Dollop of ice-cream."

Perhaps Liz's sang-froid that night provoked Al's judgment – or her indifferent response to his admiration for *Wirkorgan*, or something about her dark face, but Al, being then a very famous anthropologist, something, indeed, of an expert on Indians and shamans and such, was believed when he said, in a decided tone after Liz had left –

"Your artist, Tom, is a witch."

The two couples were settled in the sitting room, one floor lamp-lit, which made the gold in *Wirkorgan* simmer.

Tom poured a cognac for his wife, as Pat Kronen said to her husband,

"Darling, that's nonsense. She's a white woman from Minnesota, from the North Shore of Lake Superior. That's what she told me, at dinner. Farming people."

Al shook his head and sucked on his pipe. "Several bands of Ojibwe live along the North Shore."

"Thanks, dear," said Nancy, as Tom handed her a drink. She looked at Al. "I'm afraid there's no Indian in Liz," she said. "Norwegian, Hungarian, Scots, with a little English thrown in."

Tom patted Nancy's shoulder. "Well, Al, what kind of a witch is our Liz?" he asked. "Good or bad?"

"Tom, really," said Pat. She tugged at the bottom of her blue dress a little, and crossed her ankles. "Don't encourage him."

"As I said, a real one," said Al quietly.

Tom sat down on the floral arm of a loveseat. "Meaning?"

"She has force, a power. Most whites ignore it. My people cultivate it."

"She's a force, all right," said Nancy, smiling. "A force of nature."

"You mean like a witch-doctor?" Tom asked.

"If you like. Watch her. She's remarkable – and talented. But not dangerous, I should think." Al blew out thick shag smoke. "At least not to herself."

Tom believed him. So did Nancy in a certain way and a rumor fired up, spread around, ran to the City and settled in the Village. Liz Moore was a witch. When Liz did nothing to quash it, what started off on cocktails and cognac solidified into fact and would remain a fact to the day Lá Moore died.

But in April of 2002, Liz Moore, ninety-four, internationally famous, was very much alive, and en route from her estate – once her mother's home – in Lutsen, Minnesota, to New York City for a retrospective at MoMA, a send-off for the fifty-third-street location, closing that May for renovation. While East, Liz was going to visit C.C. Davis, who was, of course, no longer a tow-headed child, but a woman in her sixties.

Sitting in her own Connecticut living room with her long-ago lover, Quiola Kerr, C.C. said, "Liz's work has the magic, but I'm not sure about her."

"No kidding." Planted smack in the middle of a squat black sofa, Quiola glanced at a portfolio of C.C.'s new work, laid flat on the cedar chest in front of her.

The older woman nodded. "That anthropologist used to come and stay over with Mother and Father, every summer when I was a kid. He was bald. His wife smiled a lot."

"Al Kronen was a very important scholar. I've read a lot of his writing."

"Yes, yes he was... special. For one thing, he didn't call Indians lazy or drunks or dirty, like most folks did back then. Conquered, he said. Subjugated by an indifferent people, a ruthless people, a people with no empathy. Us. He was adopted by one of the California tribes."

Quiola looked up. "Which tribe?"

"Honestly, Quiola – this was something like *fifty* years ago, now."

"Just curious. You remember the name of your mother's perfume from those days. What did you call it? Joy?"

"Of course I remember that," snapped C.C. "She's my mother. And I also remember your grandmother's tribe. Ojibwe. I didn't mean to offend."

"Anishinaabeg," murmured Quiola.

"What?"

"I said no offense. And yes I would like coffee, sweet and black."

C.C. laughed. "Mind-reader."

"Maybe. I see you're working in oil again."

C.C. nodded an answer, and stepped from the living room out into the kitchenette of her studio, her "shed" as she called it, an old caretaker's home on a Connecticut estate, tiny, except for the converted attic-loft, where she worked and slept. Returning with their coffee, she said, "Oil suits me. The latest is unfinished and I'm having the devil of a time with it – when you look at it, you'll see why. So? What have you been doing?"

"Watercolor. Some acrylic. Pottery on occasion, too, when I can get kiln space."

"Really? Liz Moore won't approve. Do you think she's arrived yet?"

"Her flight should have landed at noon. If it wasn't delayed, she should be at the Plaza by now."

C.C. took a quick peek at an antique clock. "MoMA paid for the limo?"

"Of course, but I wish she would have let me fetch her."

"Oh no, not Liz." C.C. put both elbows in her hands, a characteristic gesture. Compact and wiry like a terrier, C.C. Davis never seemed to add or "shed" a pound. She looked almost exactly the same as she had a quarter-century ago, except for a few more lines and the fade of a blond, snowing to white.

"Liz likes being a stranger," she said.

"And hates watercolor. Loathes ceramics."

"They lack strength – according to Liz." C.C. nipped a glance out the window. That hot, hot April of 2002 had brought up early crocuses at the end of the driveway, along the old rock wall, and as the afternoon sunlight began to turn from midday, their lavender and yellow cups grew dark purple and burnt gold.

"It was always a relief, you know," said C.C. "to go home, back when we lived on the Island. The trip from the city to Montauk wasn't always easy, the traffic could get murderous, but calming, you know, like that drive out to Pete and Mark's in P-town. The road narrows, you can taste the sea. I'd love to go –"

"To Montauk?"

"No, to P-town."

"Why don't we, then? I'm sure the boys would be happy to see us."

"I can't."

Quiola's long, slim, dark hand, hovering above the portfolio, froze. She lowered her fingertips to the edge of the plastic page, then flipped it, asking, "Not even after?"

C.C.'s gaze moved to the floor. "You don't know how I – how glad I am you've come, and how sorry I am to have dragged you here on such short notice, but I wanted to see you, to talk, without static and the Atlantic between us."

"Oh no. I had a bad feeling –"

C.C. shrugged. "I didn't want to worry you –"

"You're worrying me *now*."

"Yes, I know, I'm sorry, but the tumor is large, larger than Dr. Shea supposed. I've seen a surgeon, a Dr. Wong. She says she's going to have to take the whole breast, and lymph nodes. I'll need radiation, chemo —"

Quiola grasped C.C.'s forearms across the portfolio. Smaller than C.C., her gesture took her bodily over the cedar chest. "Breast cancer," she said, "is curable."

C.C. laughed and pulled one forearm from Quiola's tight grip. She laid her hand gently over Quiola's wrist. "Where there's life there's hope, eh?"

"Bullshit," said Quiola roughly. She let C.C. go, and sat on the edge of the couch, holding onto that piece of furniture as if she might be sucked away somehow. "What exactly did this doctor tell you?"

"I have Stage IV cancer."

Quiola's black eyes glistened. "There is no Stage V."

"No. There isn't."

"Why didn't you *tell* me?"

"I *am* telling you. Don't be angry with me. I can't take it."

"I'm not, I'm not. I just thought breast cancer was curable."

"Caught early, it is. But I didn't notice until the lump was — well, noticeable. Still, I might beat it —" The phone rang. C.C.'s face sharpened, the weight and shadow of her news lifting. "That's got to be Liz!" she said. Then, swiftly, "When we see her, don't say anything. She knows I have cancer. That's enough," and she scurried to the landline.

Alone, Quiola leaned her head back on the couch and closed her eyes for a moment as a jagged tumble of thoughts jostled past one another: *she'll need help, how could this happen, why didn't I know, chemo, oh, no not chemo, she'll... she can't, I can't...not again...* meanwhile, Quiola could hear the murmur of one side of the conversation, so rather than eavesdrop, she went up the tiny switchback staircase to see C.C.'s latest difficulty.

The studio-bedroom-attic was in disarray. A pile of dirty, rumpled cotton clothes sat in one corner beside a dresser, an unmade futon sat in another. At the far end of the large space stood a long, rough-hewn table covered with misshapen tubes of paint, jars of brushes, palette knives, string, gauze, and towels. In the middle of the table sat a small aluminum easel, covered by a drop cloth, which Quiola pulled up.

"Hmm. What on earth moved you back to this?" she said.

In the late fifties, C.C. had painted a series called *Planets*: five long, narrow, subdued oils of three heavy globes, in varying tones, sensuously pungent, so eerily and erotically charged, it caused a minor scandal. And that, it seemed, was that, because – and for no reason she'd ever given Quiola – she turned to a modified, cubist realism, something that irked the boys of New York. She remained faithful to that idiom until 1971 when abruptly she'd turned to female portraits, most in morbid colors, as if the women were corpses.

The difficulty that Quiola gazed at was both new and old – the narrow canvas and the globe-shapes were back, but now in clusters, elongated so they seemed unburst rain aching to fall of thick, palette knife-strokes in gelatinous green pond scum beside cartoon yellow or contusion purple and black.

"What do you think?" asked C.C., coming up the stairs.

Quiola let the cloth drop. "Very personal."

"Exactly. It's killing me."

"Lay off, then."

"Can't."

"No. Of course you can't."

"Ready to eat?"

"Sure," she said, turning to follow C.C. back down the stairs. "How's Liz?"

"Fine. Wants us to stay with her at the Plaza. Says the suite is enormous."

"That's just silly. We can stay in Chelsea."

"No. Wants us close. Come on, I've got salmon to broil."

"You let her push you around, you know."

C.C. laughed. "Can't help it."

"She's a bully. Anyway, C.C. – this thing, tomorrow night? Makes me nervous. MoMA and all."

"I know. Try not to worry."

"And when is the surgery?"

C.C. glanced up. "In a week. Let's not talk about it –"

After supper, Quiola retreated to the guest room; when C.C. knocked, she found her ex in an old, bleach-battered XXL t-shirt, kneeling by the front windows that ran smack along the floor.

"Mind if I intrude?"

"Nope."

"What are you looking at?"

Quiola got up off the floor, and handed C.C. a black and white snapshot: a woman, about forty, wearing a checked woolen overcoat standing in am empty lot on a cold, snowy day; beside her, a young, very pregnant girl; their hair pulled back from their broad faces in a single braided tail.

"Oh," said C.C. "these two again." She examined the picture briefly, since she'd seen it many times before, while Quiola sat cross-legged on the bed. C.C. pulled the sash of her robe tight, placed the photo on a dressing table, and sat down in a chair, knees and hands pressed together, like a kid might sit. "An angry woman, your mother."

Quiola shrugged. "They do look grim, don't they? Mom used to say she had a lot to be angry about."

"And you?"

"Me? You know me. Am I angry?"

"Very funny. You burn. You hum like a wasp's nest. Now would be a good time for a cigarette," she added. "If I still smoked."

"You *smoked*? I didn't know that."

"In the fifties, everyone smoked – sometimes it was nice, you know, not to talk. Just light up and share. Simple."

"I see. What else *don't* you want to talk to me about, besides the you know what?"

C.C. laughed. "Always cutting right to the chase, aren't you?" She shook her head and rumpled her curly hair. "Nothing, really. I'm restless. I can't sleep. I hate needles. I hate going under. I loved my father, but I hate doctors."

"I know. Have you told your brother?"

"Ted?" said C.C. bitterly. "Jesus. You remember what happened the last time I talked to him, don't you? I haven't bothered to call. I won't. He can read the obituary." She stood up, folded her arms and began to pace, then stopped in the center in the dark room. "Do you

11

think you can stay with me for awhile? Just until I get through this? I'm going to fight it, I will, I promise. I know it's a lot to ask, after Luke and all, but I —"

"Hush yourself," said Quiola, "and come here."

✦

Neither the Plaza nor the Waldorf are now what they once were and, like stately matrons unable to give up their posts, they've gone shabby and gaudy. Quiola would've asked for a W or a Swisshotel, but Liz remembered them as they had been back in their heyday; she saw the Plaza as if Gatsby and Daisy, Tom, Nick and Jordan were all still in the wedding-cake suite on a hot summer night, caught in the coils of hope and betrayal. She'd insisted on staying there, for its lost glory and for its proximity to Central Park.

"Honestly," Quiola muttered at the dizzying neon mid-town display, as the stretch limo careened up 6th from Grand Central.

"What?" asked C.C., from a half-mile away on the other side of the stretch.

"Nothing."

"God it's so hot, you'd think it was August."

Studiously deaf, the driver delivered the two women to the Plaza where they found a young man from MoMA stationed at the lobby desk, awaiting the impossible, incredible Liz Moore. He'd been sent over, in person, to greet their guest and to offer her a small token, a platinum and diamond Tiffany brooch. But what Liz hadn't told the emissary was that he would wait there, at the lobby desk, until C.C. and Quiola arrived. So he'd been standing there, patient and nervous, for about a half-hour.

A long, spare drink of Minnesota water was Liz Moore as she stepped out of the elevator and made her slow way across the lobby; even with her shoulders stooped by arthritis and her strange olive eyes worn beyond worn, Lizzie was still formidable, thin-legged and rangy like an ancient Amelia Earhart, although she preferred to think of herself as Lindbergh, "the hero of my youth," as she called him. Ignoring MoMA's young man, who stood as stiff as if petrified by Medusa's glare, she gave C.C. a kiss on both cheeks, and said,

"You're looking well, my dear." Her voice carried the lilt of a Scandinavian mid-west and she wore some sort of pine or evergreen scent, as if she'd been determined to bring the North Country back east with her. "The short hair becomes you."

"And you," said C.C., "look marvelous."

"I'm antediluvian," said Liz, with slight quaver into a laugh.

"Here," said Quiola, "let me take these," as she retrieved two small bags near their feet, one her own, one C.C.'s.

"Ah, Quiola," said Liz. Her disquieting gaze softened. "Always a pleasure. I thought you were in Paris."

"I was."

"How nice of you to come, then."

"For good, this time."

"*What?*" said C.C.

Meanwhile, the man from MoMA, frostbitten by fear, smiled and smiled.

"I don't intend to go back," said Quiola quietly.

"We'll talk about that later," C.C. muttered. "Can we leave the bags here, or should we take them upstairs?"

The young man cleared his throat. Despite his excellent manners, Quiola could see his eyes shining with a reverence close to hysteria at History, the great, the magnificent, the impossible Liz Moore. History, however, continued to ignore the young man, saying to C.C., "Upstairs. We're not expected until five. There's time for a little nip." Liz tucked an arm in C.C.'s. "Come."

At this point Quiola stepped in to relieve the poor emissary from MoMA: she answered his questions, accepted his gift, and hastened him away by the possibility that his mere presence might have over-taxed History and perhaps ruined the show. When Quiola finally made it up to the rooms, Liz was chatting idly with C.C. about old friends, scattered or dead, most of whom Quiola had not known or did not know, except by reputation. She poured herself a drink, and put the Tiffany box on the coffee table. C.C. asked Liz what she thought of electronic art.

"Electronic art? There is no such thing. People may be doing it, but it isn't art. I refuse to 'e'. No email. I won't have a cell phone."

13

"But a cell can be useful," said C.C. "I keep one in the Heap, for emergencies." She shook the ice in her G and T. "Did you know that Mark Twain was one of the first people to put a telephone in his house?"

"You *would* know that," said Liz.

"Why not? His home is in Hartford. Can't say how many times I've been there, after visiting Mother. Anyway, Twain had the phone installed in its own little alcove. But he regretted it. Couldn't stand the ring."

"A man after my own heart," said Liz. She sipped sherry, then asked in a lower voice, "And how is your mother?"

"Failing, I'm afraid. I miss her. Alzheimer's is just so pitiless. I visit, but she doesn't know me and she's so…small."

"Terrible," murmured Liz. "I'm sorry." Silence took them, until Liz turned briskly to Quiola and asked, "What do you think of it? Electronic art?"

"Not much. But I'm no expert."

"Nonsense," said Liz, with a shrug and quick chop of her knobby hand. "Of course you are. All an artist needs is an eye and –"

Quiola got up and walked to the window. "It's raining," she observed.

"Good," said C.C. "Maybe it'll cool down."

But it didn't cool down. The pavement gave off steam, the temperature barely dropped, the air hung thick with moisture. Once she'd finished with her clothes and face, Liz went and sat beside the hotel window, watching vapor.

August, she thought with disgust. *This is city-August. Not April. Not like April at all.*

How many sullen summers had she spent in this City, stifling, endless in the days before air conditioning? Nights of torture, no relief, little sleep; she'd kept the kitchen window of her fifth floor walk-up open but after a solid month of it, she'd become a life form no higher or drier than a sponge. She'd flogged herself to sketch because that's why she'd ridden the rails from Minnesota to the glorious, god-awful City, but it was hard to believe it was worth the effort as grit blew in off the street, thick as week-old dust, and the pencil slicked in her hand and sharpening it raised a sweat. She'd open the window, then start the fans and everything not tied or weighted down flew about, including more grit. She wore a sleeve-protector to keep the grit off but it was awful. Desire wilted. All she could think of was a biting, icy Lake Superior bath. When the end of the heat came, it came in inches, until all at once it was freezing, and she had no money for heat.

The Moore retrospective was set to begin just after the galleries closed for the day, and by invitation only. MoMA was whitely lit and stark – to sanctify the dead, Lizzie always said. Ushered in discreetly, the three women met with the curator in his office, and then headed for the show. Lizzie squeezed C.C.'s hand, a reflex, as the curator, anxious as a park squirrel at lunch-time, hovered beside the elevator, waiting for his famous guest to walk the short length from his office to where he stood.

Liz Moore took her time. She couldn't rush, her legs were not as reliable as they'd been the first time she'd visited MoMA. No one had paid her the least mind that day, just another Jane Q. Public, drab, unkempt, hungry. MoMA became her nemesis, and her church. It had the effect, sometimes, of that cold bath she couldn't afford – *do you want, Elizabeth Sarah Moore*, she used to ask herself, *do you really want your work embalmed here? Hung on a wall where only people who can scrape up a fee can get in to see it?* That's why she'd done book illustrations – there was always the public library, open to anyone. Still, MoMA had caught her. Over the years friends donated her work, even the Davises, rot them.

Such a silly, wasteful effort, she thought, *getting the old lady all dolled up to endure kindnesses seldom bestowed on the elderly.* She should know. She'd been elderly for almost half her life.

"Just look at me," she muttered, catching a reflection off the elevator chrome. She leaned over to C.C. "Should I get my hair colored?"

"Should you what?" said C.C., startled.

"Well? Look at it. My hair. You think it could've turned a definite white like yours is doing, or a stunning gray. But, no, it's thinned and faded to no color at all."

Quiola burst out laughing, while the curator stared at the closing elevator doors.

"Well?" Liz demanded. "Color is everything. Especially blue," and she smiled, which appeared to encourage the curator. But her smile was not for him, it was for blue: midnight, cerulean, navy, cobalt, all the fragments of water and sky from the Mediterranean clarity of California midday to the ebony of indigo night.

"Never thought of you as a blue-haired lady," said Quiola, deadpan. "But if you want, I'm sure we can find a hairdresser in the City to give you a rinse."

Fortunately for the curator, the elevator doors re-opened here. Liz let C.C. have her arm, Quiola her elbow, and they made their slow way to a podium of sorts, where History was going to be enthroned for the event. As they moved through the applauding crowd Liz was glad she hadn't worn her glasses. All the faces, as featureless as a Matisse, seemed wonderfully distant.

"Who are these people?" she muttered.

"Just make nice," whispered C.C.

"No, really," said Liz, a bit louder and more annoyed. "My friends are all dead."

"Not *yet*, they aren't," snapped C.C.

Liz let herself be lowered onto what amounted to a divan, like a tough Venus on the half-shell. People nattered on at her, and she answered with what she hoped passed for polite nonsense, and was grateful when Quiola handed her a glass of iced sherry – her particular kind of sherry – along with a plate of goodies. She concentrated on what mattered: food. Tomorrow: a ride around the Park.

"I hope the goddamn weather clears," she said, to no one in particular.

Unlike Liz, both Quiola and C.C. had working obligations at the opening: C.C. had a "shed" full of things her dealer said she couldn't deal, and an installation postponed; meanwhile, Quiola shopped half-heartedly around for someone who might deal her into the humming hub of the art universe. C.C. might have helped, but the older woman thought it would be vulgar to do so, since they'd once been lovers. Liz would let no one take advantage of her belated fame, not even Quiola.

The gallery buzzed with the tense of pitch. Quiola soon ran out of gas. Deflation set in, and she longed for the one sanctuary that

Liz's fame made possible, the Plaza suite, full of chintz and silence and a wet bar. She scanned the room and found C.C. standing, alone, before one of the smallest canvases in the gallery.

As a rule, a Moore canvas is big. Sometime in the 1940s Liz went large with minutiae. Yet, unlike O'Keefe, she'd chosen minutia her generation thought unsuited to her sex: no giant genital flowers for her. Instead she'd harkened back to her childhood, when she'd been schooled to sketch bees from her father's apiary, to make the miniature sculpture of insect anatomy into arching, huge but intricate surreal abstraction.

Not everyone's taste, to be sure.

Yet her famous massive miniatures did not mean she'd given up on small. C.C. was standing in front of a sequence of a dozen tiny paintings, called the *Series B*. Liz had done one a year, for a dozen years, as a chronicle of how that particular year had been to live. She'd started the series as something between and joke and a jab in 1945, when her future husband, the sculptor Paul Gaines, complained that she was so often distracted, so unto herself, he wondered if she even knew the War was over. As a response, she painted *Series B One*. In it, a lone figure, thin and dark, dances away from the jagged teeth of a fluid architecture he also grasps in one hand, so it looks as if the figure is a matador, and the architecture his cape. The figure's other arm is bathed in light and reaches to the edge of the canvas and in that light tiny people dance, make love, fly and sing: a satiric and whimsical answer to Paul's irritation. Of course she knew the War was over.

Each of the twelve in *Series B* was painted in the same precise, intense manner, some more complex that *B One*, some less. By the time Quiola made her way across the busy room C.C. was at *Series B Three*, her face tented, unreadable. When she felt Quiola beside her she said, "I haven't seen this one in so long. My parents owned it, you know, but they never hung it. Couldn't bear it."

"I thought *Series B* belonged to the museum?"

"It does, now. Father donated it, and also his version of *Wirkorgan*, back when the Museum acquired the others in the *Series*. It was a relief to Mom and Dad to have a legitimate reason to get them both out of the house."

17

"But why? They're so lovely."

Wirkorgan and *Series B Three* are, in fact, lovely, the latter so vital and mystifyingly alive, the former showing a naked white child, fat as a cherub, who gives off a hot, blue light that graduates to rose-gold. The flaming child vaults, a diver defeating gravity, toward a corner of the canvas where stars dot space. Gracefully looped around the child's shoulders and neck is gossamer black lace. It drifts across the figure's back and vanishes off the canvas.

So why did Tom and Nancy Davis find them unbearable?

"It was a bad year," was all C.C. could say that night in MoMA.

"1947?" asked Quiola, helplessly. "I don't understand."

"Look at the lace. See?"

Quiola bent forward. "Names? A scarf of names? I never noticed before."

"You can't see them in reproductions. Liz used a magnifying glass to paint them – the names on the blacklist. She added name after name, until 1952, I think."

"Were your parents blacklisted?"

C.C. laughed a pleased laugh. "Oh, no, nothing like that. McCarthy outraged them but they had no sympathy for communism. Conservative liberals."

Quiola glanced over her shoulder. "I wonder how she's doing."

"She's fine. Look at her. Drinking it in. Who is that man? He looks as if he'd kiss her ass, doesn't he?"

"You'd think we were nothing more than country mice," said Quiola, folding her arms tight across her chest.

"Ah, but she's waited a long time for this. Let her enjoy it."

Huffing, Quiola turned away, back to *Series B*. "Her work I can stomach," she said. "Liz herself is another matter."

Series B. Critics will tell you that these Moore paintings are an idiosyncratic take on the post-war years in America. *Series B Three* 1947, they say, commemorates both American daring – Yeager's breaking the sound barrier – and American paranoia – Joe McCarthy's witch-hunt.

But in 1947, there was also Tucker.

Liz called Tuck Davis her watching child. His eyes, of no striking color, nevertheless caught you: large, and bright and watching.

Photographs show a boy whose head, adorned with hair in long ringlets, seems too big for his nose, and his nose too delicate for those eyes and his eyes too watching for comfort. In that summer of 1947, as Nancy had told Al and Pat Kronen, the Davises had vacationed in Florida. They'd camped near a small lake. Picture this, then: the family eating BBQ, and here comes Tucker up from the lakeside, his wet diapers sagging because he's running as quick as his fat legs can go and right behind him, clumsy swift, a 'gator, jaws widening and then Dr. Davis is there, his big hands slipping under the boy's arms, and Tucker swings in the air. The 'gator, discouraged, stops, snaps his jaws shut and saunters away, safe inside his ancient armor, hungry still.

Thing of it was, Tucker just giggled. When Tom saw his son's bright, laughing eyes, he turned the boy over a knee, right there, in front of everyone, lowered the sodden diaper, and whacked him until his white, new flesh reddened. Standing the half-naked child on his feet, the doctor scolded, but Tucker had become a ball of fury, a fury so fierce Dr. Davis slapped the cheek of it, and astonished, the boy sat down. Yanking his son back up, Dr. Davis carried him by his arms, his chubby legs stiff with surprise, to the screen porch. He sat him on a wicker chair and said,

"Tucker, you will sit here, by yourself, until Father comes for you. And if you so much as move, you will sit here longer. And if you mess yourself, you will get another spanking. Understand me?"

And then Tom Davis made sure that whatever the rest of his family did that day, they did it in front of Tucker's watching eyes. C.C. remembers him vividly on that porch, his face hot, baby-fat hands clutching chubby knees, his cherry red mouth set.

Three months later, that same winter on Long Island: it is a Saturday in late December. Tom leaves the farmhouse after lunch, to chop firewood. After dropping her two older kids at their grandparents' house, Nancy begins canning mint jam. Tucker, now taller, less chubby, has a cold.

"Mama?"

Nancy looks up from the hot, sweet reduction. Her mason jars, lined up like portly glass soldiers, wait to swallow their duty. Tucker, his hair in a tangle, his green flannel pajamas rumpled, stands barefoot at the kitchen door.

"Sweetheart, what are you doing downstairs?" She comes over to him, crouching down, smoothing her skirt under her. She fingers his forehead, which is cool. "Are you feeling better?"

The child nods, sniffling and rubbing his nose with the back of his hand. He reaches out to touch the top of her apron with small, white fingers.

"Well, honey, you don't have a fever." She stands up, re-ties her apron in the back, and finds him a tissue in its front pocket. "Here, now blow that nose."

Glancing up over his tissue he says, "Mama, can I get my books?"

"Of course you can. Where did you leave them?"

"In there," he points down the hall toward the sitting room.

"That's fine." She takes the used tissue and throws it out. "Tuck? Mind you should take your books back to bed. I know you feel better, but your nose is still runny, and you look flushed. All right, sweetheart?"

He nods, his big watching eyes shining, and trots off to get his sack of baby books, left abandoned on the rug behind the chintz loveseat. The sitting room is dead cold, no fire, no light in the December gloom, no people, now even lacking the artificial warmth of Liz Moore's *Wirkorgan*, which Tom had moved to his office on the promise of another Moore, a Christmas gift. Tucker grabs his sack to drag along behind him, across the braided rug, over the stone of the hearth where he stops, just at the foot of the massive fireplace. He looks around, then out the window: a red and black wool jacket bright against the thin snow, a muffled chop of the ax. Smiling a fierce little smile, Tuck sneaks over to the metal sconce of fireplace matches, and lifts one out to strike against the granite hearthstone, and again, and again before the match ignites with a hiss and flare.

Dr. Davis, being on that side of the house, sees the smoke first. Nancy, still canning, doesn't smell it, doesn't know until a shriek so wild makes her drop a jar.

"What –?" She glances up from broken glass to a mass of smoke rolling fast toward her from the hall.

Without a sound she runs, just as Tom bangs into the kitchen behind her.

"Nancy!" he cries as he too, breasts into the smoke, choking on the acrid bitters of his own house, burning. Coughing, his eyes awash in stinging tears, he moves fast, trying to beat the swift blaze until wham! he trips, down on one knee, almost on top of Nancy, passed out in the hall. Staggering, Tom lifts her up. Limp, she's hunched over Tucker, wrapped in a blanket. Somehow the doctor hoists his wife in the crook of one arm, clutches his son in the other, and staggers back through the kitchen, out into the snow. Frantic and calm, Tom the physician does what he can for Nancy and Tuck, as the entire side of the house roars, a beast, unleashed. By the time the fire engines and ambulance arrive, that side of the house is gone.

At the hospital, Nancy is put on a respirator and heavy sedation because Tom can see what she must not, yet: Tucker – his burnt, lacerated, swollen flesh, his tender lungs seared. Swaddled in bandages, tiny and inhuman behind the oxygen mask, unconscious, Tuck struggles. Tom Davis sits down on a bare wooden chair beside his son and holds one somehow whole, unaffected hand, a cruel fluke of the fire. He caresses the small fingers, the tiny, perfect fingernails, then gently sets that promising hand down upon the hospital blanket. Reaching over to the metal bedside cabinet, he picks up a bottle and needle, tapping out a double dose of morphine because nothing else can be done, now, and nothing else matters, so he does not weep as he eases the needle in. Leaning over, he kisses a damp forehead and whispers for the last time, "Good night, my son."

Later, in January, the Davises sold the property of that old, lost Montauk home, that farmhouse where a woman was first named a witch, and where a child caught fire. The new house they built for the family, they build without a hearth.

2. THE OPENING

"She was unlike any other adult I ever knew when I was a kid," C.C. would say, if asked. "Utterly unlike. She went barefoot in summer, sat cross-legged on the pavestones with you, or ate honey right out of the jar! Other adults would say don't, watch out, be quiet, be careful. With Liz it was yes, let's not tell, wait 'til I show you, no, I won't lie, cross my heart and hope to die. It was a good thing – a fine thing, for a hellion like me. She was different. She didn't believe that the right shade of lipstick would solve everything. Certainly did not believe in the power of powder or paint, unless it came from a tube and ended up on canvas."

She was also in a foul humor, after the MoMA opening. As soon as the three women got settled in the limo for the ride back to the Plaza, Liz said, "Where the hell have you two been? How could you leave me like that, fair game for the vultures?"

"Vultures? Please," said C.C.

"Since when do I enjoy flunkies?"

"They weren't flunkies," said Quiola. "You're admired."

"My foot. I'm hungry is what I am."

Quiola thought: *by the time I reach Liz's age, the Creator willing, I hope all the childish petulance I now control by the force of knowing better won't simply break through the firewall and go on a spree.* Coaxed through the excellent dinner MoMA had ordered at the Plaza, Liz subjected everyone in range – from clerk to room service and particularly C.C. – to bitter, non-stop complaint, until she went to bed, by then mollified.

"She *will* be like that," C.C. muttered, staring out at the ceaseless street, and the play of evening neon. "Shoot me, if I never get like that."

"Yes," said Quiola, pulling her XXL t-shirt on. "I mean, no. No, I don't want to get like that." She sat on one of the single beds.

C.C. turned from the window. "What's wrong?"

"Nothing. Why?"

"You sound about a million miles away."

"Oh? Oh. I suppose I am." She laid her head on the pillow.

"Where? Back in Paris?"

"Oh, no," said Quiola, brushing off that idea as if swatting an insect. "I know you and Liz love the city but, to be honest, after these last six months, I don't. I told you. I want to come home – I wish I could go back up to Lutsen."

"Lutsen? To Lizzie's Treetops, you mean?"

"Yeah. I know it's odd, since I've only been there once. But I was born by that lake, and on our visit with Liz, I don't know, I was captivated by the land. I still dream about the river otters we saw, and the horses we rode."

C.C. laughed. "We were there in May, sweetie, the loveliest month of the year. You've never been through black fly season – at least not as you'd remember. Or survived a winter. Trust me, its no paradise. Didn't your mother say anything about it?"

"Mother left," said Quiola, her dark eyes going matte. "I know there are good reasons to leave. Weather is one of them."

"See?"

"But that spring, it was so beautiful. Truly. Don't you remember?"

"Of course I remember. Daydreaming a Lutsen spring, then?"

"No. Actually, I was thinking about Luke."

"Oh." C.C. bit the side of her lip and looked away. "Do you – often?"

"No. Not so often. Not as often as I should – as he would, of me. Do you mind if I turn out the light, now?"

"Quiola?"

"What?"

"Nothing. Good night," but C.C. did not drift off easily. She lay in her hotel bed, listening to Quiola snore – she sighed and folded her arms under her head as the city murmured and beeped. Her thoughts moved over that night's celebration. Nobody had wanted, really, to talk to her. They all wanted to talk to History. Eventually, snoring melded with the ambient street noise enough to lull C.C. to sleep. But she felt lousy in the morning, and when Quiola bounced out of bed, all kinetic energy, a few tears came.

A light rap on the door and "C.C.? Quiola? You two up yet?" asked Liz.

"No," said C.C., violently, wiping her face clean of tears with both hands.

Quiola poked her head out of the bathroom, her short hair a mess and her mouth full of toothpaste. She frowned at C.C. who shrugged. Quiola turned away to spit.

"Give us a few, Liz. I slept badly," C.C. called through the door.

"Coffee's here."

"All right, all right, hold your horses. Damn."

"What?" said Quiola, still in the bathroom.

"Room service. Liz knows I can't stand cold coffee." She peeled herself out of bed like she'd been glued to the sheets.

"Neither can I," said Quiola, pulling on sweats. "You ready?"

C.C. smiled wanly. "As I'll ever be."

The weather, as it turned out, still had not broken – the heat bore a drape of humidity, hanging over the city like a drunkard. Instead of driving around the park, Liz asked to go to the Metropolitan. It took the three of them what seemed an eternity to climb the vast stone stairs, and once inside the cool foyer, Liz had to sit down to recover. People milled about while C.C. and Liz found a wooden bench.

"I used to come here as a kid," said C.C. "With Mom."

"I know," said Liz. "I took you, once."

"*You* did? When? I don't remember –"

"You wouldn't, you were not even eight. Anyway, Ted had gone to camp, and you were home and bored and Nancy was busy so I whisked you off to the city for the day, and we ended up here. You made a beeline –"

"– for the mummies. I always did," said C.C.

"And I have always hated this place," said Liz, serenely. "It's a tomb."

"You *hate* this place? Why did you drag us up here, then?"

"The garden room has a nice lunch."

"The garden room? The garden room is gone. It no longer exists. They've replaced it with a cafeteria."

"My God, a cafeteria. Blasphemy. Does your mother know?"

"Liz, Mother doesn't recall much of anything."

"She barely remembers C.C.," added Quiola.

Liz shook her head, and sighed. "My poor Nancy, it's so awful. Things like that shouldn't happen. She was so generous."

"She was," said C.C., stoic. "So. Is there some other place we can go for lunch?"

✦

Liz Moore was utterly unlike any woman Nancy Davis had ever met, either. Women, according to Nancy, were rivals. They worried about everything, fought over husbands, homes, shoes and children. But Liz seemed… "so – free," is how Nancy put it, when anyone asked her why she'd befriended someone who could wander shoeless into a cocktail party.

April 1934. Even at the height of the Depression, New York City was a busy, bustling place, the opposite of Nancy's quiet, rhythmic life out on Montauk Point. April Fool's day in 1934 found her on the LIRR, three months pregnant, uncomfortable and yet happy to be on the train into town. She was to meet Tom at the Algonquin, and they'd take in dinner and a play, stay overnight. Young, pregnant and comparatively well off, Nancy Davis felt her privilege and tried to accept it without guilt, which became harder as the train headed into a city full of thin, hungry people, many of them ragged or filthy. To distract herself, she browsed over the *Atlantic Monthly*, to linger over three poems by Mrs. Morrow. The poetry both cheered and saddened her, for what mother, or mother to be, could forget the gruesome, unresolved death of the Lindbergh Eaglet?

Poor, brave Betty Morrow! she thought. *Poor, brave Anne.*

Nancy set the magazine aside as the train came into Penn station. Walking briskly along on moderate high heels up from the steamy, smelly tracks to the equally aromatic streets above, she headed not for the hotel, but to the gallery An American Place. Stieglitz was showing O'Keefe again, and even if Nancy was disgusted by the Stieglitz-O'Keefe May–December romance – so outrageous – she still wanted to see the new work.

Such a bold vision, and a woman's vision, too, Nancy thought and was not disappointed. But as she wandered from one magnificent, lurid flower to the next, she found herself watching this tall, odd-looking girl with a boy's haircut, tears running down her dark face. She kept mopping them away on a coat sleeve that had seen better days. The tears were so genuine, the coat so torn, that Nancy said, "Can I help you?" before she could wonder whether the offer was wise.

And Lizzie Moore, at twenty-six not much more a girl than Nancy herself, but looking younger in her outgrown clothes, turned to the stranger and said, "I'm hungry."

"Then let's get you something to eat. I'm buying."

And so they left together just like that, and found a coffee shop where Liz ordered scrambled eggs and Nancy drank coffee to keep her new friend company; she was a painter, this girl-woman, and O'Keefe had made her furious.

"Furious?" said Nancy. "Or jealous?"

"Both."

"She is startling."

"She's pornographic," Liz shot back. "But what can you expect? All the critics who rave about O'Keefe, they're all men, aren't they? And they need Stieglitz, don't they? They aren't about to insult his whore in public. They do it when they think he can't hear them. But I've heard them. Some of them, anyhow."

"Like who?"

Lizzie hesitated. "Like Paul Gaines."

"Oh, Gaines," said Nancy, smiling. "Such a strange little man. Anyway, you must come and meet my husband. You, he and Paul together can decide the fate of O'Keefe."

Lizzie wiped up the last of her eggs with a corner of toast. "Oh, she'll be around forever. The talent is too great. The question is: what's left for the rest of us to do?"

"Something else," said Nancy. "Come meet Tom."

"All right."

And so the two women, now no longer strangers, went to the Algonquin. In the hotel lobby they were waylaid by a set of wild sketches: distorted limbs, club-footed dancers with staring eyes, a small, eerie exhibit. Nancy was repelled, but Liz called them joyous monsters, and that's how Tom found his wife and Liz Moore together, arguing about elephant-footed ballerinas. It wasn't until many, many years later, as C.C. was going through household things with her mother, paring down after Dr. Davis's death, that she re-discovered whose paintings her mother and Liz had seen in the Algonquin lobby: Zelda Fitzgerald's. Zelda, too, had gone to the O'Keefe exhibit that spring, and had come away thinking O'Keefe's flowers "lovely and magnificent and heart-breaking," a counter-point to Lizzie's succinct judgment of pornography, while Nancy thought them merely rowdy.

And then the years passed, years in which people like the Fitzgeralds, or Stieglitz and O'Keefe or later, even Liz Moore, were presented to Nancy not in the flesh, but in words: in biographies, retrospectives, history. Nancy retreated. All those words about people she'd known, making them over into people she had never met or did not recognize, until, slowly, she forgot them all.

✦

"August in New York," sang Liz in an uncertain, gravelly tenor. "It feels so enervati–ing." She smiled.

"That's autumn," said Quiola, "which is exciting. Or embracing. Something cool, at any rate. Here we are –" The cabbie braked. Abandoning the Metropolitan, the three women had caught a cab, which Quiola directed to Prince Street, to a bistro in NoLita. C.C. stepped out first, helping Liz, who complained under her breath about the sagging of car seats making it hard on old bones, while Quiola paid the tab.

The bistro, a long narrow nook of a place with a pebbled outdoor garden in the back, wasn't busy. The hostess led them to a table that overlooked the garden.

"Does it feel like autumn to you?" said Lizzie as they marched down the narrow aisle of floor between the tables. "No, it feels like August, in April. Disgusting. I'd much rather be sitting out there –" she pointed to the empty garden, "– but we would roast."

"This place reminds me of the Left Bank – I thought you didn't like Paris," said C.C. to Quiola as the host handed around menus.

"Impossible!" said Liz. "Not to like Paris."

"But true," said Quiola. "I hate Paris."

Liz stared, as if Quiola had sprouted horns.

"Okay, so I do love the food. That, I miss. *Où est ma boulangerie?* That's what I want to know when I come home."

"*Ici*," said the waitress.

"Of course. Right here. How've you been, Carol?"

The girl smiled. "Fine. Can't wait for the fall. My last semester."

And so the three chatted to Carol for a moment about college, her plans, the menu. When they were through with the order, C.C. excused herself to the restroom.

As soon as she was out of earshot, Liz bore down. "Quiola. I know C.C.'s lying to me. Don't lie to me."

"What did she tell you?"

"Nothing. You tell. Quick. Before that little liar gets back."

"If C.C. –"

Liz gripped the younger woman's wrist with one bony hand as if the two women were teenagers, or sisters, with secrets between them. "Don't. I have a right to know."

"Do you? Let go of me."

But Liz had other plans, and her blanched green stare make that clear. "She will die of it, won't she?"

Quiola stared back, her own gaze black and inward. "I don't know."

"Bullshit." Liz let go of Quiola's wrist. "So?" she said, as if settling a bet. "That's that, then. Tell me –"

The soup arrived, and so did C.C. and all questions were left to glitter in Liz's eyes each time she caught Quiola's gaze.

"Ah," said C.C. "Cold white wine, creamy pea soup, piping hot *pommes frites* and chicken roasted with red peppers – what more could a person ask for?"

The spark in Liz's eyes banked.

"Your flight tomorrow is at eleven?" asked C.C. "You'll let us take you to the airport, Liz. That's not a question."

"Of course, of course. But you know how much I hate goodbyes."

"None of those," said Quiola. "Not tomorrow. We'll be good."

"No, not tomorrow," said C.C.

✦

Quiola, too, had never known anyone like Lizzie either, but for a rather different reason then either Nancy or C.C. because, by the time she met Lá Moore, Liz had become an icon, powerful, comfortable with fame and quite willing to exploit it – she refused to be interviewed, rarely left her Minnesota home, and did her legal best to keep the facts of her life as much to herself as she could.

In the spring of 1983, however, Liz decided to make a rare visit to New York City, after an absence of a decade. This made several galleries, MoMA, and her agent ecstatic. The *New York Times* took note; a few old friends arranged a party. But she'd come then in '83, as she would come in '02, to visit C.C., then just back from Paris, and flush with a new love.

"This girlfriend of yours, is she stunning?" Liz asked, as they headed downstairs for an early supper at the Plaza. "Well, Charlotte Clio?"

"You are not my mother! And I've already told you, Quiola isn't beautiful. She's lovely in a way I have no words for."

"Will I want to paint her?"

"I do," said C.C. with vehemence.

Liz smoothed her graying hair. "That's all that matters, isn't it? Where did she get such an unusual name? How did you pronounce it? Quiola?"

"That's right. Her mother is Chippewa. Didn't I tell you? Anyway, her mother had an Apache-Cherokee friend at boarding school named Quiola so we assume it's Indian but I think it might be Spanish. Anyway, she is lovely but her *name* is beautiful."

"Chippewa? You mean Ojibwe? Where is she from?"

"That's the funny part. She was born on the North Shore like you, but from a town or a place called Grand Portage. I think it's a reservation. Her mother left right after Quiola was born, so really, she's a New Yorker by right."

"What's her last name again?"

"Kerr."

"Hmm. I don't know that name."

"Why would you? Oh, I see – small towns. Kerr is the father's name, Joshua Kerr. They never married, and he split early on."

"I see – and her mother's maiden name?

"I believe it was some kind of animal. Wait. Otter. That's it. Rose Otter."

"Ah."

"Ah?" C.C. narrowed her gaze. "Ah what?"

"Nothing, just ah."

"You will behave?"

Liz turned the wattage up on a stare of mock surprise. "Behave?"

"Please, Liz. Don't batter the poor girl."

"My, my these elevators are slow! Anyway, I do what I like."

"Always have."

"You should know. Putting up with me since you were in diapers. How is my sweet Nancy doing, by the way?"

"Mom's well. A little forgetful."

"So am I."

"Yes, but you wear the years more lightly than Mom. She's wobbly, and had a fall that spooked her. I'm sorry she won't come in for the party –"

Liz put her hand up in a gesture of dismissal, as the elevator opened. "No matter, C.C. None of us bops around like we used to. I'm only sorry I don't have the time to visit Connecticut, and see her myself. Now, where's your new friend?"

But C.C. was already scanning the snowy plains of the dining tables, reflected in the ice of the wall mirrors, to find Quiola sitting straight-shouldered, her gaze frozen, as if she were awaiting execution at some rococo, Italianate palace. She had good reason to be nervous. It was bad enough that C.C. doted on the woman, but Liz Moore was a phenomenon, documented, researched, revealed, in some quarters, reviled. As a college student, Quiola had studied Moore's style; she'd read the one, unauthorized biography and had bought postcards of several works, like *Rib*, for her dorm room. She was so nervous about meeting Liz that day that her hands grew damp and trembled. She tried to keep them clasped, under the table. This made eating difficult.

"So, you are C.C.'s muse," said Liz, deftly seating herself. "I'm glad to meet you."

"Likewise," Quiola managed, staring.

Liz stared back. "So –"

C.C. plunked herself down between them.

"How are you feeling?" she asked Quiola. "Better? She doesn't take jet-lag well."

"I see," said Liz, opening a red clutch for her glasses, big, black and oval. She picked up the menu. Other diners seated themselves, but then, all at once, the room began to buzz with murmurs.

"What is it?" asked Liz, looking around. "What's going on? Good Lord, it isn't me, is it? We'll have to leave, I can't bear –"

"Calm down, its not you, it's a wedding," said C.C. "There's the bride and groom." A dark-haired, youthful, well-dressed couple were just dashing up the steps and in through the brass-plated revolving doors, he in a black tux, she in white eyelet, a single, brightly-dressed bridesmaid in turquoise, followed by a single, elegant bridegroom, then, family. The party swept across the lush lobby carpet to squeeze into an elevator, and was gone to what guests could soon hear through the floors, a reception. As the faint chords of an orchestra wafted down from above, Liz turned back to the table and said, "Such a spectacle! I should be ashamed to spend so much on a wedding."

"Marriage is an institution for those who want to be institutionalized," said C.C.

Liz stuck her tongue out and wrinkled her nose. "Despite my own best advice, I married. But we didn't parade ourselves through the Plaza."

"No," said C.C. "Stone broke, the both of you. Paul had to borrow the car."

Liz shrugged, and then said to Quiola, "C.C. tells me you work in ceramics. Don't you find that limiting? I would."

"Well, I –"

"So *domestic.*" She took off her glasses and laid them on the table. "You'll never be taken seriously if you stay with clay, let me warn you. All this nonsense about finding a woman's voice, or whatever these new-fangled feminists go on about, takes the backbone out of any good artist's work."

"But –"

"Come on, Liz," said C.C. "You owe feminism –"

"I owe nothing. Not to this bunch, anyhow. The *feministes* of Paris, or the Village, I admired them – they were my friends. But these girls, all they've done is take away my privacy, and interfere with my work. Don't tell me you've become one?"

"As a matter of fact, yes," said C.C., huffing.

"Hogwash."

"Really? Your work would be right where mine is now, without feminism. In storage."

"Bull," said Liz. "If the work is good it will find an audience. Eventually."

"Thanks."

Liz glared at her. "Your work is good, Charlie. Time will out."

"I'd prefer not to die before time wills itself out."

"That happens. Can't be helped. But Quiola, you must change your medium. Paint, my girl, not pots."

"I don't make pots –"

"Doesn't matter," said Liz. "Are you a feminist, too?"

"I – don't know. Like Rebecca West once said, 'I've never been able to find out precisely what feminism is. I only know that people call me a feminist whenever I express sentiments that differentiate me from a doormat.'"

Liz sniffed. "Cicely," she said "also announced that the main difference between men and women is that men are lunatics and women, idiots."

"Cicely?" said Quiola, confused. "Who is Cicely?"

"Rebecca West. Liz knew her," said C.C., glum. "In Paris."

"Panther," said Liz. "At least, that what Herbert – oh, excuse me, Jaguar, once called her, your Rebecca West. She was Cicely Fairchild, to her family. Rebecca West is an Ibsen character."

"Liz Moore, honestly, name dropping. Shame on you," said C.C.

"I drop nothing," said Liz, primly. "Your muse, here, is the one who dropped Rebecca on my head, for daring to defy what I think is so much mumbo-jumbo. Look at you two! Just because you happen to be in love doesn't mean you also have to toe a political line. A strong woman with talent is a strong person, period. The rest are all lunatics or idiots. I leave politics to the politicians."

"Everything is political," said C.C.

"Slogans. I can't stand them."

"Just what *do* you like?" asked Quiola roughly, and then blushed. Liz eyed her.

"Well!" said C.C.

"Ah-ha!" Liz smiled. "Glad to see your muse has some spunk, my dear. I was beginning to wonder if you'd fallen for a dud."

"Liz!" said C.C.

"I like strong people, with talent," said Liz Moore, answering Quiola's question, ignoring C.C.'s protest. "And good food."

✦

The root cellar of the "shed" was the coolest place C.C. and Quiola could find, bar air conditioning, all that hot April 2002 week, as they awaited C.C.'s operation. Earth-sweet, the cellar would store C.C.'s work while she was laid up. She looked over an empty frame and asked, "Do I really want this? What do you think? Is it worth keeping?"

Quiola turned around. "Sure? Why not?"

"I don't know. It's too fancy for one of mine. Maybe Liz –"

"Keep it," urged Quiola. "What about this?" She pulled a stack of unstretched canvases from under a workbench, mussing the swept floor with cobwebs and a flurry of dust-bunnies. "They look old."

"God, the stuff I've wasted. Just put it in the trash."

"All right. And this?" She held up a small painting of a small cramped room with one open window. "Yours?"

"Mine," said C.C. taking the picture. "Liz's city studio, so tiny the paint fumes knocked you over. I doubt she ever closed that window. You know she passed out, once. Place was lousy with bugs, too, and here I was, right out of school, clean as a whistle. I bet she read my face like an open book: you *live* here? How can anyone actually *live* here?" She laughed, but the laugh caught up on a cough, lung-deep, with legs. Quiola tried to keep her face blank as new paper, while

C.C. cleared her throat. The younger woman pulled up her blue jeans a bit, then knelt in order to pull a box of dusty jam jars from a space behind the bench. Doing so sent a spider packing, and she murmured, "Be well, Grandmother Spider."

"What's that?" asked C.C.

"A spider." She stood and brushed off her knees. "Why did Liz stay in that studio for so long if it was foul?"

"It was also dirt cheap. The painted lady's lair – that's what she called it. 'Come into the painted lady's lair!'"

Quiola leaned back against the workbench, resting her elbows on it. "Did she ever mind being called a witch? She's never seemed to mind."

"Oh, no. She just laughs. Says Al Kroenen was a fool." C.C. drew herself up, as if to mimic Liz's height, and assumed a very Liz-like pose. "'That man drank too many of Tom Davis's loaded martinis, and thought I'd been making eyes at his wife. I wasn't. She wore too much warpaint for my taste.'"

"Warpaint?"

"Yeah, warpaint. What, haven't you ever heard make-up called 'warpaint'?"

"Not really, no."

"Funny. We used to call it that. 'Can't leave the house without my warpaint!' Mom would say to Dad. You know how I hate the stuff. Refused to learn how to use lipstick. Mom was so patient. Like Liz said, generous. But for all her effort, I still failed girl's school."

"You just wanted to be a different kind of girl."

"Did I ever. Let's have some coffee, eh? I'm getting tired."

"Let me brew it?"

They climbed out of the cellar, into the hot, bright afternoon.

"Why, because you think mine's too weak? Coffee snob!"

Quiola let go the heavy cellar door, which shut in an ungentle whack, making a small dust storm. "What time's our appointment tomorrow?"

"Nine. Have you ever noticed doctor's offices are all same? Not like my Dad's old office, solid and wooden. Today it's MacDoc, cheerful and subdued, those same brown or beige or aqua chairs, that same carpet anywhere USA. They must all use the same carpenter,

contractor, painters – maybe that's what I should've done, become a
house painter, like my great-uncle. Much more useful than making
pictures nobody wants."

"Nobody is an exaggeration."

"Next to nobody, then."

They were still arguing the next morning, as they sat in the
cheerful MacDoc waiting room.

"Mrs. Davis?" called a nurse.

"My mother isn't here," hissed C.C.

"She's coming," Quiola said.

"I'm not Mrs. Davis!"

"At our age, we are all Mrs. Somebody. People being polite."

"My ass."

Quiola let it go. If C.C. wanted to be cross, she had every right.
No one should have to have the kind of conversation she was about
to have with her surgeon, Dr. Theresa Wong, who said Taxol,
radiation, and then we'll see. To prep, nil by mouth after midnight.

And then they were back out in the hallway headed for the car.

"I'll go bald," said C.C. after a few minutes. "From the Taxol."

"Very lesbian chic."

For a full moment, C.C. said nothing. Then, "How about a
tattoo? Think I'd look too butch – or too old? Bald old bitch with
a skull tattoo?"

"Perfect! Let's do it. Right now. After, they won't let you near a
tattoo needle."

"Are you serious?"

"Are you?"

"Dead."

So that afternoon in New Haven, they found a barber, reluctant,
at first, to shave off a fine head of hair, but when they told him why,
he relented. Then, a tattoo parlor, a husband and wife business; he
did the hard-core, she did the students, and they both let their seven-
year-old watch as they worked.

"A dentist's chair?" said Quiola as they stepped into the place. It
was late afternoon by then, April sun sliding through blinds to pool
in slats on the linoleum. The place was scrupulously clean, one wall
lined with photos of past work, one hung with an old-fashioned

wood oval mirror. The woman who greeted them, heavy-set, dyed blonde, redolent with tobacco, laughed.

"Vintage dentist 1950s," she said. "Kinda puts you in the mood."

"For what?" asked Quiola.

"For pain," said C.C.

The tattoo artist nodded, taking C.C.'s brand-spanking new baldness in stride. "Something like that," she said. "I encourage clients to think of the tattoo as less painful than your average root canal. Hi. I'm Kate. Am I doing both of you, or just one?"

Impulse jumped up Quiola's throat. "Both."

"Now wait a minute —" said C.C.

"Guess you two didn't discuss this."

"It's all right," said Quiola. "It'll be fun."

"Fun for me, at least," said Kate. "So. What would you like, and where?"

C.C. chose a delicate blue and yellow crab design, and had it put just above the curve of her right ear, a totem for her battle against cancer. As the needle whined high to low, inking color into flesh, C.C. fought tears, grit her teeth, while Kate dabbed blood; meanwhile, Quiola drew free-hand the sleek undulating silhouette of a river otter at play and had the artist put it just above her heart, near her right shoulder. Kate's daughter watched with an intense, interested stare.

"This is nice," declared Kate, when she was through. "People sometimes choose the oddest things. But these — I like them both. Can I keep the otter for my collection?"

"Absolutely," said Quiola.

"And you've got your care instructions? Good. Nurse your tattoo, and it will be beautiful for a lifetime."

"Amen," breathed C.C. She stared at the blue crab in the mirror, a raw wound still, beaded with fine drops of her blood. "I'll beat you," she whispered. "I'll beat you, damn crab." She raised her voice. "Quiola? I'm *ravenous*. Let's grab a bite at the York, and let the bald lady scare the pants off some fresh college kids."

✦

When Paul Gaines asked Liz Moore to marry him, out on Montauk Point, five years after the War had ground to its bitter, horrifying end, she told him about what sometimes happened to her – another reason, perhaps, that Tom Davis's friend Al Kronen named her witch. She'd always treated what she called her "limited insights" lightly, but felt if she agreed to be his wife, Paul ought to know.

"Like this," she said to him, snapping her fingers. "Out of nowhere, I get this clear glimpse of some event. Not a full story. Never that. Just a snapshot image with an odd sensation, like déjà-vu, but whatever it is hasn't happened yet."

"A woman's intuition," he said. "is a precious thing."

She didn't respond. They were in her Long Island studio, on a fine, sunny afternoon. He'd hocked a few things to make the cost of the diamond, so he was feeling good about himself, sacrificing for his woman and all that jazz. But as the silence grew long between them, he began to worry a little.

"Premonitions," he said at last. "I've had them, too." He held her long, thin hand in his stained, rough fingers, kneading hers gently.

She smiled at him, but it wasn't pretty, no, no it was a cat's smile. She touched the diamond with her forefinger. What she saw was not premonition. What she saw would be. This limited view was the reason she had never run away from anything in her life – well, except from her father. But that had been another matter.

Anyway, since her insights always came true, why run? For her, the idea of luck or chance had died one Minnesota winter, out in the snow near the Temperance River. She'd been seven and had seen her first limited view; at sixteen, she'd left and never looked back until age caught her by the heels and dragged her, step by step, up to the river and the North Shore of Lake Superior, but by then her parents were dead and besides, she'd always known she'd return home, to her people, the land of her birth. That, too, she'd seen.

But on the day of her betrothal, standing in her studio by the sea in 1950, with the sun streaming on her hands and face, and Paul so ardent beside her, all she said was,

"Of course everyone has had a premonition."

He smiled. He had a goofy, lop-sided smile made sillier by his twice-broken healed-flat nose, a boxer's nose. Ten years her senior, nearly a foot shorter, Paul drank. Everyone knew he drank. But Liz Moore married Paul Gaines, knowing his ways, because she also knew he would take good care of her, and just then she wanted his care.

One June day, Paul borrowed an old, old Model T from a neighbor, filled it with gas and drove it down to the justice of the peace; they picked up the Davises along the way, to bear witness, and C.C., who was thirteen, to serve as ring-bearer, flower girl and bridesmaid all rolled into one excited teenager. Liz cut down an armful of wild flowers – Queen Anne's Lace, daisies, cornflowers – for herself and her guests, and after the ceremony, as they drove back from town, she wove a crown of flowers for her bridesmaid. Crammed into the studio, they celebrated; Paul popped the cork and sloppily served everyone; Nancy vanished only to reappear with a white-iced wedding cake, complete with the bride and groom atop a tiny dais.

That stiff-armed wedding-cake couple still stand, in all their wedded bliss, on C.C.'s desk, battered by years of rattling around from one of Lizzie's junk drawers to the next, until C.C. had asked after it. Paul Gaines, goofy smile, paint-rough hands, a gentle and foolish man, had left them all a mere decade into the marriage, an alcohol-induced heart attack. He'd been just sixty.

3. SILENCES

"Who let this woman die?"

Theresa Wong, C.C.'s surgeon, stormed out of the operating room, looking for someone to blame. But there was only Quiola, who wasn't the person the doctor wanted. She wanted a reprehensible family member who'd been derelict enough to let a mother, sister, wife, daughter, aunt or cousin skip her yearly mammogram, which would have certainly prevented –

"– the first tumor from getting so large. But I get in there and what do I find? The first one, the size of a baseball, that's bad enough but there's a second, smaller one, hiding behind the first. X-rays didn't catch it. I had to remove a sizable portion of her chest wall muscle to be sure to get it all. She'll need physical therapy. Why didn't this woman see her doctor on a regular basis?"

"I don't know," said Quiola, her voice mild, flat. She gave Theresa Wong a searching look and the surgeon, still in scrubs, pushed the green surgical cap back off her forehead. "A case like this, I'll give her *maybe* two years at best. The only thing I'm certain about is that I got all the affected tissue. Where is the family? Hasn't she got any?"

"Her mother has Alzheimer's. Her father is dead." And she didn't know what to say about Ted. She'd urged C.C. to call him, but no. She thought about calling him herself, but hadn't the nerve. She knew he had sons, but since C.C. had given up on the whole business of family after her mother began to forget everyone, Quiola wasn't sure what the right thing to do would be. Dithering, she finally called Belinda, Ted's latest wife: at least Ted would know what was going on. The ball was in his court, now, and it looked as if that's where it would stay until it had bounced itself to a roll, and rolled away.

"God," said the surgeon. "Look, I'm sorry, but your friend will need help. She's going to be weak, in pain –"

"She'll have help. Mine. When can I see her?"

In fact not immediately, but when she was finally allowed to sit beside C.C. in recovery as the effects of the anesthetic wore off, she became as stolid as a rock, and tried not to look at where the blanket flattened, on C.C.'s breastless left side.

Only half aware, C.C. kept removing the pulse-clip the nurse had attached to her middle finger. Every time she got it off, the heart-monitor went blank, sending a frantic OR nurse swishing through the privacy curtains, at first with alarm, then with annoyance. But C.C., unable to process a scolding, just kept at the clip until the nurse gave up and took the thing off. Quiola said nothing until the nurse left. Then she leaned over and gave C.C. a pat on the hand. "Good for you. Teach 'em a thing or two."

When C.C. finally came fully around, she turned into a groggy nuisance. "My mouth's like cotton," brought her a sippy cup, "It's ten degrees in here," brought her an extra blanket, "It hurts," gave her a painkiller, but "I'm hungry," had to wait until the staff were sure she wouldn't give the meal back to them in an altered state.

Theresa Wong breezed in sometime in the late afternoon, checking chart and sutures, making quiet pleased noises, but Quiola could still see the steel of futility glinting in the eyes of kindness, a fury for which she had no answer, no aid.

Later, C.C. told Quiola that she had begun to come out of the anesthesia long before they wheeled her to recovery. Disoriented, she'd found her limbs indifferent to half-hearted command. For several decades, or so it seemed, she'd lain there, helpless and thirsty. Had she been forgotten, left to die in that dim room? Her back ached. She couldn't hear anything and the cold quiet began to prey on her. Although she had a blanket over her and not a sheet she wondered if she'd died.

"I've only been to a morgue once," she said, propped up in the guestroom bed. Before the operation, she and Quiola had moved all her necessaries down from the shed's loft to the guest-room; it seemed easier for a post-op, with a bathroom close to hand, the kitchen near.

"Why did you visit a morgue?" asked Quiola, pouring a mid-afternoon green tea because the temperature had dropped. When she checked the weather, they were predicting snow. Neither Quiola nor C.C. believed the forecast until the sky blanched white and the mercury started falling.

C.C. winced, shifting her position. Her sutures pulled, and had begun, as stitches will, to itch. "My father had to identify a woman who'd been murdered in Montauk. Her name was Eva Kevechion, workingwoman, a housemaid. My parents had her in, before I was born, to help out. She'd been battered to death. Dad took us kids with him. To toughen us up, he said. It was awful."

"Tea's ready."

"Thanks," said C.C., taking her cup, her mind still in the past.

"Dad was afraid he'd coddled us too much, after – after what happened to Tucker."

"Your brother?

"Yes. Coddle me?"

"I try. But you know very well, I'm not much of a nurse."

"Fiddlesticks. You've been peachy – besides, when we first met, you were a nurse."

"Nursemaid," replied Quiola, stirring her tea. "Nursery maid."

"A 'live-in au-pair' is the way you put it, back then."

"Why not? Sounds better than baby-sitter, and I wanted to impress you."

C.C. laughed. "As you did. Ah, yes."

"Stop teasing."

"Why? You know you did. And you hated the baby-sitting."

"I didn't hate it as much as I said. What I learned was how not to be a mother." She paused, then added, "After caring for Geoffrey, I knew I never wanted to be one. Even if I was good at it."

"See? I told you. I'll be back on my feet faster than Dr. Wong thinks."

"Look!" Quiola pointed out the window. "Look. Snow. In May."

And so it was. Fat, late flakes as big as goose down were spiraling down from the whitening sky, aloft on the soft of the evening air.

✦

A different, warmer spring, in 1979, Quiola, newly graduated from college, had answered this ad:

Seeking a young woman, good manners, to take care of infant in suburb for part of the day, while academic parents work. Semi-detached room, with separate entrance for privacy, and board included. Must have references. No experience required.

It sounded ideal: she had been working a time-flex internship at the Riverbed Press in Cambridge, and now needed a place to live plus food, because the internship didn't pay and she was out of the dorm. Either she'd have to take a second job or – but the Nelsons hired her to care for their baby, who, it turned out, had yet to arrive from –

"Peru. The adoption is almost final," said Mrs. Nelson, a tall, Scandinavian-pale brunette, with sharp features and blue-gray eyes. "We're flying down next week to pick him up. We'd like you to move in as soon as you can."

"Geoffrey. We've named him Geoffrey," added Mr. Nelson. He was equal in height to his wife, thinner if possible, which made Quiola feel short and plump. "We're very excited. We think you'd be the best for him – your references are so good, and you seem so…suitable."

Quiola nodded, unsure what 'suitable' meant, in Herbert Nelson's mind. But when she took one look at the baby, she knew: Geoffrey was clearly a mixed-blood. Quiola didn't know much about Peru, but she did know those dark, "Indian" eyes. When she held him, her own skin-tone seemed browner, to match his gold.

"He was a beautiful boy," said Quiola to C.C. that snowy, post-op night. C.C. had insisted on getting out of bed to sit in her now-favorite seat at the dining table, where she could see the crocuses, still bright with spring life, even as the snow gathered.

"Who was?" asked C.C.

"Sorry. The baby I played nursemaid to, when I was an *au-pair*."

"Yes? Most babies are beautiful."

Quiola cut C.C. a sharp glance.

"All right, all right. Forgive me, O honest one, some babies look like bald, wrinkled men. And who am I to say? I never wanted one."

"Me neither."

"And why not? What was it about that baby that scared you off?"

"Oh, C.C. don't. You've never asked me that, and I've never asked you."

"No," mused the older woman. "But you've made me curious."

"When I was younger, I got asked the baby question often enough, didn't you?"

C.C. waved her hand. "Of course. Mother was worst. 'When will you give me grandbabies, Charlotte?' Thank god Ted ponied up. Got me off the hook.'"

"So?"

"So, I'm *still* curious. Didn't your mother badger you?"

Quiola sat down on the couch and folded her arms. "No. In fact, she didn't. She disliked motherhood, and hoped I'd escape. I'm not saying she was a bad mother —"

"No, you never have said anything of the sort. Sang her praises, in fact. I would've liked to have met her."

"She was frail."

"That wasn't the reason, though, was it? You never told her, did you? That we were lovers."

"No, I never told her."

In a moment, C.C. said, "I understand."

"I knew you would." She shut the muted television off. "We have snow. I don't believe it. A week ago, it was August."

"I hope the crocuses make it."

"Geoffrey," said Quiola, as if there had been no break in their talk. "Such a beautiful, loving boy. A good baby, though he wasn't at first, but how could you blame him? He had infections. He'd been circumcised in a hurry, shot up with vaccinations and brought to the states. Mrs. Nelson didn't know what to do with him, so she just handed him over to me. He wasn't even a month old, and it was my job to feed, bathe, diaper and dress him, play with him, be his mother — until his adopted one came home from work, at three in the afternoon."

"That's not right."

"No it wasn't," said Quiola. "Nothing was right, for Geoffrey. I found out that the Nelsons got him through a broker. South American babies, they were all the rage in the early eighties, remember? Wealthy Americans want infants, not children. The Nelsons bribed a judge in Peru with wine and a case of Cuban cigars. What, I thought, would the big blond Nelsons tell their short, dark-eyed, dark-haired son about himself? But they were spared the trouble of explaining."

"Quiola —"

"You knew they fired me?" she went on, heedless. "Because Mrs. Nelson comes home and Geoffrey doesn't want to go to her. He'd grip me and scream. I'd been giving him *me* for the first months of his life, what did she *expect*? I turned him against her, she said. How? By mothering the child. When you asked me should I like to travel with you, Mrs. Nelson had just fired me. I was both angry, and relieved. I had no place else to go. Even the internship was falling apart. And then, of course, there was you."

C.C. made a little, reminiscent laugh. "I was smitten. And you! You were so hard to seduce. Never quite worked so hard in my life, getting you, you little fox."

"You mean otter, don't you? Anyhow, I was terrified. I'd only been seduced for the first time that January, by that blond editorial assistant, David. I was a late bloomer. And as you well know, confused."

"Ah. I don't remember the man. Only you. So, so – electrifying." She shifted her weight. "Do you regret it? Do you regret loving me?"

"How can you ask such a thing?"

"You left, after all. And then there was Luke —"

"But you know why I left! And I admit, I made mistakes; Evelyn was one of them – not Luke, though. Don't, C.C. Please. Must we go over old ground again?"

"These are strange days. For one thing, it's hard to get used to my maimed body, and I know it's hard for you, too. For another, I've decided to unlearn silence."

"Then you should call Ted."

"Oh, no. Some silence is worth keeping."

The telephone rang. Both of them stared at it, until Quiola picked up the line. It was Lizzie. After a few minutes of polite chat, Quiola handed Liz over to C.C. who, clearly pleased, took the call in her bedroom, for comfort's sake.

About a half-hour later, as Quiola made sure C.C. was settled for the night, C.C. asked, "Did you keep up with your beautiful Peruvian boy? Did you ever find out what happened to him? He'd be, let's see, in his twenties now."

Quiola sat down on the end of the bed, and massaged C.C.'s feet through the quilted comforter. "He's dead. The *au-pair* they hired after me was convicted of manslaughter. It was in the paper. She beat the boy to death for crying."

"Oh, my God. Oh, my God –"

"It was awful. I blamed myself for a while but –"

C.C. couldn't hear the rest. Instead she heard the sirens she'd never really heard; blinked at smoke she'd never seen; put her hands over her face, as if the heat of a long-ago fire would scorch her eyes and lashes.

"C.C, what is it? What's wrong?"

"Tucker. Oh, Tuck." She groped for Quiola's hand, caught it. "We'd gone to Gramma's, Ted and me, we weren't there! If only we'd been home – the house caught fire, you see, and poor Tuck was so badly burned, just a little boy, my baby brother –"

"Oh C.C – I knew he'd died but now how!"

"How could you, when I never said, I know. I know. It was just before Christmas in 1947 – you see why *Series B Three* haunted my parents so? A burning child…her way, I guess, of dealing. She'd loved him like he'd been her own. I think that's why she took me up, you know, instead. After. But I've never talked to her about it. Can't."

"You just said you wanted to unlearn silence –"

C.C. groaned. "Sure, yeah, right! But you know damn well we *both* have a remarkable capacity for it!"

✦

A few days later, seated in yet another MacDoc's alcove waiting for her first chemo, immured in one of Quiola's wide-eyed silences, C.C. announced:

"I'm all set. Let's get this show on the road. The sooner it's over, the better."

Another patient, a hollow-faced woman with black hair so black it had to come out of a box, and skin as white as stage-paint and lips as red as lipstick could get – Snow White in the cancer ward – laughed.

"Honey," she said, "you must be fresh meat. We'll wait like good children until the vampires are ready. And you don't need to think it, because it's been said. I look like a vampire myself." She laughed again, a smoker's cackle. A few of the other patients ogled her; the rest kept their eyes on the tattered copies of old magazines or stared into space.

C.C. was so startled by Snow White, she said meekly, "Oh."

Quiola leaned over. "I like her. She has what my Mother used to call moxie."

"Moxie-schmoxie" said C.C., her attention drawn suddenly to a young woman, bald, pale-yellow to white, as if she were wax, turning.

And so they waited, as Vampirella White knew, until the chemo-nurses, three efficient, no-nonsense women named Donna, Barbara and Doris, took each patient in turn to a row of recliners under windows in the ward. The recliners were reminiscent of old-fashioned beauty parlor hair-drying stations, except each had an I.V. hook up already 'loaded' as one nurse put it, with a patient's particular mix of medicinal toxins. C.C. didn't watch as the needle entered her arm with a chill, wicked little sting, and the tape to hold it was taped on, and Barbara solicitous but firm about the red liquid that was about to drip into her patient's veins, while Quiola kept up a funereal silence.

"Say something," commanded C.C. as soon as Nurse Barbara bustled away on her silent white sneakers. "Talk to me, baby, soft and sweet."

"That's a line from an old song."

"I know. Think of something, Quiola or I'll go nuts."

"All right. I've decided. I want a horse."

"*You want a what?*"

"You heard me. A horse."

"How old are you? You sound about ten."

"If you're going to be insulting, I won't say anything."

"Fine." C.C. sighed. She was beginning to feel very peculiar. At first the chemo had been cold; now, it felt hot. "You want a horse – the wish of every ten year old girl. Do you know how to ride? I mean more than just hanging on, like I did on that trail in Lutsen."

"I could take lessons."

"You could. But why do you want a horse? Why not get a cat? Much easier to deal with, much cheaper, far less demanding."

"Would you mind, C.C., if I moved back to the states now instead of months from now? Would it be a problem? I want to come home."

"Not just because – of this –" she gestured with one had at the ward.

"No, I told you. Paris is killing me."

"You don't mean that –"

"I do. I know its sacrilege, but I prefer to be where I can stretch and breathe and wander in the woods, my woods in the US of A. Paris can be merciless to a stranger. Do you know for the first month over there, I became a deaf-mute? It was easier to say nothing. People started speaking very loudly and slowly, and became very helpful."

"But you speak French, Quiola. You read it."

"Only a little. I murder the mother tongue. I know I should be grateful for the chance to be there, and Paris has given me watercolors – I mean, the demanding speed of the medium. If you aren't in the zone, if you don't measure effect, watercolor is ghastly. There. I agree with Liz. But when it's right –"

"I know. I've seen some of your new work, remember?"

Quiola sat very still. "You do like it?"

"Much, yes. Paris. It's hard to believe you hate it. When I first went there –"

"I know. But I want a home. I want – a horse."

"And just where are you going to keep a horse, in Chelsea?"

"Don't be silly. I'd move out of the city – although people do ride in the park. I've seen them."

"You mean Donald Trump's daughter rides in the park, don't you? Where do you want to live? You can sell the Chelsea flat, that will give you a nice, tidy bundle of money – or we can sell both it and the Paris flat."

"Your money. Those properties are yours, C.C."

"Okay, let me put it this way: Lizzie deeded both places to me. I hereby give them to you. I don't need the money. I need you to be happy. Which you aren't."

"No. I'm not."

"It isn't just Paris, is it? Are you in love?"

Quiola laughed. "No. But I think I need –"

"– a horse."

"Oh, C.C. for heaven's sake, give me three seconds. I'm not as good with words as you are."

"You mean you're not as glib."

"For Christ-sake."

"How are we doing here?" asked Barbara, who'd grown used to swooping in on testy conversations. "How do we feel?"

"*I*," said C.C. icily, "feel weird. I'm not sure how my friend feels."

Barbara folded her arms. "Oh, I see. Well, I've had your kind before."

"I'm sorry. I'm feeling crabby."

"Obviously. Now, would you care to tell me how you feel, physically?"

"Fine."

"How's the drip? Too fast? Too slow?"

C.C. shrugged. "I can't tell. My first time."

The nurse picked up the chart. "I see. Let me give you some tips. To start, a first time chemo patient will be famished when the drip is over."

So, on the drive back from New Haven to the "shed", C.C. and Quiola kept their eyes peeled for The Three Bears, housed in an old colonial.

"Pasta," said C.C., after they were seated. "with a meaty sauce. I guess I'd better eat while the eating is good, before I lose my palate, along with my hair, but we took care of that, didn't we? Nurse Barbara was impressed with our foresight. On the sly she told me the tattoo was inspired."

Quiola made something like laughter. She couldn't get all the way to a real ha-ha.

"Do you like yours?" asked C.C.

"My tattoo? I love it. Otter is a family name, and otters are joyous creatures, and since he's on my shoulder, now, I hope to feel more joy. Does that make sense? Or is that way too corny?"

"Corny? Yep. But it makes sense, too."

"At least I make a little sense. Look, C.C., I think what I want is a home. A house. Not an apartment in a city, not a flat, or a condo. A house. I'm tired of living out of a suitcase, or in a cupboard. I want land. I want to plant corn, squash, lettuces, and tomatoes. Mom tried to give me a home, but all we had were rentals. Even so, she taught me how to cook with fresh everything. That's how come her restaurant did so well. She grew her own, before it became all the rage. Now I want to do it. I want a home, a horse – and cat, too."

"A cat I can understand. They're no bother. What kind of a cat?" Quiola's cheeks colored. "Siamese. Actually, I've already found one."

"You have, have you? That's funny. Did you know Liz used to raise Siamese?"

"No! Did she actually breed them?"

C.C. nodded. "When I was a kid. She had about twenty at one point. Kind of scared me, all those tiny pairs of wide blue eyes. Where did you find your baby?"

"Online. While you were recovering, I spent some nights on the Internet. Just to pass the time. I couldn't read and I didn't want to bother you with the television, so I surfed. Eventually, she found me."

"*She* found *you?*"

After they made their order, Quiola explained. "Petfinder is a website that searches rescue shelters and such, by preference. I decided I wanted a Siamese kitten. So I just kept typing in my preferences until Amelia's face popped up. She's perfect, just three months old."

"Of course. Everyone's cat – or dog – is perfect."

"No, she's really –"

"You *are* in love, aren't you."

Quiola made a sheepish grin. "Guess so. I can't get her until she's old enough, and the shelter spays her. That'll be next month."

"Well, now that the question of the cat is settled, I think we're going to have to find you that horse, hmm?"

And so they talked about pragmatic matters, how much they might get for the City flat, what to do with the Paris one, and what they might expect to buy in Connecticut because Quiola wanted to be to hand when C.C. needed help. Tacitly they avoided talking about the real nitty-gritty of what kind of help but soon got a taste of it later, when the younger woman was jolted out of bed by C.C. crying, pitiful and terrible – "Quiola! Quiola – Oh god –"

Quiola bolted downstairs from the loft, her heart-valves shutting like a submarine in dive. Breathless, she found C.C. kneeling on the tiled floor of the bathroom, cradling the toilet, as if drunk. The floor was lousy with vomit, pasta marinara redux. Quiola put one hand on the older woman's shoulder, while her other hand felt for fever. But C.C.'s forehead was cool.

"Can you stand up? Has it passed? Is it over?"

"Oh, god, oh god –"

"Okay. Just rest. Tell me, when you're ready to get back in bed. Tell me what you need. When you can."

"Jesus," said C.C. violently. "Look at that. Would you look at that?" She lifted her head, and pointed in the toilet. The water was a bright, fire-engine red.

"You're bleeding? Where's the damn phone, I'm calling 911."

C.C. blinked, like someone coming to from a coma and started to laugh.

"C.C., what's *happening*?"

C.C. put her arms around Quiola's waist. "Oh God, I thought I was bleeding too, and the sight of it scared me so much I puked my guts out. But you know what that is? Not blood – it's the dye. From the chemo. Nurse Barbara warned me about peeing red, but I forgot." She smiled weakly. "Silly me."

✦

"Would you have enough space, here, do you think?" asked the real estate agent, Molly Limon, had already shown Quiola two weeks worth of properties.

"Best we've seen so far," she said, but she wasn't impressed. She'd miss the City flat, right in the middle of Chelsea. The well-seasoned wood floors, warmed by an old oriental rug, and the kitschy plastic beads of the kitchen entry reminded her of San Francisco. By contrast, everything she'd seen in Connecticut was fatally suburban. She didn't say so to either Molly or C.C., but her nerve was beginning to fail. Leaving Paris was one thing. Selling the Chelsea flat another. There'd be no going back.

"It's not encouraging, Molly. This place."

The real estate agent cocked her head. "No, I agree with you. Well, I have one more condo on my list today. It's a little more irregular than this place."

"It's all just so ordinary. Plain but not simple. Why would anyone want it?"

"Security," said Molly, gathering up her papers. "It looks just like every other place. People find that comforting. But you're different. Come on. I think you'll like the next one."

Molly was right. Quiola decided to make a bid, even before they set foot inside the place, but not out of passion, out of practicality. The two-bed, one-bath condo was five minutes, if that, from C.C.'s "shed", plus the place was new, yet designed to look old on the outside. Inside, it had high ceilings and plenty of light. Within the month, she had the keys. When she walked over the threshold for the first time, she had her new kitten, Amelia, in her arms. The day after the movers had come, Quiola, on her knees in front of her coffee table, exclaimed to C.C., "Would you look at this! It's cracked and they didn't bother to tell me."

"You've got to expect damage. When Mom and Dad sold the farmhouse, they lost a hallway mirror that'd been in the family since the last century. Shattered to bits."

"Seven years bad luck. How are you feeling?"

"Lousy." C.C. sat down on the sofa. She tucked her feet up under her. "I'm tired. And the chemo goes on until November! Then, radiation – god knows what that'll be like. Honestly, I don't know if I can stand it."

"But you will."

"Will I?" C.C. closed her eyes. "I sometimes wonder if it's worth it."

"Don't say that. C.C.? Please."

But the older woman had fallen asleep.

Later that week, C.C. told Quiola: "Look, why don't you take the day off? I can drive myself to chemo."

"I don't think so –"

"I do. I'll be fine. It doesn't bother me so much now, I told you."

"Yes, but you're tired all the time. You sleep in a wink."

"I'll be fine."

And she was. Confident from her smooth ride up to New Haven, all chemoed up, C.C. marched back from St. Matthew's to the Heap, pleased. She started the car, which belched as usual, and backed out, slipping easily onto the highway. The miles zipped by until, just as her exit was at hand, C.C. noticed that the sunlight was getting a little dim, then dimmer, then suddenly –

"Hey –" she said, and aimed at the exit ramp. The next thing she knew, a car horn was blaring in her ear, and a worried man's face peered through the windshield, which seemed to have grown a crack.

The man had to shout over the horn. "Ma'am? Ma'am? Are you all right?"

"I think so. I don't know." She moved. Nothing hurt. "Can you get the door open? Open the door! What's the matter with this dang horn –"

The door opened, and she popped off the seat belt. The Heap was smaller than it should have been, and she had to crawl out the half-crumpled door, into the stranger's arms. He helped her stand, and looked her over.

"My cell's in the glove box," she said.

"I already called it in. Saw you fly off the ramp like the car had wings." He shook his head. "Never seen anything quite like it – like you was heading for the woods on purpose. I thought for sure you'd be –"

"I'm fine," she said and repeated this to the paramedics, to the emergency room, and once again to Quiola, who showed up at St. Matthews, furious.

"You said the same thing this morning. From now on, I don't believe you. And you're not driving yourself anywhere."

C.C. stood up. "Let's go. The less time I spend here, the better." Then she made a wry face. "I'm not driving, without a car. You should have seen the Heap. Crumbled like tin foil. Totaled. And I couldn't have been doing more than thirty."

"What happened? They didn't tell me, other than that you were all right."

"Stupidest thing. I feel so dumb. I was driving back home. I was fine. I mean it. At our usual exit off the highway, I just passed out. Next thing I know, this nice man is talking at me but I can't hear him over my horn. It was stuck. So was the car. I'd driven right off the ramp and into a tree."

"Jesus."

"Wish I could've seen it," she added. "Must have been a sight!"

"You," said Quiola, pulling on to the highway, just as C.C. had done earlier. "You are a menace."

"Only to myself. I'm grateful you weren't in the car. You might have been hurt."

"Me? If I'd been in that car with you, I would have been driving and none of this would've happened. Where'd they take what was left of the Heap?"

"Over to Mike's garage. He'll be impressed."

"Or pissed. He's worked hard to keep that old thing running for you."

"I'll miss her, won't I? Never find another Heap like that."

"A blessing, if you ask me. That car was twenty years old."

"I like them well-seasoned."

"Yeah – unlike your girlfriends."

Stung to quick tears, C.C. said, "Where did *that* come from?"

"Sorry. I really am. I just – you've scared me. First you say chemo isn't worth the effort, and then you fly off the road. I just – it just came out."

"It was cruel."

"I know."

For a few moments they drove up the highway in a guilty, bruised silence. As they neared the off-ramp where C.C.'s car had died that morning, Quiola picked up speed. Neither of them spoke again until they were off the highway and pulling into the shed's drive. That's when C.C. said,

"Of course it is also true."

"What is?"

"What you said. Cruel or not, it's true. All my girlfriends were young. Including you. Not well-seasoned at all."

Quiola smiled, leaned across the gearshift and gave her ex a long, reminiscent kiss. "There," she said. "A bit of spice."

C.C. laughed. "Yowza."

✦

"I've never done this before," murmured Quiola, her long hair veiling her face. April 1978. After a Legal Seafood supper, and several drinks, C.C. finally persuaded the young editorial intern she'd been wooing to come over to her large studio on the first floor of a Cambridge brownstone, not far from the Riverbed Press, then in it's heyday, which is why C.C. had introduced herself to Arthur Rivers, owner and publisher, on Liz's behalf. Rivers had agreed to arrange for a Moore catalogue raisonné, along with a short biography Liz would commission – if she was going to discovered at last, she said, let someone get the story right. The instant C.C. had laid eyes on Quiola, she'd begun a strategic seduction: after hours, a casual drink; a week later, a select luncheon spot; tonight, champagne (which she'd been chilling for almost a month, in hope). She sat down on the only place anyone could sit in that apartment, on her large caramel-colored sofa bed. She toed off her loafers, kicked them out of the way, and tucked her feet up. She'd worn khaki pants and a black blouse because she thought the trousers made her look trim, and the blouse flattered her full breast. She'd wanted to look sexy and smart.

At first, Quiola just wandered about, sipping champagne and looking at the things C.C. had chosen to hang: a Moore, a black-and-white version of *Rib*; two small canvases of her own, both landscapes, Montauk 1 and Montauk 2; a Ga'g print. They talked about painting, and about the class C.C. was teaching at Boston University.

"Sit," said C.C.. She patted the sofa next to her. "Stop fluttering."

"C.C., I –"

"I won't hurt you."

Quiola finally landed on the couch.

"There," said C.C. She leaned over for a kiss, spilling champagne. Which is when Quiola murmured, "I've never done this before."

"You've never been kissed? Sure you have. I can tell."

"Not by a woman."

"Lips are lips. A tongue is a tongue."

Quiola sighed from behind her hair. "But –"

C.C. leaned across the couch for another kiss; this time she flicked the end of her tongue hard against the younger woman's lips, as her fingertips drifted across a blue-jeaned thigh, firm and light. She unbuttoned the fly, unzipped the pants and ran one fingertip from belly button to the elastic top of the panty line, and then back up, and under Quiola's shirt around to the bra hook.

"Come here," she murmured.

"I don't know. I don't think I can do this." Quiola looked up with an intensity that made C.C.'s ears drum so hard she thought she'd go deaf. Kissing a cheek, an earlobe, she whispered, "I love you. I want you."

"But I'm afraid."

"Of what? Of love?"

"I don't, I mean, I'm not –"

C.C. brushed Quiola's long hair back from her face and tucked the ends behind each ear. "In love?" she said. "Aren't you? I am." She began to unbutton Quiola's shirt. When she had all the buttons undone, she stood to undress. White and naked in the semi-dark, she tugged a blanket off the back of the couch and curled up, resting her cheek against Quiola's arm. Then she just waited, in silence.

She didn't wait long.

PART II

BEAUTY AND THE BREAST

4. POISON

During C.C.'s first weeks of chemotherapy, when she wasn't asleep or sick, she watched birds: robins, a blue jay, blackbirds, a sparrow. But it wasn't the cardinal at his bath, vivid against a sky-blue bowl, or the titmouse clutching beanpoles or the wren gathering moss from her hanging baskets – these didn't really catch her. Flight, however, did. The aerial choreography of barn swallows, the long glide of an occasional gull come inland, the ominous heavy flap of crow's lift-off, the cardinal's bright dart. She took to watching flight at inopportune moments, say, during a phone call, after which she'd have the devil's own time remembering with whom she'd just spoken.

Quiola didn't worry about the birdwatching, until C.C. became unreasonably exasperated when a pair of cardinals built a nest in an azalea at the shed's front window.

"It's too low," she said one morning, peering out. "Some cat will get them."

"What's too low?" asked Quiola. She'd driven over from her own place, supplied with Tupperware full of soups, and microwaveable meals, and was storing them in fridge and freezer, labeled, ready to heat.

"That foolish bird," C.C. said, pointing. "I can see right down into the nest. And if I can, so can some cat."

That was bad enough, but the next week when Quiola made her Tupperware run, C.C. started ranting about DDT.

"Yes I know DDT's been banned for years," she said, looking up from her book, "but how can we be sure? It's poison. You know what it did to the peregrines, don't you? And the bald eagle," she added, pushing her chair back from the kitchen table. "Ha! We kill our own."

"America has been a slaughterhouse since Europeans started mapping. We've a talent for killing each other, always for good reasons. But we're not really talking about DDT, are we?"

"No, we're not. Chemo is poison, and I fail to see how poison is a good thing. I don't think I'll mind the radiation so much. It leaves a little burn mark, which heals up fast. Or so I'm told. But chemo is just poison – it's murdering me slow, from nerve to nail. I feel like the goddamned peregrine, doomed to extinction."

"Radiation isn't benign either. And a poison depends on the dose. People used to take arsenic for their health, after all."

"Fools."

"Chemotherapy is –"

"– a crude poison," interrupted C.C. "It just blasts through, killing willy-nilly and you hope it takes out the cancer, before it, or the chemo, takes out the species."

"You do not, by yourself, constitute a species."

"How do you know? Maybe I am the last of my kind – the Last of the Mohicans."

"Not funny."

"Well? Second wave feminists are a dying breed – literally. We're soooooo over, we're soooo old, if you talk to anyone under thirty. I hear there's a third, even a fourth wave, but I don't see it. What wave are you riding on? I mean, you were still teething when we all started raising our consciousness, and protesting the war."

"I was ten or so. Hardly teething."

"Too young."

"Well," said Quiola as she leaned against the sink near the pile of dishes C.C. had left, "we now have the War on Terror to keep us all busy."

"God help the young. I remember the day the Vietnam War ended. I thought I'd see peace forever."

"Peace never lasts long."

"What are you, a prophetess?"

"No. But I can read history – or maybe I'm the one who's a witch, after all."

"Boo," said C.C. sourly. "Anyway, what am I going to do about it?"

"About what?"

"Those idiot cardinals. Late-nesting in my azalea."

"Oh, not them again."

"Well? They've put themselves in harm's way. I'm sure that orange tom down the block has the chicks staked out already."

But the orange tom had other fish to fry. As one week moved into the next, and C.C.'s treatments dragged on, baby cardinals took flight.

✦

"Poison," said Quiola to a sleeping C.C. one evening in the "shed" after supper, "is a woman's means of murder. Hard to diagnose. Sly. Bella Donna." But C.C., wan and wasted, slept on. Quiola left the bedroom to sit down at the kitchen table, which was covered with insurance, doctor and clinic bills, sorted into piles – all of which said C.C. owed someone, somewhere, and eternally, it seemed, for the privilege of being poisoned. Quiola stared at the papers for a few minutes, then got up and fixed herself a drink – and soon started drinking with an earnest drive to pass out, which she did, on the couch beside the fireplace.

Sometime later, in the dark, C.C. shook her shoulder.

"Wake up."

"Go 'way."

"Quiola, wake up – its past midnight. What about Amelia? Doesn't she need to be fed?"

That brought her up from the bottom of Gin Lake. She pushed herself to a half-sitting position and waited while the spinning room settled. Cotton-mouthed, unable to focus properly, she stared at the worsted couch fabric in the faint light.

"Might puke," she said.

"What? Are you all right? What've you been doing?"

Quiola laughed and hauling herself into a sit, lugged her legs off the couch and looked up at C.C., luminous, bald and thin in her flannel nightgown, a blue blur, her face framed by concern.

"Quiola –"

"Leave me alone."

"You're drunk."

"Whoopee. Don't worry. I'm going."

"Are you sure you should drive? Maybe I –"

"Doan' be dumb. Look at you. Can't drive. Sheesh. Move over. I'm goin' home, ha-ha, home. To condo heaven." Squinting malevolently at C.C.'s several faces she said, "I'm never going back to Paris. Neve'." She pushed herself to her feet and although C.C. tried to stop her, she left the "shed", banging the door behind her, then, in the car, she wove along pitch-black back country roads with the intense concentration of a very, but not entirely, drunken drunk. With care she rolled quietly into the condo's lot, shut the headlights, and staggered up the walk. Insects hummed in the July night. She dropped the keys, picked them up and fell down. Giggling, she got back on her feet and inside to find the poor cat beside herself with kitten joy. Quiola cried a little as she spooned out cat food, then made herself stop.

"Self-indulgent brat," she said, dropping the used spoon in the sink and putting Amelia's dish on the floor. She watched the kitten devour it, and then lay down on the linoleum and fell asleep.

Some hours later, a ringing, ringing, ringing brought her around. Fumbling up from the floor, she answered the phone – "Hello?"

"What the *hell* do you think you're doing?"

"Hello? Who is this?"

"You know damn well who it is. And I want to know what the hell you think you're doing?"

"*Liz?*"

"Oh, Christ, what – are you still piss-ass drunk?"

"Well, hello Minnesota. I gather C.C. told you about last night."

"Damn right she did. Weeping into the phone at five a.m., of course she knew I'd be up but what can I do? I thought you were looking after her –"

"I am –"

"How? By getting pie-eyed?"

"No, I –"

"– and just what kind of half-ass excuse do you have?"

Silence.

"None," said Liz. "Thought so."

"I'm tired," said Quiola.

"*You're* tired?"

"Yes me, I'm tired. Besides, I don't see you here, filling Tupperware with soup or making the chemo pilgrimage to New Haven."

"Oh, please. Just what kind of help would I be? If you hadn't noticed, I'm not exactly *young*."

"Neither am I."

"*Please*, save me the pity-party. Just wait till you hit my age."

"If I should be so lucky."

"Oh, you'll be around," said Lizzie, sounding grim and sure. "Long, and I mean long after C.C. and I are dust, so you might do a little better at taking care of her while you can."

"Look, Liz, I don't need a scolding. I feel bad enough as it is. Okay? I don't have an excuse. I know it was wrong — but you try sitting around for hours watching other, sick bald, people get chemotherapy. It's worn me down. C.C. hates the treatments, of course, but she's a trooper, she's built up a rapport with the nurses, she swaps stories with Snow-White the Vampire —"

"Snow White the Vampire?"

"Another patient. Anyway, I'm just *there*. Like furniture, like I was for Luke, sitting there, watching AIDS eat him to nothing, it — hurts. It hurts, to just watch, helpless, as C.C.'s pumped full of poison. I can't explain — I know I'm being selfish. You don't have to tell me."

"Quiola."

"What."

"Call Ted."

"Don't you think I have? I call his wife every week. She's been very polite. I have no idea if she passes this information on, but I keep the Mrs. informed. She thanks me. That's about it."

"Ted was such a good boy. Nancy would be unhappy, if she knew."

"Thank God, then, that she doesn't."

"Have you seen her lately?"

"Nancy? Yes, although C.C. was in an agony of distress about being bald. Her mother didn't even notice, which made it worse."

"Quiola."

"What."

"You can't take care of someone else if you don't take care of yourself."

"Yeah, right. I know."

"Do you? C.C. told me her chemo is almost over, isn't it? Good. Take a break. I told her you needed one. She's too focused on the present misery to notice, and you can't blame her, but you have your own life, too. Are you listening to me?"

"Yes, Mother."

"Well, everyone needs a mother now and then," said Lizzie sharply. "I'm not much of one, still, when C.C. tells me you've been drinking rot-gut, I think: poor child. I love C.C. but she's demanding. Remember, I've lived with her."

"I remember."

"So – are you all right now?"

Quiola chuckled. "I've a sledgehammer of a hangover, if that's what you mean."

"Take care of yourself, then."

"I will. I promise. Goodbye, Liz. Call you in a few –" and she hung up.

✦

Dead calm, the Sound barely sounded, a murmur like a hem of silk, as a brisk breeze offered no hint of winter's coming. The sun hid behind a scrim of summer cloud, which dulled the July heat. Quiola trudged across the grainy sand, each step jarring. Aspirin, coffee and a soft-boiled egg on dry toast had done little to cut the pain ringing her eye-sockets. She carried a water bottle and drank at it half-heartedly, walking out toward Meig's Point until she found a secluded niche, a driftwood log, nothing special unless you'd been there again and again, which she had. Swinging the backpack off her shoulders, she unzipped it and unfurled a striped beach towel, which she laid out flat then planted herself on it before the wind had other ideas. She sighed and drank little sips out of the water left in her bottle.

"Must rehydrate," she admonished herself and then closed her eyes, shaking her head, muttering something about old ladies who natter to no one.

Her cell-phone rang. She stared at the back-pack, hoping the cheery little Mozart air would stop, but it didn't, so she unzipped the pocket, flipped open the phone and said,

POISON

"Hello."

"Where are you?" asked C.C.

"On the beach."

"What beach?"

"Meig's Point."

"Fuck that —"

"Charlotte Calliope! I'm shocked."

"Where are you, really? I've called the condo twice."

"I told you. I'm at the beach, out on Meig's Point. Really. It's lovely this morning."

"Are you all right?"

"Yes and no."

"Just how much did you have last night?"

"Why? It was mine, I paid for it."

"You can drink me out of house and home, for all I care."

"I'm paying for it now, if you prefer."

"I see. Call me back, when you're ready to talk," she said, and hung up.

Quiola snapped the phone shut. Then, she opened it, and shut it off. She watched a dog attached to a family, vainly chase one seagull after another, unfazed by failure, while kids tossed a ball between them in the water. Getting to her feet, she walked away from her niche, off toward the breaker, down to the sea. Lemony late sunshine sat like custard between puffs of gray-blue rain clouds soon to burst over Meig's Point.

✦

Luke O'Connor, thin and gaunt, sat in the front seat of the rental car with an alpaca throw across his knees and an old ski-hat tucked over his ears. "Where are we going?" he asked as Quiola pulled off the brake and eased onto the street.

"To the beach. For the weekend. I've packed for both of us."

"Packed? The weekend? You know we can't afford it."

"We don't *have* to afford it."

"What do you mean?" He turned to eye her. "What have you done now?"

65

"Don't sound so suspicious! I haven't done anything except ask a favor."

"Oh, no. Not from C.C."

"Well? Look we both need a break, and the beach is only a few miles from her little house. Besides, she's not really living there right now, she's moved in with her mother until she can find a good nursing home."

Luke turned his paling face away, to look out the window at the passing city. "You should've asked. You should've asked me first. You know how I feel about – that. C.C. And it isn't as if she has much regard for me, either."

"Oh, Luke."

"Well? It's true."

"But I care for you both."

He closed his eyes, and rested his temple against the car window. "Do you? Must I share you, always, with her?"

"What do you mean by share, Luke?"

"You know perfectly well what I mean."

"Listen," she said, although she'd said it before. "I am *in love* with you. In love. With you. I love C.C. I am not in love with her."

"You were once, weren't you?"

"Maybe," she said, biting her lip. "We had sex. We lived together. You know this. You knew this when you married me. But I was a kid! Just out of college, green as corn. I didn't know what I wanted and besides it was a long time ago."

Luke ran his index finger slowly along the window edge. "It's hard," he said after a few minutes. "Maybe if I weren't sick, I wouldn't care so much, I don't know. I didn't care when I proposed to you. I swear I didn't. *So what?* I thought because by the time you get to be our age, if you haven't fallen once or twice for the wrong one, well, that's not a surprise. But now, when there's no future –"

Quiola caught her breath. "Honey, none of knows if we have a future."

"Oh, sure, we could both get hit by the next crazy on this highway. Right. I know. Hey, let's stop at the beach first. I mean before we get to the house. It's a beautiful day. I'd like to sit by the water."

"I'm there before you," she said, smiling. "I packed us a lunch."

The sun seemed desirous of shining hard as if just for Luke, who soon fell into a doze and only woke again when Quiola swung off the ramp, through the stoplight and into the park. Off-season, no guard was on duty; the winding road of marsh and tide was empty; dry, burst cattails shook in the light, chill wind. The parking lot, too, was empty and the winter beach entirely theirs. Draping his alpaca throw across his shoulders, Luke let Quiola help him out of the passenger seat, and together, with their lunch in a red cooler and a heavy woolen Pendleton blanket, made their way across the weathered boardwalk, to the sand.

The grayish Sound, so much calmer than its cousin the Atlantic, rippled quietly a few yards from their picnic. They didn't speak as Quiola unpacked lunch, but when she handed Luke his wax-papered egg-salad sandwich and bag of chips, he said, "I will die soon, you know. I feel it in me, Qui. I feel… different. Lighter."

She could not take his gaze with her own, so kept her eyes on the sandwich they both held. "I don't want you to leave me," she said. "Don't."

"Oh, no," he said, his voice suddenly Luke's old voice, real, firm, and warm. "Are you kidding me? Not when there's egg salad and chips!"

✦

At Liz's suggestion – her insistence, really – when C.C.'s chemo treatment ended, Quiola took a break: a week in New York, talking to gallery people about a possible show for C.C.; two weeks in Paris, closing up the studio cleaning it out, making it buyer-ready.

"By the time you get back, I'll be well," said C.C., watching Quiola haul a black nylon suitcase out the back of the closet; she put it on the bed, unzipped it. Amelia leapt up from the floor to investigate.

"Promise?" asked Quiola as she rummaged in the bag.

"Yes. By then, the radiation will be done – hey, what have you found in there?"

"An old postcard."

"What does it say?"

"Nothing. It's blank. But it's – here, look," and she handed it over to C.C.

"It this a joke?"

The lurid red, green and beige card was titled **INDIAN SYMBOLS** in bright red, bold capital letters; it was subtitled **And Their Meanings** in lower-case brown type. An illustration of a Hollywood-type Native American in red-feathered war-bonnet was super-imposed on what seemed to be a dried buffalo hide. Written on that hide were tiny black symbols followed by English interpretations:

✛ PATHS CROSSING
➤ ARROW…PROTECTION
✸✹ SUN SYMBOLS…HAPPINESS
⟋ LIGHTNING…SWIFTNESS

"Might be a joke," said Quiola. "It could also be, well, just American kitsch. The colors and typeface look fifties, but I think the card's a replica."

"Where'd you get it?"

"Somewhere in Paris."

"Says here it was published by Petley Studios, Albuquerque, N.M."

"Helpful."

"Why did you buy it?"

Quiola put her hand out for the card, and smiled. "Because it's so awful. And because it's so – so –" she shrugged. "So American." She folded the card inside a shirt. "I was homesick. When I found the card, it made me laugh, so I tacked it up over my desk – I know, it's weird. But in Paris, it seemed less so. I mean, whenever I'd run across another American – even a loud, fraternity kid – I'd practically throw myself at them because I *am* American. I'll never really be anything else. Even if I know that postcard is twisted, just plain wrong, I also think it's typical, so American."

"I see what you mean. Like those shops you find near a beach or a lake somewhere, Indian Trading Post. Genuine Indian trinkets."

"Yeah. I was confused by those places, as a kid. I also wanted the doll and her papoose. Mother eventually broke down and bought me one, but she also taught me how to bead the old-fashioned way, so I could make myself, and my doll, more beautiful things that the crappy stuff it came with."

"I've never seen you bead, or even wear anything beaded."

Quiola sat down on her bed next to the suitcase. "No. I haven't done that since I was a teenager. I stopped because everybody back then wore beaded flower necklaces. It was the '70s, after all. Flower power. I remember, though, one Halloween, I dressed up like what I thought an Indian Princess would look like, and I made a beaded headdress but that pained Mother so, the next year I was a flapper. I had a straight white dress with fringes all over it, and an elastic headband with a feather in front – my Indian princess headdress from the Halloween before, worn backwards and covered in gold sequins. That was first time my Mother let me wear makeup like a real woman, with the lipstick and the eye-shadow where they were supposed to go. I had worn lipstick a few Halloweens before, when I was really little, but it was in a straight line from the side of my mouth to my chin--blood dripping down the side of a young vampire's face. Anyway, flower-power, when it took over, never appealed to me. I didn't want to be a flower child. I wanted to be a robot."

"A robot? Seriously?"

"Seriously. It would be cool to be mechanical. So lean and chrome. Looking back, I suppose it was self-defense. A robot can't get hurt."

"It can break down."

"Of course, but they can also be fixed, like a toaster or a car. That's what I thought. But even mechanical things sometimes can't be fixed."

"Like the Heap. Like me."

Quiola rested her hand on top of the suitcase and gave C.C. a look that said, without speaking: *and this is why I have to leave, for now. When you say things like that.*

"Well? It's the truth, isn't it? I'll never be entirely the same."

Quiola stared at the wood floor, silent.

"Goddamn it, Quiola. Can't we even talk about this? I'm not the same, I'll never be the same, and there's no guarantee I'll even make it. You ask me to promise to get well, but you can't really ask me, for your sake, to believe in a miracle, can you? You can't just ignore the fact that I've been bent, spindled and mutilated, that I'm sick, and that you're leaving."

"I'm not leaving, leaving. I'm coming back. Three weeks."

"Fine! I stand corrected. I'll be alone for three weeks."

"But you won't be alone! There's Margaret next door, and then Valerie will be here – and you said you'd be all right, you said it was a good idea! I can cancel my trip –"

"No. That would be a mistake." She glanced up warily. "For both of us."

"Yes, it would. I need to get – I'm sorry, C.C. I need a break. I'm not perfect."

"Neither am I," said C.C. quietly. "Neither am I."

✦

"Mom." Her long, thick dark hair in a single braid down her back, Quiola stood solemn, a point of stillness in her blue Catholic school uniform. The cramped kitchen bustled, as the first wave of the dinner hour swung into tempo at *Rose Garden*. Tucked into a corner of the Lower East Side, the tiny restaurant had grown hot as a furnace with local traffic. Rose Otter turned away from the gas stove she'd been supervising at the sound of her daughter's voice. A spry woman, Rose Otter was just thirty; her employees called her Mrs. Dynamo.

"What is it, Quiola? You can see how busy we are. Why don't you go upstairs and start on homework? Then come back in an hour or to help us out. Tonight looks like a rush already. But then it is Friday –"

"Mom, I – I don't feel well."

Rose frowned. She touched the shoulder of the woman standing at the stove beside her. "Britta? Can you handle this by yourself?"

"Sure, no problem – it's early yet. Go on."

Rose wiped her hands on her chef's apron, and laid a palm against Quiola's forehead, her gaze full of concern. "I don't think you're running a fever."

"No, it's not like that," said Quiola lowering her voice to no more than a whisper, which got lost in the clamor of pots, flares, chopping, dicing, the fragrance of onion and garlic, vegetables simmering, meat sizzling.

"Hey," said Rose to a young man. "Watch how much of that oil you use! I'm not Mrs. Gotrocks, ya know! So tell me, Quiola, how don't you feel well?"

"I'm sick."

"To your stomach?"

"Not exactly. Maybe. Please, Mom, can't we talk about this upstairs?"

"Have you lost your mind? Do you see what's going on here, hmm? Dinner. I can't just leave and you know it. Quiola, honey, what is wrong with you? Do you have a headache? I don't think it can be flu, you aren't running a fever and you don't look flushed."

"Order up, number nine!" cried Britta. "Now, George!"

"Never mind," said Quiola. "I'll go up and lay down."

"Do you think aspirin would help?"

Quiola gave her mother a tragic look. "No."

"Honest to Peter, Quiola, why won't you tell me what's wrong?"

"I can't. Not here."

Rose folded her arms and looked her daughter over. "All right, then, let's go. Britta? Be back in five?"

"No problem, boss."

Nodding, Rose threaded her way through the orchestra of preparation that was her restaurant's kitchen ballet, to a set of back stairs that led to her apartment. Quiola followed, watching her mother's small back and slightly hunched shoulders, wondering how to say, how to tell her mother what she knew: she was dying.

Once they'd gotten inside, and the noise from below muted to a distant rumble, Rose felt her daughter's forehead again, and took a bottle of aspirin out of a kitchen shelf. She filled a glass from the tap, gestured for Quiola to sit at the little kitchen table beside an open window, and sat opposite to her. "All right, honey. Tell me. What's wrong?"

Quiola shook her head, then lowered it, to stare at her feet.

Rose waited. After a few more tense moments she said. "It's not a boy. Tell me it's not a boy? Not that no-good Romero you went around with last year?"

"Mom, we were just friends. He's funny."

"Funny or crazy. Depends on how you look at it but I say friends like that one you don't need."

"Well it's not him. It's not a boy. You've warned me a thousand times –"

"With good reason. You don't need to make the same mistake I did."

"Fine. That's not it, anyway – I – I think I'm dying."

"You think… for heaven's sake, Quiola what a thing to say to your mother! Why do you think you're dying?"

"I'm bleeding and it won't stop. I've soaked right through the toilet paper I stuffed…up…there…I'm dying, Mama. I couldn't tell the nuns – it's too awful to be bleeding…."

"Down there? Oh, sweetheart, it's all right. You're fine! You're not dying, you're just growing up. Don't you remember I told you about the flower – the monthlies. I told you it would probably start soon, just a few weeks ago."

Quiola stared. "But you said it would just be a little – not like this, I'm *bleeding.*"

Rose stood up. "I thought you would be like me, a little trickle at first. But of course we aren't all the same. Some of us start with a flood. Your grandmother did – but she had her old-fashioned ways of handling it, and said it just made her proud. Proud! Of the curse? Let me get you what you need – you've seen my pads, haven't you?"

"Curse?"

Rose turned around. "Don't you think so? Most of my friends call it the curse. A mess like that, every month and for what? To have a baby – thank god you're bleeding and not pregnant is all I have to say."

✦

Paris, 1960. C.C. traveled aboard a steamer, to live in the City of Light for a while, with Liz Moore. Paul had willed Lizzie everything, having no one else, which included a Paris studio he hadn't used since before the War, and it was in that one, high-ceilinged room, the kitchen a mere hotplate wedged into a closet with a sink and a glass fronted door, so the 'kitchen' could be closed off from the 'dining room' and miniscule bathroom, that she'd found a certain peace about his passing. Not an entirely peaceful peace, lined like a too-thin linen garment with a sheer slip of fear: what would she do now, without him?

Yet more immediately that summer she had another question: what was she going to do with Nancy's daughter? Twenty-four, all grown but as far as Liz could see, Smith College hadn't changed the Davis girl much, though it had given her the veneer of a sophisticate – she smoked, drank martinis, wore the latest, no matter what it was – but then again, most middle-class American girls in 1960 feigned so much world-weary sophistication. C.C. was no different than the rest: she arrived off ship with a Samsonite set, complete with pert little make-up bag, though Liz knew C.C. never made up.

Must be Nancy's doing, she thought, as she gave the girl a customary Parisian kiss; predictably, C.C. found the unfashionable 11th arrondissement studio appalling. It took her a week to give up her white gloves, and she never quite stopped walking on her toes in the morning, sure the place had mice: it didn't. What it did have was birdsong in the bathroom, some kind of acoustic trick that funneled the lark and pigeon tweets down the roof and into the bathroom, as if the birds had nested in the pipes.

One Sunday morning found Lizzie with *Le Monde*, late coffee and oranges in a sunny chair on the enclosed patio. The cracked cement floor was as dingy as the dead delphinium and sagging clothesline, but she was reasonably happy. She restricted her view to the oranges and the dark sweet coffee or, better still, when she leaned back, to the sky, past the backs of the apartments with the shuttered Sunday windows, their mute façades. She'd taken, lately, to watching birds, an idling sort of interest, born of loneliness.

"What are you doing?" asked C.C. from the solitary window that looked out on the front patio.

"What does it look like? I'm writing a piano concerto."

"It looks like lazy to me."

"And just what should I be doing?"

C.C. stepped out onto the patio, barefoot, wearing a man's shirt, her hair braided into a knot at the back of her neck. She looked every inch a well-scrubbed American.

Lizzie regarded her houseguest appraisingly. "Lovely."

"Do you think so?" C.C. made a quick pirouette.

"Of course. I've always thought you were a pretty child."

"I'm not a child."

Liz tipped back her chair. "Aren't you?"

"No. I wish you'd stop treating me like one. I want to go out to the bars and cafés at night. I want to hear jazz, and dance. I want to meet…" she hesitated, her glance on the ground. Then she gave Liz a frowning look. "I want to meet a girl."

Liz sat very still, tipping the chair back into place. "What sort of girl?"

C.C. said nothing. Slowly, she sat down on the stoop.

"I see," said Liz. "Have you told your mother?"

"Oh, no. Not Dad, either. I can't. They'd be so – shocked."

"You'll have to tell them someday." Liz folded the paper. "Sooner or later. I won't lie to them. I couldn't. Not to Nancy."

"I know."

"And are you sure? Sometimes, you know, it passes, that feeling. You're young."

C.C. laughed. "I'd be lying if I said I wanted a boy. I've tried. I dated a couple Amherst guys, my freshman year, whooo, what a mistake! I couldn't stand them, not at all, the very idea of petting made me queasy. I couldn't get away fast enough. I thought, of course, that there was something wrong with me, but to whom could I spill the beans? Then one night, late, I was talking to this other girl in my dorm – we were in French class together – and I told her, well, I told her how much I couldn't stand boys and the next thing I know, she's kissing me. And I liked it. I liked it a lot. We became roommates. Her name's Susan Perry."

"And you fell in love with this Susan Perry?"

"Yes."

"And where is she now?"

C.C. pouted. "I don't know. When she found out I had a ticket to Paris she threw a fit. 'You're not going without me!' she kept shouting, but how could I bring Suz? I couldn't ask Mom and Dad for another ticket, and I couldn't see myself asking you to put us both up. I haven't heard from her since I left the States. I wrote. Nothing. No offense, Liz, but I'm –"

"Horny," said Liz.

C.C. blushed, then, to the roots of her pale hair and stared at the concrete floor.

Liz stood, and smoothed out the front of her summer dress. "We need bread and cheese for lunch so I'm going to run up to the bakery. Why don't you get dressed? After lunch we can go by that gallery I told you about. Tonight you can go wherever you please. I won't ask too many questions."

C.C. looked up, almost in tears. "But…I wouldn't know where to go!"

"You don't think I would know, do you?"

"You knew Gertrude Stein."

Liz laughed. "Knew? I met Stein, once, a long time ago. If you were an American artist in Paris at that time, you ended up at 27. But believe me, she had no use for any girl other than that Alice, whose job it was to shoo all the wives and women into a corner under those goddamn floating doves or love-birds on the wallpaper, while Gertrude held forth to the men. I believe she was of the opinion that women weren't really artists, which made my blood boil. Besides, that was a long time ago and, well, a different world. I wouldn't know how to locate – what you're looking for."

"Me and Suz found a bar in New York."

"Of course you did."

"But here – I don't know. I don't know –"

"You don't know the territory," said Liz. "Well, honey, neither do I. But I do know how to manage the baker. So go get dressed. Maybe between the two of us we can dope something out and come up with a solution."

Which turned out to be a round-trip transatlantic ticket for Susan Perry. Liz didn't want C.C. wandering about or sitting in some bar, hoping to meet some girl, when the person she really wanted, after all, was Susan.

5. RUN AWAY

On the concrete patio of the Paris studio, under a cloudy sky, Quiola finished a cup of black coffee. At nearly two o'clock in the sticky August warm, the day dragged. She pushed back from the small wire table, hunted up an umbrella and then, locking the studio's grille behind her, walked to the 20th arrondissement.

Cimitière Père Lachaise, the largest garden in Paris, is renowned for its eclectic mixture of famous, infamous and obscure dead, all jammed together in a miniaturized version of the city. Americans often make a pilgrimage to Jim Morrison's grave, but not Quiola. Striding off the broad, living street and through the high gateway in the graveyard, she hurried past tourists. The Avenue Principale, lined with marble coffins and mausoleums, some neglected, some with flowers or new glass, set among headstones and trees, is one of the least narrow. Sunlight dappled cobbles as she approached the Monument Aux Morts, with its sobering and weird sculptural reminder of the direction we are all headed in; then she took a series of cement stairs, winding her way past tombs wedged shoulder to shoulder, over to the Avenue de St. Mary to stroll beside Etienne Godde's elaborate cement coffins for Molière and La Fontaine. But she had a destination: the Gassion-Piaf Famille's granite gravestone.

Standing beside the high-polished marble memorial, sweating in the heat, she wished to hear the singer's voice again. But she hadn't brought any Piaf overseas with her, and buying anything, from a newspaper to supper, was so unnerving she wouldn't dare try for a CD. No matter how many times she visited France, no matter how long she stayed, a command of anything remotely like spoken French eluded her. She could read, she could understand, but she could not make her tongue or lips serve the soufflé of vowels and sibilants with the proper lift. No matter how wonderful the bread, she had never managed the alchemy that made the French word for it, "pain," translate into anything other than the English word, pain.

After a few moments, she walked out to the shady Avenue Circulaire, to the very minimal concrete slab for Gertrude Stein. The newly mown grass was sweet, and someone had left a fresh rose. She tried to remember Liz Moore's pithy account of Stein, but failed.

"I'll have to ask," she murmured aloud and walked on.

Lingering in the city of the dead did not bother her as much as did all the shuttered tight, forbidding second and third story windows she passed as she re-entered the Paris of the living. The absolute refusal of those dark evergreen shutters saddened her, as did the rain, which came down all at once, as if in a hurry to drench pedestrians. She had to leap over a massive puddle gathered at a street corner housing a tiny children's park, complete with a carousel of rocketships to ride. Close to the studio, she gave up on a meal out, and went home. Slipping off sodden, grayed-out tennis shoes, rolling off damp cotton socks, she tiptoed across the cold wood floor to the calendar tacked on the wall beside the desk and crossed off the day.

✦

C.C. opened the squeaky condo door to find Amelia, sitting in the hall, blue-eyed, statuesque, imperial and hungry.

"Always know when its suppertime, don't you?" she said to the cat, who arched her back, curling a chocolate tail into a perfect question mark. The condo was quiet with only Amelia in it, not exactly eerie but flat and mournful, empty shadows behind shadows. C.C. switched on a hall light, and another Chinese-inspired lamp in the living room, then went to the kitchen, Amelia hopping before her in a rabbit-like gait. Tuna yesterday, today liver and beef. The phone rang over the electric grind of the can opener, but Amelia got her dinner before receiver left cradle.

"Hello?" said C.C.

Nothing.

"Hello?"

"Quiola?"

"No, I'm sorry, she's out of town. Can I take a message?"

"Out of town," repeated a woman's voice. "Where?"

"Who is this?"

"An old friend."

C.C. crossed her ankles and leaned against the kitchen sink. "Who is this, please?"

"Who are you?"

"An old friend," she countered. "I'm taking care of Quiola's place while she's away. Now. Who is this and can I take a message?"

"Charlotte Davis? Isn't it? This is Evelyn. Evelyn Porter."

C.C. gripped the phone. "Oh. Hello. What do you want?"

"Where is Quiola?"

"In Paris."

"At the studio?"

"Yes."

"Are you fucking her again?"

"None of your business," snapped C.C. and slammed the phone down, muttering, "bitch." She slid to the floor and clasped her arms around her knees. Amelia, done with the beef and liver, padded over.

"So long ago," C.C. said to the cat, touching the brown, dry triangle of a nose. "Why do I still care, hmm?"

✦

Summer, 1982. Paris sweltered, and Paul's old studio felt airless, stifling.

"The chickens are dying," said Quiola. Lying naked on the unmade double bed, she tried not to move.

"What did you say?" asked C.C. from the tiny bathroom. She'd filled the chipped claw-foot tub halfway with cool water to soak her feet. Sitting on the tub's rim in a sleeveless t-shirt, she wiggled her toes and draped a soaked towel over her shoulders.

Quiola raised her voice, "I said, chickens are dying – in the paper this morning. They don't really sweat, and since the temperature stays high, they can't cool down like normal, so they're dying of heat stroke."

"Me, too. Tonight we go some place with air conditioning. I can't stand it. I need a good night's sleep. I'm not as young as you are, remember."

"We could find a restaurant that has air."

"That, too. Dinner, and a hotel room."

No response.

"Quiola?"

"How much will it cost?"

"I don't care. In fact, let's make it *très* expensive. We need a treat. A night at the Ritz or something."

"I don't have a lot of cash, you know."

"Doesn't matter. I do." C.C. lifted her blistered feet out of the tub and set them down on a dry green towel she'd spread on the gray tile floor. Pentagon-shaped, the cool tiles beaded water. "People at the Ritz know my family. My parents used to stay there whenever they came over, and Ted still makes a yearly trip *en famille*. I can already feel the air conditioning. Not to mention the sheets."

"I thought the Ritz was being renovated."

"Yeah, when Al-Fayed took over. Doesn't mean the place is closed."

"Who?"

"Mohammed Al-Fayed. Didn't you see *Chariots of Fire* last year?"

"Sure. Why?"

C.C. stepped out of the bathroom. "One of the producers was Mohammed's son, Dodi al-Fayed. A controversial family; I think they came from Egypt. Anyway, they bought the Ritz and have been renovating it bit by bit. But we can still stay there. Let's do it now before I melt."

"I don't know –"

"What's the problem?"

"I – it's just not right."

"What's not?"

"You paying for everything."

C.C. as sat down on the edge of the bed. "I have enough money for both of us."

"Yes, I know you do."

"Well?"

"Maybe you should go. Get a good night's sleep, as you said."

"Are you nuts? Why would I want to go there by myself? Come on, Quiola, you didn't mind so much when we were in Italy."

"I did mind. I just didn't know how to tell you. I don't like being kept."

"Kept! I'm not keeping you, I'm sharing what I have. We've been sharing with each other, haven't we?"

"But it's not an even exchange. I can't treat. I can barely pay for my half."

"I don't care."

"But I do."

"This is ridiculous. This whole argument is ridiculous." She stood, picked up the phone and rang the hotel.

Three hours later, the two women and one suitcase were dropped off at the front door of the Ritz in the Place Vendôme. Vast, imposing, the old hotel stood like a well-proportioned stallion, regal, quiet, and muscular, as if always awaiting some royal rider. Such grand architectural repose made Quiola panic.

"I can't go in there," she said, tugging at C.C.'s sleeve.

"Of course you can. Just walk."

"But look at me! Look at my clothes!"

C.C. stopped at the curb of the cobble-stoned street, and turned. "I am no fashion plate myself, am I? We have a reservation. My American Express card is just itching to be run through. If you really want new clothes, we are certainly in the right part of the city for it. Didn't we just pass Dior?"

"Stop that. Stop teasing."

"Then you stop being a baby and follow me inside where there is air conditioning before we are so drenched in our own sweat we'll look even more down on our luck, and smell worse." And with that, she marched up the street and through the revolving doors.

✦

Smack in the middle of a Minnesota snowstorm, Liz Moore borrowed – as in stole – a threadbare flannel shirt, faded cord trousers, a floppy hat and a thick old torn sweater, one from each of her brothers, then snuck out of the family farmhouse in the dead of freezing white night.

It was 1924. She was sixteen, furious, and lucky she didn't die.

It started this way: there was a local buzz about some soldier-boy from her neck of the woods, who had been publishing these racy stories in the *Saturday Evening Post*. Stories about young people, people from Liz's dream world: fast, audacious, beautiful girls who did what they wanted, with whom they wanted. A friend from school stopped by the farm that afternoon to loan Liz Mr. F. Scott Fitzgerald's first two novels.

The Moore place wasn't big, but big enough to have three separate barns: far-barn, near-barn and the tiny Father's barn. She stuffed the first book under a coat, told her mother she needed to curry the new mare and headed across the pasture.

"I thought," she said to C.C. and her girlfriend Susan Perry, as they sat over coffee in a pastry shop one afternoon in the fall of 1960, after Liz had paid for Susan's passage to Paris from the States, "that no one would be in there. But I was wrong. I saw Father before he saw me, so I ducked into an empty stall and peered through the bars. He was on one knee, reaching under a rickety wooden shelf. It was dark, and at first I couldn't see what he was doing. Our Sally, the barn cat, was squalling and then I figured it out – he was shoving her litter into a burlap sack. I screamed at his shoulders. He just stood up with the creepy crawling sack, looked and me and turned his back. For some reason, that was the last straw. I ran. Bobbed my hair for money, bummed my way to Minneapolis, then New York, London, finally, here, Paris."

"What happened to the kittens?" asked Susan. A tall, stoop-shouldered girl, she'd folded herself into the corner seat of the table.

Liz blinked. "Why, I'm sure he drowned them."

"I don't want to think about that," said C.C. She'd pulled her wire-back chair as close to Susan's as possible, which made Liz feel a little like she was holding court.

"A working farm is a cruel place," she said. "He'd drowned a litter of Sal's before. Anyhow, I never went back. I made it here, to Paris, with nothing more to sell except myself. But I wasn't going back."

Susan's eyes went round. "Did you?"

"Sell myself? No. I dressed like a boy. If I had sold myself, some john would've been very angry." She shrugged, smiled and added, "or maybe not."

Both girls giggled nervously.

"Besides," said Liz, "I was bare bones. I'm not proud of some of the things I did, but I survived."

"And?" prodded C.C. "What *did* you do?"

Liz reached into her jacket pocket for a pack of Lucky Strikes and lit a cigarette, blowing smoke out fast. "Things. But one night, I didn't care about anything at all except this one particular man."

"A man? What man? Not Paul."

"Want a cig?" asked Susan.

"Sure. Light one for me, would you?" C.C. narrowed her eyes. "Who did you fall for, Liz? What man?"

"All of Paris fell, all the world, really. We all fell in love that night. We knew he was coming, but so many had failed, everyone held their breath. France was mourning their own, lost somewhere off Nova Scotia. This young American – a Minnesota boy! – was flying solo. I heard people call him a fool, a kid with a watery grave. But there we were, and so far as anyone could tell, he was going to land, as he said he would, on the field at Le Bourget."

Susan blinked through the thickening cigarette smoke, and handed C.C. one she'd lit. "Who?"

"Lindbergh," said C.C. "Of course."

"Lindbergh? But that was a million years ago."

Liz laughed. "Not quite. I'm not that ancient, even if Lindbergh was the hero of my youth. I hitched a ride, walked when I had to, and got to Le Bourget as a crowd was gathering in for the night. After a while, it got very quiet and my heart went dead: was the adventure over? Had he gone full fathom five? And then we heard it, that buzzing hum, the sound of war, the sound of a mail drop – a plane. He'd made it. In an instant the field broke into a sea of whooping Parisians. I caught a glimpse of him as he climbed up out of the cockpit, squinting into the headlights, utterly shocked. In an interview I read later, he said he'd expected to land in the dark with a few mechanics about, so was puzzled, then downright alarmed, by the crowd of cars, all beaming the joy of their headlights into his face. He called us the Reception Committee of Fifty-Thousand, and said we were probably the most dangerous part of the whole flight."

"Nearly ripped Lindy, and his plane, to bits," said C.C. She'd heard the story a thousand times.

"They did. Souvenir hunters. But I thought: this is the new world, this world of flight. We won't go back, never go back to rules and earthbound things. I was young. But a part of me can still feel the blood of that moment, the soaring visions of – what?" Liz fiddled with the white pack of cigarettes, making a crinkled corner dance.

"*Pluck?*" asked Susan, naming the Moore C.C. owned.

Liz shrugged. "I wanted to paint the unseen. My whole life changed as the world changed, because after Lindbergh flew the Atlantic, time telescoped. I remember thinking that if I could hitch a ride home, I'd be in the states in three days, rather than three months. Now that, my dears," she said, smiling and flicking ash into a glass tray, "was something to think about."

"But he didn't fly back, did he?" asked Susan.

Liz fanned smoke from her face. "No. He was snapped up by the American ambassador and whisked off to see Important People. Me, I hitched a ride back to town, and sort of staggered to the atelier I was sharing with two other painters. Dirty and tired, I just crawled into my gear and slept."

"How long did you stay in Paris?"

"A couple years. There were a lot of Americans here in twenty-six, twenty-seven, and that summer, after Lindbergh's flight, I fell in with a group, students and would-be writers, many drunk on Hemingway and living like the *The Sun Also Rises*. A lot of girls in the Montparnasse cut their hair short, drank, smoked. When I found a tiny studio I could afford, I turned from a boy back into a girl. Later, after my work was beginning to sell, an older woman I'd met at a gallery took me over to the Rue de L'Odéon. I was too shy to go by myself so Rebecca West took me over, introduced Sylvia Beach, bought Joyce's newest, and left me to wander about by myself. That Beach woman was nice. You know, C.C. you remind me, a little, of her. "

"I do? How?"

"Your hair, for one, and she was –"

"Did you meet Hemingway?" interrupted Susan.

Liz shook her head. "Not exactly."

"Not exactly? Like you not exactly but actually met Stein?" asked C.C.

"Did you really meet Stein?"

"Suz, I told you before she met Stein."

"Excuse me?" said Liz, stubbing out her cigarette. "I'm still here, if you please. Yes, I really met Gertrude Stein. I disliked her. Hemingway – I had no idea that the man with the beard I saw one day was or would soon become the Papa – I never liked his work, either, so I paid no mind. Besides, what I remember most from that summer was painting, Picasso, a parade, a funeral, and riots against the Americans – but by then I was more French than American, so I got away easily enough."

Both girls looked puzzled, so Liz added, "Sacco and Vanzetti were executed that summer – a shoemaker and a peddler. Most Frenchmen thought they were innocent. Working men attacked Americans in Montparnasse – a few of my friends got hurt, and the gendarmerie had a devil of a time keeping order. To make matters worse, that September the American Legion paraded down the Champs-Élysées. What a day that was – rain steady, Isadora Duncan's funeral in Lachaise, the crazy loud Americans on the street. I admired Duncan, so I was upset. Such an awful accident."

Susan giggled.

Liz's eyes narrowed. "What's funny?"

"Nothing," said Susan, blushing violently. "It's just –"

But Liz plowed over the girl. "Remind me, Susan Perry, to laugh at your funeral."

"Hey!" said C.C., as Susan burst into tears. "Come on, Lizzie!"

"Your *friend*," said Liz, wrinkling her nose as if a foul odor had crept in upon the pastry shop, "is cruel."

By now, Susan was sobbing. C.C. had an arm around her girlfriend's shoulders, and an angry bead on Liz. "Enough! We sometimes make jokes about Duncan. You can't be pious all the time. Wearing a ridiculous silk scarf so big and long it gets caught in the wheels of a car is funny. It's also vain. She was kind of odd, wasn't she?"

Liz folded her arms. "She was a genius. And it was a horrible death. Violent, sudden and –" she stopped, gazing at the two girls. Susan had laid her head on C.C.'s shoulder. " All right, and silly.

But she was still a genius. Come, let's pay the piper and go. I've had enough of the past, haven't you?"

✦

Nancy Jones Davis stood in the lobby of the Paris Ritz, waiting for her new husband. He was asking the concierge, in halting French, what might be the easiest way to get to a bookstore his wife wanted to visit. Barely twenty years old, married a week, she'd already begun to take the measure of her husband, only to find his sleeves, as it were, a bit short, and his trousers a bit too long. Her infatuation with the young doctor had begun to mellow out into affection. She stood, nervous and a bit impatient. Her French, learned first in boarding school and then at Smith College, was better than his. And besides, she knew exactly where the Rue de L'Odéon was, she didn't need directions. But he had to ask.

She tugged at a glove, touched her hat, and settled her clutch a little more firmly under her arm. Tom headed across the rich red carpet to her. With his needle nose and already thinning hair, he wasn't a beauty, but he was funny, and such a dedicated doctor, her heart made a little surge of *he's mine*.

"Darling," he said, slipping a hand to her elbow. "Are you sure you want to go to this bookstore? I think it must be a tad disreputable."

She laughed. "Of course it is. Every artist I know talks about it."

"Rue de l'Odéon. Is it in a poor neighborhood?"

"Come on, Tom. Paul would be mortified if we didn't go."

"Do you want a cab?"

"No, let's walk."

"I thought it sounded far," he said, glancing behind him.

"Oh, Tom," said Nancy merrily. "Nothing is ever that far in Paris."

He smiled in a way his bride would come to understand as both apologetic and annoyed, and followed her lead.

Cold and clear, the flat, unruffled cerulean sky arched over the Seine as they crossed it, two young Americans between the wars, burnished by the armor of a yet untarnished love. They said little. The light was too perfect, the city too various, all of it new to Tom, all of it beloved by Nancy. While he took note of streets Parisian, she drank in the comfort of sunflowers or daisies sold in dull silver pots, ivy and architecture, the winter's sharp metal air. She wore a cloche she'd bought yesterday, one with a small brim, and a fur trimmed coat from Revillion & Cie, 89 Rue de Petite Champs, bought with her mother's money and at her mother's insistence, though the extravagance made Tom wince. When Nancy caught a glimpse of herself in the bookshop's plate window, she felt, well, quite modern.

"Is this it?" asked Tom, squinting through the glass.

"There's the Bard," she said, pointing to a portrait of Shakespeare hanging above their heads from an iron rod. "Yes, this is it."

"What did Paul tell you about this place?"

"If you are an American artist, you must visit."

"But we're not artists."

"Oh bother. You read, don't you? This is a bookstore, isn't it?" and she stepped up into the shop. Tom doffed his hat and followed. Once inside, he relaxed. He was, after all, a reader, and the shop was crammed floor to ceiling with books. Several walls hosted black and white framed portraits of men and women, only two of whom Tom knew, but if you were living in or near New York, as Tom and Nancy were, it would have been hard not to know the Fitzgeralds. The papers followed the couple as they tore around town.

Two women were standing beside the marble fireplace, underneath about a dozen or so of the framed portraits. One wore a neat tweed jacket and skirt set, with a round white collar and a soft, striped silk bowtie, her thickly curled brownish hair bobbed to the earlobe. The other, younger woman, also in a short, dark bob, wore a green drop-waist dress and leaned against the top of the hearth, writing something on a small white card. Both women had strong features, the kind dubbed handsome rather than pretty.

"There —" said the younger woman. "Now I'm one of the Company, too."

"I'm glad," her companion said, taking the card. "Is there anything you'd like to take today?"

The woman shook her head, just as a man stepped in from the street, or rather blew in at a clip that was almost a dash. Nancy worried about the possibility of books flying off shelves as he whisked by the laden tables to claim the younger woman by slipping an arm around her green drop-waist. The older woman said something low, which made the big man laugh and in another moment, the couple left.

A rough, Nancy decided, and went back to her browsing. When she heard the woman in the bowtie sigh, and say, "Poor Bumby," she felt confirmed in her opinion of the one-man windstorm.

"Who was that?" asked Tom, suddenly at Nancy's side.

"How should I know?"

"He looked familiar."

"All Americans look familiar."

"Oh? And how do you know the man was an American?"

"He looked American."

Tom laughed and Nancy smiled. "Well, he did," she said, putting the book she'd been looking over back on the shelf. "Big galoot like that."

"Want to bet on it?"

"Why? We both thought he was an American."

"Hmm," said Tom, rubbing his earlobe. "True. I'm going to ask, though. I want to know." And he stepped over to the woman in the bowtie, who was filing library cards. "Excuse me, Ma'am?"

The woman looked up. "Yes, may I help you find something?"

"No, thank you. I do have a question, though – if I may ask, was that man who just left an American?"

Which made Sylvia Beach laugh outright. "Why yes," she said. "Oh, yes. I don't think there's anyone so American as Hem. Would you like to see some of his work? These short stories are his –" and she reached for a small pile of books on a table, a small pile of *In Our Time*, by Ernest Hemingway.

"Never heard of him," said Tom, looking over the slim volume.

"You will," said Sylvia Beach. "Trust me, you will."

✦

"I read somewhere," said Quiola, sitting on the blue and gold floral brocade spread of the king-sized Ritz bed, "that after WWII, Ernest Hemingway was greeted by the doorman at this hotel and asked if he'd come to pick up his trunk. They'd kept it safe for him, during the War. That's why he wrote *A Moveable Feast*, finding all his old stuff in that trunk."

"Yeah? Have you read it?" One by one, C.C. hung their few shirts, two pairs of blue jeans and a light zippered jacket in the closet, unpacking their shared suitcase. The Ritz had given them a two-room suite, with a sitting area, a desk and a bathroom.

"No. Should I?"

"It's mean. He savages the ex-pats, especially Fitzgerald. Who, by the way, drank himself silly downstairs at the bar. With Hemingway."

"The place is too much," said Quiola glancing over to the gilded hearth. "It's all so, I don't know, gold." She shivered at the stately, ornate, impersonal pomp of the room.

"Ritzy?" C.C. put the empty Samsonite on the floor of the closet, next to two pairs of loafers and a pair of once-white tennis shoes.

"Our clothes look sad and lonely in there."

C.C. turned around and put her hands on her hips. "Would you just stop?"

"Sorry."

"Aren't you pleased we're not melting anymore?"

"I guess."

C.C. rolled her eyes, stomped one foot like an enraged elf, and marched off to the bathroom. "I'm taking a shower," she called over her shoulder. "A *cold* shower."

"Okay." Quiola got up from the bed and went over to the unusable gilt hearth, upon whose marble mantle sat a fat gold clock and two twisted gold-plate candelabras. Behind the clock and candelabras was a long plate mirror, which reflected her and the room, the brocade bed with its assortment of tasseled throw pillows, and the heavy, matching brocade curtains. Quiola examined her face briefly, for blemishes. Finding none, she tucked a strand of hair behind her ear, and wandered over to the window, which had a view of Place Vendôme, the vast square of grey cobblestone surrounded by a certain architectural uniformity, dotted with iron streetlamp trees, each one sprouting three lanterns, dead quiet in the daytime, all sight lines leading to a central spiraled monument, the Colonne de Vendôme, atop of which stood Napoleon. Quiola thought it probably the ugliest thing she'd seen in Paris, and when she read in her guidebook that the artist Gustave Corbet had helped tear it down during the Commune in 1871, her heart went out to him. Unfortunately for Quiola's sense of beauty, the column had been restored by 1874.

"What are you moping about now?" C.C., finished with her shower, was mummified in white terrycloth, head to toe.

Quiola turned away from the window. "Grandeur."

"Parisians are good at it." She unwrapped her hair, shook it out and toweled the curls. "Hungry?"

"Not really."

"Well, I am. Let's go down for a drink, and see what's on the menu."

"You want to eat here?"

"Why not?"

"I don't know. I thought we'd go out."

C.C. sat down in one of the brocade armchairs and crossed her ankles. "We can do that, if you like. Where?"

"Oh, come on C.C., I don't know Paris the way you do. What about that café where we had the chicken and pepper thing? Or that Vietnamese place near the studio?"

"We've been to that place three nights out of five."

"So? It's good."

"It's also cheap. Don't make me fight you every single step. Let's just relax. Go downstairs. I'm sure there's something tasty at the Club."

Early the next morning, Quiola snuck out before C.C. woke, after collecting a map, her room-key, sunglasses and enough francs for brioche and coffee. The lobby was abandoned, the doorman invisibly visible. She left and practically dashed to the Rue de La Paix, only to find herself in front of a dark and empty Tiffany display window. Ducking her head, she marched forward. No one was about. All the expensive storefronts were locked tight, alarms at the ready and although the sun had only just risen, the heat was already wet and palpable.

As often happens to anyone who simply wanders Paris without a clear destination, Quiola ended up along the river. Book-sellers and such were just opening their wooden stalls; flowers and fruit, old movie posters, old, tattered *Life* and *Look* magazines and the like were being hauled out of their nightly storage, arranged and re-arranged. At one booth, for sale in small wooden cages, tiny birds, cinder gray with heart's blood wingtips and tails, hopped from post to swing and back. She watched the creatures for a few minutes, just for the sheer beauty of their feathers, until the vendor, chatting at her, began to extol them as highly decorative, undemanding pets.

✦

Pacing around her San Francisco apartment, her heart beating a two-step of pure fear, Quiola sank into the deep middle of a full-blown panic attack. Her hands shook. Sweat beaded her dark forehead, and the salt stung the cut below her bruised eye. She paced back and forth in the bedroom, back and forth, her gait unsteady.

"What am I going to do?" she murmured, glancing at the closed bedroom door. "What, what –?" She paced over to the window, but the fog that morning was dense and so the world seemed nothing but full of swirling gray, which almost made her stop breathing altogether. She turned away and threw herself on the bed, crying with the sorrowful intensity of an infant, shaking the bed.

Suddenly she sat up, listening. "Hello?"

Nothing.

"Evelyn? That you? Evelyn?"

Silence.

"Evelyn!" she shouted, hoarse. "Answer me!" She went to the bedroom door, closed her hand around the doorknob and then just stood there, as if frozen. She stood there, unable to open the door, for long enough for her neck to stiffen, long enough that the knob grew slick. Then she let go to pace again but after a few steps inside the cage of her head, words burst open like flares.

You cannot let them win. Even after they've stolen everything from you, you have to push on. Do you hear me, Quiola? Take it from a woman who knows. If you fall to the bottom, look up.

"Mom," she whispered. "Mama? I've hit bottom."

Okay, then, look up.

RUN AWAY

Quiola stood still. Stiffly she marched to the bedroom door, yanked it open. The living room was as she had left it last night, tidy. She said, "Evelyn?" into the silence, and when only silence answered, she saw her mother's old steamer trunk, and knew what to do. She took all the things off the top of it, magazines, mail, an empty vase, then dragged it into the bedroom. Frantic and yet precise, she folded her clothes – all of them – into the steamer, and then went about the apartment, sorting, separating her self from Evelyn by the magic of things; she slipped these three necklaces, one of her mother's, one a gift from C.C., one she'd bought herself into a velvet bag, took *Collected Poems*, her talismanic *Ariel*, *Moby Dick*, and *The Awakening* off the shelf; put all her work into a portfolio, then brushes, tubes of paint, into the trunk. Feeling like a surgeon, she severed the violent nerves and joints of fear and desire that knitted her to Evelyn, bleeding inside but determined that morning to push on, to get out of that place that she'd come to, and be free once again.

✦

An evening in the City of Lights, C.C. always said, was always supposed to end on a piercing bright aesthetic note, not simply fade like an old TV. But Quiola had never felt the spike, not back in 1982, not last year, not now. It was after eleven, and although the restaurant was full of diners, she also felt as if she was the only real being in a colony of merry, contented ghosts.

Or maybe it was the wine. She wasn't sure.

"*Un autre?*" asked the barkeep, and it struck her that he was being irresponsible. She'd had enough.

"*Non, merci. S'il vous plaît?*" she asked, gesturing with money since she'd forgotten the word for bill.

Leaving, she stepped into the warm, lively night street and walked back up the Rue de Roquette to her flat, her hands in her pockets. It was raining lightly. It had been raining on and off. It would go on raining, after she left. She only had one day more, now, in Paris, and she was counting the minutes. Nothing, not even the pleasing solitude of her last week, could make her feel happy. Certain places had grace, yes, and beauty inhabited even the headstones at Père Lachaise, yes. But all she wanted was to go home. For good; she would never return to Paris – she would never live in a city again. All the years of her childhood, moving from apartment to apartment, each smaller than the last seemed to be crowding her. She wanted air.

A letter was waiting in the box at the flat, and since she was not expecting any correspondence, the sight of the slight blue note resting by itself sideways in the mail slot alarmed her. She hurried inside and switched on the light. The envelope had been typed, and there was no return address. She ripped it open with haste, worried, illogically, that something might have happened to Amelia – but *C.C. would call, not write*, she thought as she unfolded the single page.

> *Quiola:*
> *Knowing you are half a world away, I am comforted. I am comforted by that distance & hope with all my heart that you decide to stay there, for good.*

Quiola sat down.

> *Years ago, you broke me. You know it. When I came back to San Francisco and found that you'd gone, just left our place, gone, I collapsed. I dropped to the floor, and lay there, sobbing. Was that what you wanted? Did you care? I don't, anymore. I've finally managed, after all these years, to burn anything you'd left, everything you'd ever given me, anything you'd even touched. I built a bonfire in the backyard last night just like you said Sylvia Plath did, burning Ted Hughes's leavings. I chanted at your evil, and prayed you ill.*
> *Never come near me again, you witch. Ever.*
> *I will kill you.*

She – Evelyn – hadn't even signed the letter. Quiola felt a rush, then it passed and she was left holding a thin sheet of angry paper which she folded up and left on the kitchen table. She "shed" her damp clothes, got into sweats and a t-shirt, crawled into bed.

She didn't turn the lights off.

From the kitchen table, the paper sat, not quite mute. She stared at it, and could not sleep. Sometime around dawn she got up again, lit a match and burned the letter in the bathroom sink. Her hands shook. Evelyn never did anything small, and now, what had started out on the rocket fuel of lust was still flaming, flaming hatred.

When Quiola woke again, she felt groggy. She flipped over onto her side, slipping her hands under her cheek. Gray light filtered in the studio front, half-shuttered window. Without moving, she let her gaze cross the familiar space, already half-stripped of the personal, prepared for new paint and new owners, young Parisians who'd never heard of Liz Moore, let alone Paul Gaines or C.C. Ryder –

"…or me," she muttered. "Ha."

She sat up, pulling the blankets with her, to clasp her hands around her knees. "No one will ever hear of me," she said to herself, and got out of bed. She stepped into the bathroom. Ashes of Evelyn's note still smudged the sink. She washed them away and ran the shower. Pulling on a thin cotton robe, she went to the kitchen-space and made coffee, taking her cup with her, weary already, back to the shower.

Later, as she walked home from the grocers with her dinner in her cotton mesh sack, Quiola made a slight detour to stroll beside the Seine and found that they were there, still, not of course the exact same birds, nor the same vendor certainly, but yet the same sort of gray and red-tailed tiny birds in wooden cages for sale as she'd seen in 1982, busy grooming powdery dove-gray feathers, tipped in a deep sparkling red, like snake's blood.

6. MAKE-UP

LaGuardia was crowded. Quiola thought her baggage lost, but it made an entrance at last, flapping through the black plastic curtain of the conveyor belt. She shouldered her duffle, flipped the handle up on her roller, and, mowing back through the throng of travelers for the taxi line, nearly ran C.C. over.

"Good lord, what –" said Quiola. "What is that on your head?"

"A turban. Valerie helped me pick it out. What do you think?"

"Stylishly bright." She eyed the flaming orange and white cotton thing hugging C.C.'s bald head. "Ugly as sin."

"The other one is purple."

"Grand. I'll never lose you in a crowd again – and just what are you doing here?"

"Hug?"

Quiola put one arm around C.C.'s thin shoulder, brushed her lips against a pasty cheek and stood back. "A turban?"

"I got tired of being the scary bald lady. Playing at being a one-breasted Amazon sounds romantic, but trust me, it gets old fast."

"What about your tattoo?"

"I still love it. I just don't like the sight of my naked skull. Come on, let's get out of here."

"I could've caught the train home."

"I know, but I bought a new car. You don't mind a lift, do you?"

"New car? You bought a car *new*?"

"No, of course not. I'd never. I bought a new used car, a real humdinger."

"I've heard that before – what sort of trash heap this time?"

"Not a heap my dear," said C.C., as the two women headed for short-term parking. "I bought a Volvo. In other words, a tank, one of those boxy 1996 Volvo 960 station wagons, white, slightly dented about, but quite solid. I call him Moby. My own private white whale."

"More like a white elephant." Quiola left her suitcases beside a wheel and walked around the Volvo, checking it out. "Does he have airbags?"

"Yes." C.C. opened the rear.

Quiola folded down the roller, stowing both duffle and suitcase in the wagon. "I'm driving," she said. "Hand over the keys."

"Why? I've been well, well enough to shop for a turban and to buy Moby. Besides, you'll have jet-lag."

"That'll hit tomorrow. Hand over the keys. I want to put Moby through his paces, and I don't fancy sailing off the highway ramp. Keys, please."

"Yes Cap'n Ahab, sir."

"Don't try me," she said as she slid behind a rather large steering wheel.

C.C. snapped her seatbelt on. "I *can* drive."

"Of course you can. How's Amelia been?"

"Lonely."

Quiola started the car. "Poor thing. I missed her, too – those two weeks in Paris felt like a decade. I am so glad that's over and done with."

"Didn't you enjoy any of it? Take a left."

"Yes. I loved walking in – the gardens. Do you have a five?"

"Here."

"Thanks. Besides, I got a letter from Evelyn that shook me up."

"She phoned."

"Evelyn did?" Quiola braked, rolled down the window, paid the short-term fee. "I can't believe it. What did she say?"

"Nothing. I was feeding Amelia, the phone rang, I answered, it was Evelyn. She asked for you, I told her you were away, and then I hung up on her. Want to take the Merritt? It will put a half-hour on the trip, but it's much prettier. So, what did Evelyn's letter say?"

"That she would kill me."

"You're kidding. That's crazy talk."

"Well, she's bi-polar, among other things."

"Great. Other things, such as?"

"Such as being a prescription drug addict."

"Oh. Why haven't you ever told me this before?"

95

"I couldn't. I felt like a failure. I was ashamed."

"Oh, please. Her problems aren't your fault."

"She thinks they're all my fault. Anyway, her letter was creepy, so I burnt it."

"But you don't believe her? She wouldn't —"

"I don't know what she'd do. Honestly. She's made of steel and she's capable of brutal things when she's angry. Once, she cut up some Christmas ornaments my mother had sewn into a million little pieces, with a pair of pinking shears."

"But that's just spiteful. Small."

"And emotionally brutal. Nothing can replace those ornaments."

"Are you afraid?"

"Maybe." Quiola frowned. "Yes. Yes, I am."

✦

In early 1986, several weeks into the spring semester at Berkeley, Quiola went to get her long hair cut short for the first time ever and on a whim. She chose a salon on Shattuck Avenue, quite near the University, an easy walk to after class. Squaring her shoulders, she pushed open the glass door. Tech-Tops was a big place, with twelve stylists, bleach-blond hardwood floors, potted palms, pink sinks and black stations. She asked the receptionist for the first available stylist. Which is how she met Evelyn Porter.

Meanwhile, C.C., back in New York and feeling lost without Quiola, stewed about how things between them had gone south. By the time she collected enough nerve to phone, singing, "I left my heart in San Francisco —" Quiola had been seeing Evelyn for almost a month.

"Oh, please!" she said. "I've only been out here for a little while, and you've never even *been* to the West Coast for a visit. Not once."

"Details," said C.C. She sat down on the couch in the Chelsea apartment, figuring the time difference, embarrassed she hadn't thought of it before picking up the phone. "How was the move?" she asked.

"It was a move."

"And how do you like it out there?"

Quiola took a blue metal folding chair and sat on it backwards.

"I love San Francisco. But Berkeley is something else again. The department is small, competitive. I feel left out."

"Come home, then."

"I am home." She smiled across her apartment's small living room; her mother's old steamer trunk served as coffee table, she had an easel, four empty jars full of various sized brushes, a drop cloth, a framed Moore, a gift of C.C.'s and Evelyn, a tall, square-shouldered brunette dressed in faded straight-legged jeans and a striped t-shirt.

"I'm sorry," said C.C. "You never will be a California girl. You're a New Yorker as much as I am."

"But I was born in Minnesota, just like Liz."

"Details. Anyway, I don't see the point of taking a degree. It's silly. You're an artist, you practice – it's your work. School is a waste of time."

"Not to me. With a degree, I can teach anywhere."

"You can always teach."

"It's not the same. A degree gets you more. Why don't you visit? The weather is phenomenal. I've never seen the sky so blue as this spring. And the flowers! In Berkeley, everyone's garden seems overrun by bougainvillea."

"By what?"

"Bougainvillea – it's a flowering vine. Lovely." She glanced over to Evelyn again and mouthed silently, "*you* are lovely."

Evelyn shrugged and left the room, her black stiletto heels tip-tapping.

"And is Frisco as dyke-friendly as people say?" asked C.C.

"Absolutely. Hey, that reminds: have you heard about this thing, this gay disease they're calling AIDS?"

"The gay cancer?"

Quiola shifted the phone from one ear to the other, and frowned. "Last summer, I think it was, the CDC named it 'acquired immune deficiency syndrome'. I don't know much about it – guess I've been too wrapped up in my own stuff. But it seems to be fatal, and the men here are scared."

"Why? You can't catch cancer."

"I don't know, C.C. but a lot of gay guys I know are sick with fear. People have died. I've heard people say it's a gay epidemic that will wipe out all the queers and clean up the streets. You know? Vile stuff."

"Then be careful."

"I'm not the target – the guys are."

"When people get vile about sex, they get vile. How are things otherwise?"

"Fine, really."

"You do sound well."

"I am."

Evelyn came back into the living room from the kitchen with a container of strawberry Dannon yogurt.

"But you're not sure about Berkeley," said C.C. "The program, I mean."

"I've made friends outside the program. In fact, one of them is here now, so I should hang up before I bore her to tears."

"Not a student?"

"No. A hairdresser. Evelyn. Evelyn Porter."

At the sound of her name, Evelyn turned and mouthed, "*Hang up that phone. Now.*"

"A hairdresser? How useful!" said C.C. "Then again, what can she do for you? All you do is make one big braid out of that glorious mess you call your hair."

"I know. Gotta run."

"All right. I'll call back in a few days. Don't get into trouble."

"I won't. Bye." As she eased the phone back into its cradle, Evelyn walked over and said, "I'm bored. Come here and make love to me." She pulled Quiola roughly to her feet, kissed her, hard, then half lifted, half-carried her to the bedroom. Panting and nearly ripping her t-shirt as she yanked it over her dark head, she pinned Quiola to the futon, clumsily unbuttoned her shirt, kissed the base of her new lover's neck, then nosed her way past the shirt collar to bite down, breaking tender flesh.

✦

A warm, single light beamed from the shed's living-room window as Quiola drove Moby up the driveway, the tires crunching gravel; she pulled on the brake. "Home, almost. I'm starving."

"Well, Amelia isn't. I fed her before I left to pick you up."

"I really should go and –"

"Not without eating. Amelia's fine."

"How has your appetite been?"

"Better." C.C. opened the car door and stepped out into the warm August twilight, the rich summer smell of mown grass on the dampish air. "I'm so happy to have you back!"

"I'll just leave the bags in the car. Okay?"

"Fine with me."

"I'm sometimes amazed," said Quiola as C.C. unlocked the chipping white-painted front door, "that the 'shed' doesn't just fall down around your ears."

"Here we are –" and C.C. stepped inside, letting out a wash of cool air.

"You're running the AC?"

"For you – welcome home." The dining-area table had a vase of sweet-smelling hyacinth on it and was set for two: jaunty blue and yellow stripe place mats and napkins.

"Oh, C.C., you shouldn't have bothered yourself so much!"

"Not a bother. Cheap and cheerful seemed the way to go, like the turbans."

"And how was Valerie?"

"Older – as are we all. It was nice to spend time with her. Lizzie called every Monday, to check in, and I've been keeping tabs on Mother, although I haven't had the heart to go up there but once. Poor Mom. She enjoys the visit, but hasn't a clue who I am. Let's get dinner up and running."

In a few moments, the microwave whirred and binged, filling the small house with the mingled fragrance of garlic, tomatoes and basil. C.C. cut lasagne squares, retrieved two small salads from the fridge, while Quiola opened a bottle of wine. When they sat down, C.C. said, "So I've decided. I want a wig. Is the pasta hot enough?"

"Plenty. Why do you want a wig?"

"Because the turban is okay at home, but I want hair."

"I truly thought you didn't mind bald."

"I didn't, when it was my choice. It isn't a choice anymore – I'm smooth as an egg, I don't have an eyelash in my head, I look like an alien. I want to look semi-normal. And I want a breast to replace the one they took from me."

"A breast? Have you talked about this with Dr. Shea?"

"Uh-huh. She'll write me a prescription."

"For a breast implant?"

"No, silly. I don't want any more surgery, and I don't fancy putting anything like silicon into my system." She took a sip of wine. "Chemo was rough enough. No, I want a fake to fill me out."

"You are too much."

"More like my old self, anyway."

"Amen to that." Fingering the glass stem, she lifted the wine for a toast.

✦

In pigtails, C.C. put a scabby elbow atop her mother's scarred vanity table. Nancy brushed out her own curls, tamed by nightly rollers so that she had a gentle wave many women envied – which she well knew. It was one of her secret prides.

"Charlotte, how old are you now?"

"You know, Mommy."

"Of course I do but tell me anyway." Static electricity snapped as Nancy brushed.

C.C. rubbed one eye, pushed an errant curl from her own damp forehead and said, "Eleven."

"A big girl."

"Yes, Mommy."

Nancy opened one of the vanity's side drawers to select a lipstick, one so well-used the gold fill of the casing was worn to a dull brass. "Would you like to try Tangee?"

"No – ick!"

"Don't you think your mother is pretty?"

"Oh, yes, Mommy, yes. I think you are the prettiest of them all."

"And don't you want to grow up to be a pretty lady, like your Mother?"

C.C. picked at a scab. "Do I have to?"

Nancy laughed and, leaning into the mirror pursed her lips, smoothing on the Tangee. She puckered, blotted and said, "Well, sweetheart, I don't know if you have to. What do you want to grow up to be?"

"I want to be a painter. Like Aunt Liz."

"Charlotte Clio! And here I thought you loved me best."

"Oh, Mommy, of course I love you best."

"But you enjoy your drawing lessons, hmm?"

"Oh, I do. Today I sketched Nadine." Nadine was one of Liz Moore's three Siamese queens. "Tomorrow, I'll try my feet."

"Your feet?"

"From life, my own bare feet."

"Well," said Nancy, turning back to her mirror to powder her face. "Liz does favor bare feet. I suppose you take off your shoes, when you're up at her studio?"

"Sometimes. Not all the time. Where are you and Daddy going tonight?"

"To the Finn's, for dinner. We won't be long. Aunt Liz will be here. You will mind what she says?"

"I will," said C.C. sliding one foot forward and back against the hardwood floor. "But sometimes Ted doesn't."

"Oh? And what about Tucker?"

"Aw, Mom, he's just a baby."

"I see." Choosing a large, beveled bottle of Joy perfume, Nancy slipped the stopper off and dabbed at the back of her ears, then her wrists. "I'll talk to Ted."

"Don't tell him I tattled, will you, Mommy? Please?"

"Of course not. Now, come here —" Nancy opened her arms and took her daughter gently by the shoulders, making the girl walk close. "Let me see you. Sweetheart, you are pretty, but you are going to be a very pretty young lady. Let me show you something —" and as she said this, she began unraveling her daughter's pigtails, loosening the braids carefully until she could brush through the kinks. "Close your eyes," she said, and began carefully making up her daughter's face, with a touch of rouge, a dust of powder, light eyeliner, mascara and Tangee. Smoothing the girl's hair away from her cheeks, she turned her daughter to the mirror and said, "Now open your eyes."

C.C. stared at her transformed face, polished like an old-fashioned porcelain doll.

"What do you think, sweetheart?"

"Mommy, I look like that man."

"A man? What man?"

"The one with the big, sad lips and the red nose we saw at the circus."

"Oh my dear!" Nancy snagged a tissue from a box and carefully wiped away the make-up on her daughter's lips and face. "You mean Weary Willy? Oh, honey. You don't look like anything like a clown."

"Yes I do," said C.C. through the tissue. "Just like that man."

✦

"You are such a clown," said Liz as she put on a pair of canvas gloves.

Paul stopped dancing with the Siamese Tom, Schmoe. Schmoe's version of dancing was to rear up on his hind paws and slash out at Paul, who dangled a string. The only male Liz owned, Schmoe was spoiled and he had a thing for string. That afternoon they were out in the potting "shed", a lean-to with a green, corrugated roof, attached to the back of Liz's dove-grey saltbox studio on Montauk. Because of that roof, everything inside the lean-to on a sunny day took on a sickly cast.

"When is C.C. coming over?" Paul put down Schmoe's toy, and leaned back against the warped wooden potting table.

Liz separated seedlings. "Soon. I decided on cherry tomatoes this year. And I want to try corn. Nothing tastes so fine as fresh corn. And strawberries, and sugar-snap peas, maybe lettuces."

"Good thing you've got all these cats prowling about. Otherwise a bunny might devastate the pea patch."

"Where is Schmoe?"

Paul thumbed over his shoulder. "I saw him heading for Nadine out by the oak."

"Good. Anyway, just what do you think of *B Two?*"

He sniffed. "I haven't seen it yet."

"Yes you have – I caught you sneaking a peek."

"What about that other sketch – the bright burning child?"

Liz frowned and said slowly. "I don't know what it is, yet. The image just came to me – maybe it's for next year. And *B Two?*"

"It's sad. Dark and sad."

"I worry."

"That's obvious. Should we also worry about C.C.? Isn't she late?"

Liz glanced at her watch. "Not really but she'll get here when she gets here."

"She seems fond of you."

"She's a sweet kid."

"And her mother, too, is fond of you."

"As I am, of her."

"How fond?"

"Paul! Do I detect jealousy? You know she helped me out when I was down."

"And didn't I gain by it? Your friendship, I mean. Gaine's gains."

"Well, sir I suppose you did, since she introduced you to me and me to you. Which I suppose means I 'gaines' two friends."

"Uh-huh. Two, for the price of one. Or three, if you count Tom."

Liz chuckled, watering a flat of parsley. "Tom is a good man – cuckoo, but a good man." She straightened up. "However did you two meet, anyway?"

Paul folded his boxer's muscled arms. "I didn't meet him. Like you, I met Nancy. She was a regular at my gallery in the Village, so I took care to meet her. Here was this well-heeled young lady all by her lonesome asking after my work. Of course when I found out she was married – what's wrong? Hey, are you all right?"

"No –" she breathed, her face white to the lips. She was staring over his shoulder through the window, so he turned around, but all he saw was little Charlotte Davis, dawdling with the two cats, who'd come away from their tryst to meet her.

"Good God, Liz, it's only C.C. Who'd you think it was, a ghost?"

"Why is she bald?"

"Bald?" He turned around again. "What the – she's not bald."

"But −" Liz put down her spade and walked briskly around to the outdoors, where she could see in an instant that the child wasn't bald. Yet she'd been so sure − "What happened to your pigtails?"

C.C. looked up from the cats, and reached back to touch the French roll her mother had, by force and hair spray, shaped her kinky hair into, then turned her head to show Liz. "Do you like it?"

"Very smart."

"Mom thinks I'm too old, now, for pig-tails."

"I see." Liz folded her arms. "Pearls, furs and high-heels are next?"

"No. I like me the way I am."

Paul came out of the lean-to laughing. "Me, too, sweetie pie," he said. "I like my girls just the way they are."

✦

Armed with a curly blond wig and her brand-new breast, C.C. stepped out of the cab at the corner of 50th and 5th, Quiola behind her. The cab was instantly re-occupied. The two women made their way from the crowded, sunny street to the grand old plate-glass windows and revolving doors of Saks Fifth Avenue.

"I haven't been here in a donkey's age," said C.C., glancing up at the phalanx of American flags waving over her wigged head.

Inside, the air was sweet with perfume. They stood for a moment next to winter hats and wool scarves, looking down the hard-wood floor corridor at the oak and glass cabinets, those graceful old display cabinets inside which, on one side of the aisle, jewelry sparkled in the department store lights and on the other side, cosmetics and perfume. People, lightly bundled up against the early winter chill, rushed in behind them, then slowed as they made their way into whichever section of the store they'd chosen as a destination, or simply wandered up the center aisle.

Quiola took off her hat, stuffed it in her handbag and took C.C. by the elbow, steering her to cosmetics. "Which do you prefer? Estée Lauder? Or Prescriptives?"

"No more prescriptions, please! Wow, this place hasn't changed in thirty years. The last time I was here, I think it was the seventies.

That's right, the late seventies. Mother needed a new dress – I don't think a single item has shifted since that day."

"Of course it has. I don't see any side-burns or 'fros."

"In *here?*"

"Yes in here. Now, come and choose a brand. You said you wanted a make-over at Saks Fifth Avenue, so, let's get cracking."

"I swear this is almost unbearable. Do you think if I wait long enough, Mother will emerge from the handbag section, carrying one that will just suit me?"

"Honestly!" said Quiola, huffing. "Look, all these nice make-up girls are waiting for your decision and if you don't decide soon, we're going to be doused with that perfume –" A young woman in extremely high heels was busy spraying wrists – or white cards, if one preferred – with a bright floral fragrance.

"I'll be old-fashioned and go with Lancôme," said C.C.

"French. You would."

"My choice."

The Lancôme counter stood a little over halfway down the main aisle, nearer the elevators than the front doors. Dodging the fragrance lady, Quiola and C.C. headed for the Lancôme chair into which C.C. hopped.

"When was the first time you came here?" she asked Quiola.

"*This* is the first time."

"Today's your first time? Are you kidding me?"

"May I help you ladies?" asked the not-so young woman behind the counter.

"Yes," said Quiola. "My friend would like a make-over."

The woman eyed them both through her heavy mascara. "What kind of a make-over? Wedding? Daily? Evening?"

"A chemo make-over," said C.C. cheerfully. "I'm just *dying* to look my best. Something light to go with my fake hair."

"Oh, brother," said Quiola.

The Lancôme sales woman seemed unimpressed. "I'll show you our suggested day-color combinations, and you can choose one." She walked through the interior of the counter to the other side calling out to Quiola, "Miss? Please, could you come around here for a moment?"

C.C. folded her arms. "Don't be long," she admonished, as Quiola made her way around the curved glass to the far side of the counter. The saleswoman leaned forward and whispered, "She is very ill?"

"Yes."

"I am so sorry."

Quiola nodded, not really knowing what to say.

"All right then," said the saleswoman and briskly removed a display case bringing it back to C.C. through the little work area where the sales people keep receipts, telephone, coffee and Danish, leaving Quiola to take the long way back around.

"I want," said C.C., gazing over the color combination samples, "to look as normal as possible."

"Of course."

"But this stuff always makes me feel like Bozo the Clown."

"Let me give you a face," said the saleswoman "and you can judge." She took the samples chart, turned around to open some drawers and began applying foundation to C.C.'s face with a make-up wedge. When she was done, the saleswoman stepped back rather dramatically nodding to herself as she fetched a large hand mirror which she handed to C.C. saying, "Much improved. I think you'll be pleased."

Quiola was, but she held her tongue until C.C. could look herself over.

"Well?" asked Quiola at last.

"I can't believe it! I look almost well. Thank you!"

"You're welcome. Shall I put together a package? Yes? Good."

And so C.C. left the make-up counter nearly a hundred dollars out, but feeling more like a million than she had for months. Back on the chill and busy Fifth Avenue, Quiola pointed to the soaring spires of St. Patrick's. "Do you mind if we walk in?"

"To the church? Why?"

"To light a candle, for my mother."

"You don't practice."

"No, but it meant something to Mom. Whenever I venture mid-town, I stop in and light a candle. At first it was just for all souls, something Mom did but after she died, I do it for her."

MAKE-UP

"You go to a church you don't believe in but you never stepped over to Saks?"

"Nope. Not until today."

"Sometimes you baffle me."

"I don't like to shop."

The plentiful steps up to the Cathedral's entrance gave C.C. a little trouble, but she got to the decorated bronze doors without pausing. "It's all so much," she said. "This place – all the tracery, these doors, the height."

"It's a cathedral."

"It's just big," said C.C., hushing her voice as they left the sunshine of the early winter day for the dim, cold interior of the church, where incense mingled with candle smoke and melting wax. Sound moved through the vastness of the nave as echo, every cough or rustle magnified by the soaring height of the ceiling. Most of the people in St. Patrick's were walking up and down the perimeter of the church, looking over the marble statues of saints, shuffle, shuffling, whispering. Here and there someone sat in a pew. One elderly woman in black was on her knees, her forehead against folded hands, from which dangled a white plastic rosary.

Quiola genuflected between the two last pews, made the sign of the cross and led the way around the back of the pews to a statue of the Virgin, in front of which was a wire rack of small white candles. About half of them were burning and smoking; Quiola dropped some change into the metal slotted box welded to the front of the rack, took a long match, lit it, and chose her candle.

"Come," she whispered after she'd finished. "Let's sit for a minute."

The two slipped into the nearest pew; C.C. placed her Saks bag on the floor beside the brown padded kneeler. For a few seconds, she gazed around at the distant altar with its snowy white clothing and high-polished gold fittings of the tabernacle. Then her cell phone started to vibrate. She leaned over and whispered to Quiola,

"Meet me outside when you're done?"

"Okay."

Quiola sat on the hard wooden pew for a few more moments. When she came back outside she found C.C. near the massive doorway, her newly made-up face green beneath foundation, powder and paint. "It's Mom," she said. "They're not sure she'll make it through the night. I have to go. Now."

"Look – there's a cab. I'll dash, you follow –"

C.C. nodded as Quiola ran down the church steps, two at a time.

PART III

TREATMENTS

7. CHANGE

Ted Davis showed up at Hartford Hospital an hour after C.C. and Quiola arrived from the City. He walked into his mother's quiet, dim, and cluttered IC room, so angry it was as if he carried a blazing torch.

"What happened?" he demanded. A big man, he crowded the already jam-packed space. Easing past various machines, he walked to the opposite side of the room to where his sister sat beside the wheeled bed. He gently lifted his mother's hand.

"Get out of here," said C.C.

"Right," he said, then lowered his voice a bit. "How is she doing?"

"Badly. She's dying."

"Nonsense." He loosened his bright yellow tie, and then took the measure of his mother's weak, irregular pulse.

"You're not her doctor," said C.C.

"No, dammit, I'm her son. *And* a doctor. Just shut up, would you, Charlie?"

"Stop," whispered Quiola. Upon Ted's arrival she had receded, like smoke, into a corner of stillness. Now, she stepped to C.C.'s side.

Ted leveled his brown-gray eyes at her. "Who are you, to be here, now? I thought this one had ditched you, Charlie, way back in the eighties. Broke your heart, didn't she? I don't see why she's here."

C.C. stood up. "Get out, Ted. You're a monster."

"Me? I'm the monster? You'd better look in the mirror."

"Homophobe."

"You can call me any name you like," he replied, running one hand over his gray curly hair. "But you can't make me leave. I have every right to be here."

"Fine," said C.C. as she sat back down. "And ditto. You can't make me leave, either. Or Quiola. Who has every right to be here if I say so."

"Where's Cosgrove? I want to speak to him."

"Be my guest. See if you can change his diagnosis."

Ted turned on his heel and left the room. As the door swung slowly closed behind him, Quiola whispered, "Hell."

Tight-lipped, C.C. said, "See? He's impossible."

"He didn't even ask how *you're* doing."

"Of course he didn't. I told you, he just doesn't care. He thinks of me as some aspect of the past, like a theory or an algorithm of family ties."

"It's terrible."

"But true." And, having come to this, C.C. had long ago released the strings of her affection for him, and let it drift away. She reached over the silver metal safety bars and lifted her mother's cool, limp hand. "Mom," she whispered, but there was no response except the light beep of the heart-monitor.

Quiola sat down and clasped her own hands together nervously. She had never been at a deathbed before. She saw C.C. shoulders tense; the heart monitor kept to a quiet blue pulse, but when she glanced over at Nancy's face, it looked drained, all the wrinkles and creases smoothed flat. Her gaze skipped away and she could not force herself to look again, her mind wandering off to the afternoon she'd first met Nancy Ryder, and to the first warm touch of her smile.

"C.C.," she whispered, leaning forward, keeping the tears out of her voice. "I have to go for a minute," and she stepped into the institution-bright hallway, jumbled with empty beds, equipment, equipment, a lost pen. She nodded to one of the night nurses, who nodded back, then leaned against a wall, took a deep, deep breath, and walked down to the windows. The night sky was just beginning to blue, and the well-lit parking lot below was empty; then she went to the ladies room beside the nurse's central reception well, where the night staff ate pizza. She washed her face, scrubbing with her palms to make her cheeks redden a bit to mask the reddening of her nose, which always happened when she cried. Squaring her shoulders, she left the bathroom, but as she turned the hallway corner, saw Ted and Dr. Cosgrove moving with swift purpose ahead of her. At the sight, in reflex, Quiola murmured, "Our father, who art in heaven, hallowed be thy name. Thy kingdom come..." but the words began to die, and in their place rose a mournful song, soft and quiet, a song her mother made her memorize, syllable by meaningless syllable, a chant composed in a tongue lost to her.

✦

In Minnesota, just before the Christmas holidays, Liz found herself rolling around Treetops like a lost marble, jittery in a way she couldn't explain. When the doorbell rang that afternoon, she was grateful to have a destination and company – her niece, Beth.

"Aunt Liz! Here I am, as requested."

"Oh, I'm so glad you could stop by," she said, opening the door wider to let Beth in, bringing with her a gust of pure ice air. Unpeeling layers of wool, shedding cap, mittens, coat and snowy boots, Beth Moore, a strongly built woman, was yet a half foot shorter than her Aunt Liz, so she was always gazing up, as she did now. "How are you feeling?" she asked, hanging her things on a clothes tree.

"Odd. Never felt like this before." Liz, who wore a large, hand-knit sweater, put her hands inside the sleeves. "On edge."

"Maybe you're coming down with something?"

"No. Let's go to the kitchen. I'll make tea."

"Well then," said Beth, who followed Liz across the living room with its vaulted ceiling and massive crossbeams, past the fire in the fireplace, to lean against the lintel of the kitchen door. "What sort of odd?"

"I don't know, just odd. And I keep dreaming about Paul. I haven't dreamt about him in years. It's very disturbing." She put a kettle on to boil. "You never met Paul, did you?"

"No. Are they bad dreams?"

"Not bad. Strange. Seeing him again. I wake up and I'm alone. It's disorienting."

"Do you want me to come stay over a few nights?"

"No," said Liz, her voice breaking a little. "Here, I'll take the pot if you can take the cups." She lifted the delicate white pot from the counter, as Beth collected the matching cups and saucers, and then they both went back into the bright living area, to a generous picnic-style wooden table near windows. Outside, new snow was piled on the deck. Lizzie clasped her knotted hands together, sighed and said, "Maybe it's losing Nancy Davis."

"Remind me again? Nancy Davis?" Beth blew on her tea and sat down with her back to the windows. Even through her flannel shirt she could feel the chill outside, trying to get in.

"Nancy was an old friend, terribly generous. She gave me – *gave* me, mind you – my studio on Montauk. C.C.'s mother."

"Oh, yes. The girl in pigtails – you showed me old pictures. She's ill, isn't she? I thought you said she was ill."

"Cancer. Nancy introduced me to Paul, you know."

"Really? This was in, what, the forties?"

"No, earlier. I met Nancy before C.C. was born – something like '35."

"The year I was born?"

"Oh, no – must have been '34, then, because Nancy was pregnant."

"With C.C.?"

"No, with her brother, Ted. C.C. was born in '36." Liz smiled. "So you and she are almost the same age. How funny. I never really thought about it before. You seem younger than that."

"Maybe because you lived in NY, and we all lived here."

"We all? I see. And I never visited, did I?"

"Not when father was alive." The fire snapped. The two women regarded one another, until Liz said, "Well, I'm here now, aren't I? What's left of me, at any rate. I do wish I could shake off this odd feeling."

"When did your friend pass away?"

"November. November 12. Less than a month ago, but it was a mercy, really. She had Alzheimer's. Everything she'd lived for, everyone she loved, just gone. Oh. Oh, my goodness! November 12. No wonder –" she stopped and shook her head.

"No wonder what?"

"A child's birthday. November 12. I'd forgotten."

"What child?"

"It doesn't matter, Beth. Truly, it doesn't. Coincidence. So, how is Sara doing?"

Beth smiled. "Well. Her business is good, but I wish, for her sake, she'd find somebody to share it with. I can tell she's still not over Terry. Five years. I hope she can climb out of it."

"Poor thing – tell her to drop by. We can sit and have at life, the two of us."

Beth laughed. "Fix the world."

"Yes. Want another cup?"

"No, thanks, I should be getting along. You need anything? I'll come back in a couple days, so if you need anything –"

Liz clasped her hands together again and muttered, "Nembutol. Valium."

"What?" Beth collected the tea things, and took them into the kitchen.

"Nothing, my dear. Think I'll try a nap." She stared down at her knotted, liver-spotted hands. "A nap. Without dreams, please. I've had enough to last forever."

"What did you say?"

"A nap," said Liz, raising her voice. "A nap!"

Beth returned from the kitchen, and began re-dressing for the cold. "Are you sure you want Sara and I over for Christmas day? It's not too much?"

"Of course I'm sure. What a question."

"All right, then, we'll bring a turkey, and all the sides."

"Turkey? Not turkey. Duck. Goose. Even chicken. Not turkey. I don't see why you make such a fuss, anyway. Christmas is just like any another day, number three hundred something."

"Honest to Pete you're annoying. I'll call you tomorrow."

With Beth gone, Liz went into her bare master bedroom – an old-fashioned iron bedstead with a blue and white herringbone quilt, two square bedside tables on either side, both with iron lamps and on one, a single round alarm clock, bakelite blue. She'd hung the startlingly silver-blue version of *Wirkorgan* over the bed, which made the room even colder, the ovoid blue to silvery shapes frigid as an interior ice storm. On the oak dresser, reflected in the mirror, was a small, flat green box, and a spool of plaid ribbon. Although her hands trembled, she cut the ribbon on a clean diagonal, and managed a careful bow.

"There," she said, placing the green box inside a brown one stuffed with newspaper, packing it up for the post. Finished, she stepped under the staircase outside the bedroom and opened the door to a small elevator-seat, a device she'd put in some years ago, after she'd fallen and feared stairs. She sat down, shut the door, pressed the button and the seat rose to a corresponding door on the second floor. She got out and stepped into the one large loft room, her studio now. Switching on a light, she went over to her immaculate workbench – everything tidy, awaiting deployment. She sat down and eyed a blank canvas, envisioning a self-portrait of the artist as a young woman.

"There," she muttered, choosing a brush. "Conjure the past."

✦

On Christmas morning, C.C. stayed in bed long after she heard Quiola slip downstairs. Her hands clasped behind her neck, she stared at the white painted tongue and groove ceiling, feeling light, washed out, as if relieved of all flesh. When the aroma of coffee overtook the slight, persistent odor of linseed oil in her bedroom, she wriggled back into the flannel nightshirt she'd yanked off in the middle of the night, and sat up. She slipped off the head-sock she wore to keep her skull warm but her head felt…odd. She laid her palm against her scalp.

"Is it possible?" She swung her legs out of the sheets and tiptoed to a mirror hung by a beige ribbon on the wall near the stairs.

"Fuzz?" She gazed at her head. "I have fuzz! I'm fuzzie wuzzie." Slipping her feet into clogs, she opened the top drawer of her dresser, took out a small wrapped box, then clomped downstairs. Although she'd been protesting for weeks that Christmas felt nightmarish this year, she was glad now that Quiola had decorated the "shed" with armloads of pine and ribbon and lights, mistletoe. Redolent with coffee and the sharp clean fragrance of evergreen, the "shed" seemed like a kid in a new overcoat. C.C. came down the stairs into the morning's thin light to slip the box she held under the tree. A pinecone snapped in the tiny hearth.

"Fire's lovely," she called into the kitchen.

"It was an icebox in here when I got up. Coffee?"

"Love some." A tiny thump-thump-thump told C.C. that Amelia was coming downstairs after her. The cat skittered past into the kitchen.

"Your familiar is hungry," she said.

"I know." Quiola came into the living room with two mugs of coffee.

"Guess what?" said C.C. bending her head. "Look – can you see it? Peach-fuzz."

"It's finally growing back? Hooray!"

C.C. sat at the table. "I'll hardly know what to do with it. Hair. Just imagine."

"Merry Christmas," said Quiola, picking up the cat.

"Merry to you, too. Wonder how long it will take to look like something other than fuzz. Wonder when I should make an appointment at the salon! Oh and Quiola – thanks."

"For what? You haven't opened a single gift yet."

"For this – for Christmas. It would have been worse, I think, to skip it."

"Your parents always made a big deal of it, and Mother did, too, so it just seemed wrong to let it go."

C.C. went to the tree, looked over several boxes, shook one, put it down. "There are so many! I thought you hate to shop."

"One's for Amelia. And that green box arrived from Minnesota."

"From Liz? Hell!" C.C. leaned over the box with its jaunty plaid ribbon. "What do you think she's up to? Always said a gift shouldn't be an obligation. If obliged, she gives food. Or flowers. Anyway, things that don't last. That box doesn't look like either food or a flower." She glanced out the window just as a pair of chickadees landed on the large wooden spool on the back porch to hop about strewn sunflower seeds. "Monks," she said. "Chickadees. With their brown caps and white cheeks. Do you believe in God?"

"Whoa – I haven't had enough coffee yet for a question like that!"

"Mom and Dad were agnostics. Mom had been, once upon a time, a Quaker."

"So?"

"So I know you've *said* you don't believe, but I say once a Catholic always a Catholic – isn't that true?"

"Maybe. Come on, let me just put on some Judy Garland or something."

C.C. sipped her coffee. "I've just been thinking – and not about Mom, if that's what *you're* thinking. Mom left a long time ago. I haven't had her as I knew her for so many years that the woman who died was almost a stranger."

"You don't mean that."

"But I do."

Quiola sorted through the Christmas CDs, stored in a shoebox only hauled out for the season. "Your mother was dignified."

"A Boston Brahmin is always dignified – all that Harvard Yard. Or Radcliffe. She loved Judy Garland," C.C. added, as the singer's voice came up over the stereo. "Have yourself a merry little Christmas."

"So let's see what obligation Liz has sent, shall we?"

C.C. put her coffee mug down and picked up the green box. "All right. I hope this thing isn't cursed."

"Maybe it's a pearl button."

"Why would it be a button?"

"Open it."

"But why would it be a pearl button?"

"It's too large. Come on, C.C. Just a joke. Open it." Quiola sat down next to C.C. on the couch. "Come on, open it."

"I don't get the joke." She pulled at the ribbon.

"It's a line from a poem, a poem about a gift. 'I would not mind if it were bones, or a pearl button.'"

"Morbid."

"Plath."

"As I said, morbid. What is this, a wallet?" She lifted a leather case from the box, and opened it. "Oh no," said C.C, staring at an old framed, black and white photo, two women with a girl in pigtails.

"You're cute as a bug!" said Quiola. "And Liz is so young!"

"I remember that day. Paul took the picture." Shutting the leather case, she put the picture aside. "Open something else, Quiola. Quick. Open anything."

✦

"Hello?" Nancy Davis pushed open the door of Liz's Montauk studio. "Hello, Liz? Paul?" It was the summer of 1944. Nancy, wearing a housedress, no make-up, hair pulled back in a ribbon, walked over the rise to invite her friends down to the farmhouse for breakfast. There was no phone in the studio, and never would be, so if she wanted her friends' company, she had to take a stroll. During winters, in the city, Paul and Liz rented the floor of an old warehouse, for canvases and sculptures, although Paul was given to slightly more moderate-sized works than Liz, and really didn't need so much floor-space. Still he liked the expanse, and when he got frustrated he walked the full rectangle of the place, smoking.

"Anybody home?" called Nancy.

"Out back," came Liz's muffled voice.

Shutting the slightly warped door firmly behind her, Nancy walked through the length of the house, from studio space, past a tiny half-bath, through the kitchen and out the back door to find Paul and Liz at their easels, each trying a portrait of the other. Walking from easel to easel, shaking her head, Nancy said, "This is crazy." She put her hands on her hips.

Liz wiped her brush with an oily rag, and gave Nancy a hug. "Good morning. What brings you up to the lair so early?"

"Breakfast."

"You've got to be kidding," said Paul. He took a drag on his cigarette, let the smoke drift, and stubbed out the butt. "Sweetheart, you're not going to find a single egg in this place, let alone bread or jam. I think we've a couple stale rolls stashed somewhere. If you look hard."

"Oh, Paul," said Nancy. "I meant for you two come over to us."

Liz stared at Nancy as if the invitation was a nasty surprise.

"She's not a cow, Liz. Why are you giving her the once-over?"

"Because she's glowing. Aren't you, Nance? Don't tell me, I can see it for myself. You're pregnant."

"Uh-huh." Blushing to the roots of her wavy hair, she made a coy face. "I'm four months along, so I thought it high time to let you two in on it."

"Why, congratulations," said Paul and hugged Nancy gingerly.

"She's not going to break," said Liz. "If you're four months or so —"

"The doctor says November 12, or thereabouts. Oh, dear," she said, puffing out her breath. "I'm so excited. I mean, I didn't think

Tom and I would do this again. But —" she shrugged. "We told Ted and Charlotte last night."

"And how do they feel?" asked Liz.

"They're fighting about it already. Ted wants a brother. Charlotte wants a sister."

"And what do you want?"

Nancy laughed. "A healthy baby."

"Boy," said Liz, suddenly and sharp. "It'll be a boy."

"If it is, we're going to name him Tucker, after his great-grandfather. Tucker Mason Davis. If it's a girl, Tom wants to name her Nancy, but I don't, so we'll see. And we want you to be the godparents. I mean, we're not religious and I know you two aren't, but we still want godparents. Will you?"

"Of course," said Liz. "So long as I don't have to take any silly vow."

"Silly vow?" said Paul. "What about 'to have and to hold, till death do us part'? Is that just a silly vow?"

"Extremely silly —"

"Mom! Mom, where are you?"

"We're out back, sweetheart. What is that child up to? I told her to start the bacon."

C.C. ran, breathless, into the yard. "Mom!"

"Charlotte Clio, I thought I told you —"

"Dad's got the bacon on," she said, gulping air. "He wanted me to come get you because there's been a phone call for Mr. Gaines. A lady."

"Well," said Liz, dropping a cloth over her painting. "I didn't think you knew any ladies, present company excepted."

"I don't." Paul stood. "Who did we give the Davises' number to, I wonder?"

Liz shook her head.

"Mom? Did you tell them?"

"Yes, sweetheart. Liz says it will be a boy."

"No!" said C.C., stamping her foot. "I want a sister!"

"We will all just have to wait until November 12, now won't we? Paul?"

"What, my love?"

Liz rolled her eyes. "Go fetch the camera. Let's have a picture, just us girls." And as he headed off, Liz called after him, "Before we find out who your mystery lady is!"

He swatted away the insinuation, while Nancy quickly re-braided one of C.C.'s loosening pigtails. "Honestly," she said, "I haven't been out of the house ten minutes, and you are a mess, Charlie. When are you going to learn how to stay tidy? Did Daddy mention this lady's name?"

"No."

"How odd," said Liz. "I can't imagine who would've called."

Paul, ducking back out of the house with his new Eastman-Kodak Brownie Target-16, said, "All right, girls. Give me a nice pose."

Liz, as the tallest, stood in the middle and crouched a bit, so she could put an arm around Nancy's waist, and hold C.C.'s hand. The child squinted into the sun as her mother laughed. "Do you know how to work that thing?" she asked.

"'Course I do," said Paul, peering down the lens. "Smile."

Once the picture was taken and the camera stowed away, the group walked back to the farmhouse. As they approached the kitchen door, as the aroma of coffee and bacon drifted to them on the warm summer air, C.C. sprinted and banged through the screen door, over to the stove.

"Hi Daddy. Can I have a piece?"

"It's too hot. Where's your brother?"

"I don't know."

"Well, go find him."

"Daddy –"

"Now. Skedaddle."

"Darling?" said Nancy, holding the door open for her friends. "Who called?"

Tom turned around and wiped his hands on his chef's apron. "Glad you two could make it," he said. "It was Georgia."

Liz pinched Paul's arm. "Liar," she said.

"Ow, stop it. Why would Georgia call here? I didn't give her this number. Alfred certainly didn't have it."

Tom looked about to see if any children were near. Then he lowered his voice a bit and said, "He's gone, Paul – very early this morning – a stroke. I think he was at Doctor's Hospital. Georgia wanted her friends to know before tomorrow's papers."

"Gone? He can't be. I just saw him in the city last week."

"He was eighty-two," said Liz.

"He seemed fine to me, the usual Alfred."

"Oh, dear," said Nancy. "How did Georgia sound?"

"Okay. I took her number, Paul, if you want to phone her back. It's on my desk in the study."

"Yeah, okay, I should do that." He put a hand to his forehead, and then wandered off for the telephone.

"The City will seem empty, without him," said Liz. "Without the gallery."

"Maybe Georgia will keep it going?" asked Nancy.

"I doubt it." Tom whipped eggs in a bowl. C.C. came in from the hallway, without her brother.

"Ted doesn't want to get out of bed."

Nancy sighed. "I think Ted resents the idea of another child in the house."

"Nonsense," Tom said. "He's just being Peck's bad boy. If you'll finish scrambling these, I'll go make our son march." He held out the bowl while Liz sat down at the kitchen table and asked Nancy, "Do you mind if I pour a cup for myself?"

"Not at all. You know where the mugs are –"

"I'll get it for you," said C.C.

"Well," said Liz. "How lovely of you."

At that point, Paul reappeared, hands clasped at the back of his neck. He shook his head, unclasped his hands, looked at Liz and said, "It's so hard to believe – he was a genius. There isn't anybody like him, not really."

"No," said Liz. "That's true."

8. FLINCH

Quiola stepped back from her worktable, put two brushes in the mayonnaise jar beside a crumbled pack of Camels. April sunlight filtered through the window as she massaged her stiff neck. The room she'd made her studio was warm, and she was tired. She opened the window, then turned back to her watercolor, whose abstract lines of force and collection meant to convey an impression of her first canter on Splash, a paint and warmblood cross. She'd started dressage lessons at a nearby farm just after Christmas.

Her cell phone rang. Sighing, she flexed her fingers and picked the phone up off the worktable. "Hello?"

"It's for sale! I can't believe it!" said C.C. "The house! I went for a walk, starting jogging when I saw the realtor's sign. If it suits me, I'm going to buy it. I've already called the realtor. We can see it tomorrow."

"Tomorrow? When?"

C.C. coughed so hard she had to put aside the phone to clear her throat. "You have a lesson at ten thirty, so I made the appointment for 3. Give you plenty of time for a ride, a shower, lunch and so on."

"Yeah, that should work." She tucked the phone under her chin, picked up the pack of cigarettes. "How much do you think the place will cost?"

"In this neighborhood? Five or six hundred thousand – maybe more, depending on what kind of shape its in. I'm just guessing four bedrooms. Maybe."

Quiola lit a cigarette, quietly blowing smoke.

"That's an odd sound."

"My phone's been acting up. Want to watch my lesson tomorrow, before we see the house? I'm told I'm getting pretty good."

123

"Not really, no. I don't like horses – big clumsy prey animals that flinch at the drop of a hat? No. I don't want to see you go ass over tea-kettle."

"That sounds like experience."

"It was. Dad gave me lessons for my birthday when I was twelve. I only took two. On the second, the horse sent me over his head. I looked like a punching bag for a few weeks. I know you should get right back on, but I didn't. Horses are just unpredictable."

"Oh, phooey. People are unpredictable. *Amelia* is unpredictable."

"Amelia does not weigh over a thousand pounds."

"Neither does Splash. He's big, but not that big."

"Okay, nine hundred and ninety pounds. If he throws you, you'll know it."

"Everyone falls. Sooner or later."

"And they get hurt. I'll see you tomorrow, what, around two-thirty?"

Quiola closed the phone, took another drag, and wondered when C.C. would just come out and say: *Why are you doing this to me? Why are you scaring the bullshit out of me? Riding horses, at your age!* How could she explain?

Splash touches the back of my neck when I tack up with his softly blowing nose, taking in my human scent, licking me until it tickles so, I shy away.

✦

"My father," Liz said, "lived an unflinching life. Most of us flinch." She stood at the windows overlooking the deck of Treetops beside her grandniece, Sara. "He drew up the plans for Treetops," she continued, "even made a scale model, but year after year, the family stayed on the farm, with all its maples, waiting to be tapped, and all the bee-hives waiting to be harvested."

"Everyone says he was a hard man."

"I used to walk all about those halls of that scale model, through phantom doors – he never even broke ground." Wrapped in her heaviest flannel bathrobe, Liz gazed through the stand of evergreens, down to the lake's cold and moody waters.

Sara, built like her mother but tall as well, put her hand on Liz's shoulder. "Ready for that bath now, Gran?"

"Oh, yes." Liz took Sara's arm; together they went to the bathroom, where the younger woman began to prepare the bathtub by setting out a jar of salts; the tubs itself was custom made, and let Liz walk into it through a door that would seal and she could sit on a platform rather than try to get all the way down – which she simply could not do.

"Thank God," she said, taking off her flannel robe, "Mother took matters into her own hands, and just built this place. It gave her last years some ease."

"Yes. I love this house."

"I know. That's why it will be yours, soon."

"Gran, please. I hate it when you talk like that."

"I'm almost a century old, my dear. Can't go on forever."

"But I don't want the house. I want you."

"My father used to say: 'Life's too short to hesitate.' He knew what he wanted and men admired him because he'd target, zero in, close for the kill and sometimes I've wondered whether it wasn't, in fact, a perverted thing of grace he had. His own artistry, the precision of a big cat."

"Come sit."

Once Liz was settled, Sara turned on the taps, balancing hot and cold, and water pooled around her great-aunt's ankles. Scattering a handful of the salts, she swirled the water with her fingertips. "How's the temperature? Hot enough? Too cold?"

"You're such a good girl. I could never be so patient with an old biddy like me. Just let it rise as high as it will go."

"Shall I stay or leave until you're done?"

"Give me a half hour, dear. I should be even more a prune, by then."

Sara laughed and left the bathroom

Liz stared at the water about her waist. *Suppose I just slipped in? How easy it would be to mistake for an accident? If I wait, what sort of thing will I be?* She'd seen enough of age. She wanted to know the end – and did not. Her limited view had never gone to that place, the last place. One thing she did know with certainty though: if she decided to take the plunge one day, she wouldn't flinch.

✦

125

Quiola patted the side of Splash's neck, slipped her right foot out of the stirrup and swung into dismount but the stirrup bumped against the horse's wither, as if in a kick, and the horse began to move forward. Her teacher, Megan White, a trainer at Flash Farm, tried to steady the horse but something about the unfamiliar situation got to the gelding, and he took off, yanking Quiola forward and down to her knees. She let go of the reins and the horse, neighing, trotted off, leaving Quiola to stare at her hands, planted in shavings and soft dirt. She dusted them off and rocked back to her feet as Meg went to get the mount, who, being well trained, had only trotted off a few feet to wait for a human to come and fix things.

Another instructor ran out of the tack room. "Are you all right? What happened?"

"I didn't feel like I was going to fall."

"You fell off Splash?"

"Not really. Not all the way. I was halfway to the ground before he bolted."

"Can you stand?"

"Yeah," said Quiola, taking his offered hand. But her legs shook.

"You'd better come inside."

Unsteadily, she followed him into the barn, and into the darker darkness of the tack room, where there was a small desk and chair. She sat down. "My knees hurt, but I'm okay. Except for this –" she gazed at the underside of one arm, where a buckle shaped welt was beginning to form. "I must have hit myself on the stirrups."

The instructor, Mike, looked over the bruises with care. "The skin's not broken. That's good. People will wonder what you've been up to."

"Well, I'm not known for kinky, if that's what you mean."

"Make 'em wonder, I say."

"Really, Mike!" She touched the bruise. "What the hell, huh? Everyone falls, sooner or later, right?"

"Part of the game."

Megan led Splash, once again his placid, schoolhorse self, into the barn, where she undressed his face, slipped a harness on, cross-tied him and unbuckled the girth. Expert and efficient, Megan could tack up and down faster than most could mount or dismount. Watching her, Quiola said, "I envy you, Meg."

"You shouldn't. I've been doing this since I was nine. You've been doing it, what, a few months?" Meg set the saddle down on a stand, then patted Splash's arched neck. "He rarely does that. I think he heard something. Are you all right?"

"I'm fine. Is he all right?"

"Oh, sure. You want to give him a bath? Or are you feeling too messed up?"

"Physically or psychically?"

This made Mike turn away from cleaning tack. "Uh-oh," he said.

"I'm going to look at a house this afternoon," said Quiola. "A big house."

"To buy?" said Megan. "But I thought –"

"– that I'd just moved into a condo not too long ago? Yes. But C.C. wants this house. She's wanted it for years, and if she buys it, I know she expects me to move in."

Megan shrugged, and tapped a cigarette out of its box. She lit it and blew a stream of smoke before she said, "You don't have to move, do you?"

"Can I bum one?"

"Sure," Meg held out the box.

"Okay then, time for a break," said Mike. He put down a sponge, capped the leather oil, and fished a box of cigarettes out of his front pocket.

Splash sighed a mighty horse sigh, which made Meg laugh. "Humans boring you, old man? Here –" she opened a tin named "Treats" and found a peppermint.

"No," said Quiola. "I don't *have* to move. But C.C. will make me, as the saying goes, an offer I can't refuse."

"Ominous," said Mike.

"What sort of offer?"

Quiola inhaled, blew out and leaned against Splash's bulk. "No more mortgage, insanely reduced living expenses, half or more of the house for my own use, a studio and so on. I could afford to ride everyday, quit one of my teaching gigs and still be ahead."

Mike whistled. "Sweet! What's the catch?"

Quiola closed her eyes for a moment. "I'm afraid."

"Of what? Not C.C.," said Megan.

"No, not of C.C. I'm afraid of what's ahead." She pulled off her riding gloves, folded them in half and tucked them into her black carry-all. "It's not just the cancer. She's got this cough, too."

"What does the doctor say about it?" asked Meg.

"I don't know. I don't know if C.C. has told her about it, or if Dr. Shea has heard it, or if I'm just hearing it because I'm worried and its nothing more than a cough. And then there are those days when I wonder which one of these awful things – cancer, Alzheimer's, you name it – is aiming down the pike at me."

Mike shook his head. "I try not to think about it. You think about it, you get stuck in it, and then what? You worry. I say, just live. Besides, you won't ride well with mortality on the brain."

"Isn't that the truth! Sorry, guys, I'll lighten up."

"No problem. We all have worries." Megan gestured with her cigarette at Splash. "Do you have time to give the old man a bath?"

Quiola smiled. "Absolutely."

✦

"Quiola? Where are you?" C.C. said as she hung up the black rotary phone, and got off the sofa as her Cambridge living room darkened and shadows grew long on the hardwood floors. It was a fine September evening, a couple months after they had started seeing each other, on the sly. Quiola didn't know what Arthur Rivers might think, and she wanted to keep her internship.

"I'm in the kitchen!"

"Just got off the phone with Mother."

"What? I can't hear you –"

"I said," C.C. raised her voice as she stalked through the swinging door into the kitchen. "Mother just called."

"I just can't get this right," said Quiola. Standing at the yellow-tiled counter near the stove, she was mixing something in a glass bowl. She looked over her shoulder at C.C., making her long hair swing. "Corn fritters. The dough is too doughy."

FLINCH

C.C. leaned one hip against the counter, crossing both her arms and ankles. "You cook like my mother, and here I am, twice your age and I can barely boil an egg. That was Mom, on the phone. She wants us to come down next weekend for a party. Can you get away?"

"To Connecticut?"

"Mm. My niece turns three and Karen's about to pop, so Mom's throwing the party – but they'll be plenty of adults. We won't be run off our feet by the kids."

"Your whole family will be there?"

"Yes, silly. That's the point, isn't it? I'd like you to meet them."

"And they know?"

"Know? Of course they know. My parents have known since I was twenty-five."

"Your brother, too?"

"Ah, well, Ted." C.C. peered into a grocery bag. "These need shucking."

"Uh-huh. So? What about your brother?"

"Ted will be there, of course, he is the proud Dad, after all. Don't worry, I'll try not to shriek." She took several ears of corn from the grocery bag. "The last time I heard from him, it was Christmas. He wanted me to go in on a gift for Mom and Dad. Like he doesn't have plenty of money, the old turd."

"Is he that bad?"

"See for yourself, when we get there."

Rather than bother with a rental car, C.C. and Quiola took the train down from Boston to New London. Standing in the dim, echoing stationhouse, waiting for Tom Davis to pick them up, Quiola checked on her duffel bag.

"Off to the ladies," said C.C. "Be right back."

"What if your father shows up?"

"Say hello."

"But I won't know what to say besides hello."

C.C. laughed. "My father will do all the talking."

Left alone with the suitcases, Quiola clasped and unclasped her hands, gazing back and forth between the station doors and the ladies.

"Hurry up," she said in the direction of the bathroom as the station door creaked open, letting in a streak of light. An elderly man in a fedora stepped inside, stood still for a moment, let his eyes adjust to the gloom. Then, he smiled and said, "You must be Quiola?"

"Yes, sir, Mr., I mean Dr. Davis."

He shook her hand. "Tom, please. My daughter's in the can, I take it. She never could hold it. Made car trips loads of fun. These yours?" He reached down for the duffel.

"That's all right," said Quiola hastily snatching the duffel before he could.

"I won't hear of it, young lady. Hand it over."

"Dad!" cried C.C. as the bathroom swung closed behind her. "Dad for gracious sake, we can carry our own."

He turned and held open his arms and C.C. walked across the station, into the hug, kissing her father on both cheeks. "It's good to see you."

"And you, darling. You see I've met Quiola. Shall we? Mother's waiting, and you know how she gets."

Tom's 1965 VW Beetle was parked at the corner. Stowing the bags inside the hood, he unlocked the doors for the two women. Once they were well on their way home, and smaller inquiries asked and answered, C.C. said "So, is Ted home yet?"

"Not yet. But Karen's here. Ted couldn't get away until tomorrow."

"Karen drove herself, in her condition?"

"No, Charlie. I went and picked her up."

"Dad, you spoil Ted rotten."

"I spoil both my children. Besides, he's got a busy practice. You know that. I don't see how he handles it, quite frankly. How is your job going?"

"I don't like teaching."

"You don't?" said Quiola, from the back seat. "I thought you did."

"And you, Quiola?" asked Tom, glancing up into the rearview. "Do you like being a student?"

"I did. But I was ready to graduate."

"And you work, Charlie told me, at Riverbed Press?

"It's an internship, and it's almost over."

"We have a plan for after, don't we?" said C.C.

"Oh?" said Dr. Davis as he pulled into the blind driveway, hidden behind a wall of bushes too high to see over. Having moved to Madison, Connecticut, from Montauk in 1971, the Davises lived in a house they dubbed Gardencourt. "What kind of a plan?"

"An escape plan. We're leaving for Paris. Lizzie gave me the keys to Paul's studio. I figure we can live cheaply there for a couple years, really paint."

"And just what about your work, Charlie? I haven't heard or seen anything for months on end."

"Oh, Dad, you don't expect to read about me in the *Times* or anything, I hope."

"I read about Lizzie," he said.

"Of course you do." C.C. opened the door. "And I expect to wait as long as Liz has for anyone to notice. It's still a boy's club, you know. Art. It still belongs to the boys."

"Isn't that the truth," said Quiola.

Dr. Davis looked puzzled. "A boy's club?"

"Come on, Dad," said C.C. popping the front end for the suitcases. "Art has been a boy's club for a long time now. The girls make coffee and the boys make art, with a capital A."

"But I thought you girls were all liberated now. Gloria Steinem and all —"

"Huh. I've been told and more than once a serious artist has to be big, bold and brash, which means a guy."

"Nonsense," said Dr. Davis. "Oh, here's Mother."

Walking down the slate path from the house to the detached garage, Nancy waved and called out, "Charlotte!"

"Mom —" and C.C. left her bags to dash up the path for a hug.

"Honey," said Nancy, taking her daughter's face by the chin. "You look lovely."

"Even without a stitch of make-up?"

"Well, I always say a little lipstick wouldn't hurt."

"You don't give up, do you?"

Nancy put her arm around her daughter's waist, and beamed at both her guests. "Of course not. Now, are you going to introduce me to your new friend?"

"Mrs. Davis, thank you for inviting me," said Quiola politely, and she remained polite while meeting Karen Davis, C.C.'s sister-in-law, and Anne, her niece; remained polite throughout dinner, polite over coffee, polite about retiring to her guest bedroom, polite until C.C. snuck out of a second guestroom to join her, which is when Quiola, already in bed with a book, let go with "I thought you said they *knew*."

C.C. sat cross-legged on the white-flocked bedspread, her back against the baseboard. "They do. But we don't talk about it. Never. They accept me, they love me, and they will love you, too. But they're also old-fashioned. They knew all sorts of artists and such, but they're conservative. Surely you can see that?"

"And which part do they disapprove of most? The painter, the lezzie or the dirty half-breed?"

"That's not nice."

"This situation is not nice. I don't feel comfortable."

"Why? They've been nothing but sweet. Even Karen has been a honey."

"Sure, because we're *friends*. That's what you told them, isn't it, that we're just close friends?"

"Mom and Dad know perfectly well that any woman I bring home is my lover. I don't know what Karen knows, and I'm not about to rock that boat."

"So why the separate bedrooms?"

C.C. burst into laughter.

"What's so funny?"

"How sweet!"

"What is?"

"You," said C.C. "Goodness, Quiola, if either of us were a man, we'd sure as hell have separate bedrooms. We're not married, are we? No. Now, if I brought home a boyfriend, do you think my parents would let me share his bed? Of course not! Like I said, they're old-fashioned and they aren't about to change."

✦

C.C. walked down the gravel drive away from the house with more spring in her step that Quiola had seen in many months. "It is, of course, perfect," she said, stopping to gaze back at the rambling home that the realtor named The Carriage House. "Four bedrooms, two full baths and it looks so humble from here."

"Yes," said C.C. rubbing her hands together. "I hope they'll jump for it. If not, I'll just give them the full asking price."

"Stone in the kitchen, pot-bellied stove, airy bedrooms – everything perfect, except for the wall to wall shag rug in the family room."

"I'll rip it up. Put in hardwood." C.C. had reached the road. She could just see the driveway of the "shed" from there. She turned to face Quiola and asked, "What the hell have you done to yourself?"

Quiola lifted her arm to look at that morning's bruising. The purpled pattern in one soft place under her forearm replicated the shape of a flattened buckle. "Nothing serious," she said, lowering her arm. "A bruise."

"That's more than just a bruise. You fell off the damn horse, didn't you?"

"I fell. Not far." She gazed back at the white house with its black shudders and trim. "It is perfect – except for the rug. I wish someone knew more about the history. The whole place must have been really big, if the 'shed' was for the gardener, and that was only the carriage house. I wonder if the real main house is still standing?"

C.C started up the country road again with Quiola behind, her gaze resting for a moment on C.C.'s hair, thick now, and styled once again. The spring air, as the afternoon waned, began to chill, bringing goose bumps up on C.C.'s neck. She shivered a little, and coughed.

"Have you talked to Dr. Shea about that cough?"

"It's nothing."

"Are you sure?"

"Of course I'm sure." At the shed's mailbox, C.C. put down the flag and took her mail, then let them in to the house "When do you think I'll hear from the realtor?"

"Not now. It's nearly six."

"Not tonight, then. You're sure you're all right?"

"Me?"

"You fell. Off the horse." C.C. sat down at the dining table, her mail still in hand. "I said you'd get hurt."

"It's just a bruise. I'm fine."

"And you've started smoking, haven't you? Quiola? Haven't you?
I can smell it through the mint. I was a smoker. I know all the moves.
And it's a devil of a thing to quit. I've been wondering, too, what's
gotten into you? Ever since you took up with this riding business,
you've been, I don't know, distant. Different."

"No I haven't."

"Yes you have. Do you have to ride? Why? And why are you
smoking? It's not good for Amelia, quite apart from everyone else."

"I don't smoke a lot, and riding takes my mind off other things. I
like to learn something new. It's a challenge."

"You mean you like having a teacher, that's what you mean.
You've always liked having a teacher. What's her name again?"

"Meg White. She's great. Patient, smart – I like her."

"Oh, I bet you do."

"What does that mean?"

"You heard me."

"Oh for chrissake! Meg's married and has two kids. You want to
come out to the farm and see?"

C.C. hung her head. "No."

"Good. I ride because I want to."

"What if I don't want you to?"

"Don't ask me to stop, C.C. just don't. I need to do this –
for me."

"It's dangerous."

"No more dangerous than driving Moby."

"I'm a good driver."

"So am I. But who knows about the guy on the other side?"

"All right. All right. But why smoke? You can't tell me smoking
and riding go together like a horse and carriage?"

Quiola fidgeted with the string ties on her jacket, and didn't
say anything.

"Hmm?"

"No, not exactly. I – " she shook her head. "You're right. I should
quit."

"Why in heaven's name did you start?"

"I don't know. It just happened."

"Oh, bullshit," said C.C., slamming an open hand down on the mail she'd just placed on the table. "I see what you're doing, and I don't like it one bit. Courting death. That's what it is. I've had my brush, and now you're courting it. Of all the crazy idiot things to do to me, Quiola."

"Courting death? No I'm not."

"Riding. Smoking. What'll it be next, sky-diving?"

"I'll stop."

"Which? Riding or smoking?"

Quiola glared. "Smoking, all right? Smoking."

C.C. closed her eyes and put her hand to her forehead. "Go home, Quiola. Please. Just go on home."

✦

When the Christmas holidays of 1944 had passed, and the children went back to school, Ted Davis's teacher became so concerned about the boy's behavior, he asked to meet with Dr. and Mrs. Davis.

C.C., only seven, didn't quite understand and she told Liz that she was –

"– scared." It was a cold, cold February morning. Liz was still dozing in the guestroom, having come out the night before from the city after she and Paul had quarreled so she'd asked Nancy, you know, with the new baby and all, if she might need any help around the house?

C.C. climbed up on the bed, and Liz rolled over. "What are you scared about?" she said, turning back the quilt so C.C. could crawl in.

"Everything."

"Oh, no, not everything!"

C.C. nodded. Her unbraided hair, wild, stood out like a blond halo around her head. "Everything's so hard."

"School?"

"Yeah."

"What grade are you in?"

"Aunt Liz, why do you keep forgetting?"

Liz laughed. "Because I'm old."

"Oh, well. Second grade."

"I see. Reading? Math?"

"I like reading. Math is yucky, and I can't tell time. I just can't."
Liz patted her arm. "You will. Just give yourself a break."

C.C. made a face, then said, "I'll tell you a secret. A secret
secret."

"Ah." Liz folded her hands under her head. "I'm ready."

C.C. elbowed up to look into Liz's face. "You promise not
to tell?"

"That's our deal, isn't it? With secret secrets."

C.C. flopped back down. "Okay. I was mean to Tucker, when
Mom first brought him home. I didn't want another brother. I
have one."

"I know. But he's a cutie, isn't he?"

"Now he is. When he was littler, he was all red and scrunched up."

"All babies are like that. You were red and scrunched up."

"No I wasn't."

"Yep." Liz rolled a curl of C.C.'s hair around her finger letting her
finger slide through the curl. "I hope you weren't too mean?"

"I pinched him. Hard. When nobody was looking. I made him cry."

"Did you stop?"

"Yeah. I got used to him, and then I felt bad 'cause I was so
mean."

"Ah, you weren't too mean. Besides, you said you stopped. He's so
little, he won't ever remember."

"I know. But I still feel bad."

"Well, you told me, didn't you? So you don't have to keep your
secret-secret all bottled up."

"I guess."

"That's not the problem, is it?"

"Maybe." She shrugged, staring at the quilt's pattern. "Aunt Liz?
What would be really mean, to do to a baby? Pinching's not so bad.
What would be really bad?"

"A lot of things. Babies depend on us. You see how your Mom
and Dad take care of Tucker – or me, if I'm holding him we are, all
of us, very gentle, very careful. Why? C.C.? Come on. What's the
real secret-secret you haven't told me yet?"

"I'm scared," she said, her voice down to a whisper.

"Of everything, you said so three minutes ago. Everything and what else?"

"Ted."

"Ted? Why?"

"He hates Tucker."

"No he doesn't. I'm sure."

"Yes he does. He told me. He told me he was going to get rid of him. He said Tucker had an evil eye, and we had to protect Mom."

"Oh, bother," said Liz, more to herself than to C.C. "And just how was he going to get rid of Tuck?"

"I don't know," she almost wailed. "That's why I'm scared. And then his teacher called – maybe Mr. Gentry found out. What will they do to Ted, for being so mean?"

"Hmm. You know I haven't talked to your mother about that meeting yet."

"Don't tell her I told you! Ted would kill me."

"Honey, calm down. I don't go back on secret-secrets. But if Ted's teacher is involved, then maybe it'll all just be over, and your secret can be buried in the back yard, with that other one we fixed. Just let me talk to your mother first, okay?"

"Okay."

✦

Seated on Dr. Shea's examining table, dressed only in a blue paper gown, C.C. drummed her heels lightly against the cold stainless steel, waiting, waiting. When someone knocked on the door, she said, "It's okay. I'm ready."

Dr. Shea came in, with a thick manila folder under one arm. "How are you?"

"Good. Fine. How are my x-rays?"

"I just want to take a listen, first." She put the folder on her chair, adjusted her stethoscope, and gently folded back the paper gown. "Take a deep breath? Out. In? Good. Another? Out. Good." Dr. Shea hung the scope around her neck and sat down, laying the folder in her lap. "I've got bad news, I'm afraid."

C.C felt as if her oncologist had just socked her in the mouth. "But the x-rays were routine, weren't they? What could be bad about my lungs?"

"I'm sorry to have to tell you this, but the breast cancer has metastasized to one of your lungs. I'm surprised because you've responded so well to the Herceptin, I just didn't think – but I have to help manage your emphysema, too, and when I saw the pictures, well, I called in a radiologist, to be absolutely sure. We need to talk about your options –"

"Options? No – wait, wait. I can't. I can't do this. I can't – I need time. Not chemo again. My hair just grew back!" she said, grabbing a handful of it. "Fuck."

"I know. I know. Did somebody come with you today?"

C.C. shook her head.

"Shall I call your friend? I don't think you should be alone."

"I don't want anybody. Not yet."

"Shall I just tell you what course of therapy I think you should follow?"

C.C. crossed her arms and her ankles, rocking herself gently. "No. I want to ask you first, point blank: can you cure it? Will I ever be cancer-free?"

Dr. Shea's whole face softened with regret. "No, C.C. All I can do is try to control it. But that doesn't mean you can't live a full life. That's what I'm here for: to help you survive, to keep you comfortable, to help you make the most –"

"Stop. Please just stop it!"

"Are you sure I can't call your friend? I really think –"

"No. I need to be alone. I need to think. I don't have to decide right this minute, about anything, do I?"

"Not right this minute, but soon. Give me a call in the next few days." She took a card from her front pocket, and wrote on the back of it. "That's my cell. Don't hesitate to use it, bypass the office get straight to me. As soon as you can? Please? You're sure you're okay to drive?"

"Yes. I am, thanks. I'll call. Soon."

Dr. Shea nodded, and left the room, closing the door softly behind her. C.C. stared into space for a few seconds, then shook herself and began to dress. Somehow, she got out of the office, paid her co-pay, and drove herself to the "shed" where she sat down on the couch, shivering and sweating.

"Fucking crab," she muttered and then shrieked, a long, loud mad sound that made her own ears ring.

9. RETURN OF THE CRAB

When C.C. showed up at the condo late that afternoon, Quiola was deep into packing for another move; open boxes, stacks and balls of newspaper, twine, tape and in amidst it all, the cat.

"She's been in kitty heaven," said Quiola.

"So I see. You're making good progress here – better than I'm doing with the "shed". But I just called some local movers to finish for me." She sat down on the edge of the couch. "There's no good way to put this, so I'll just say it: the crab is back. I thought it was a routine x-ray for emphysema."

Quiola turned away from an open box. "What emphysema?"

"Dr. Shea says I've a touch of emphysema. I don't believe her – it's just a cough."

"What do you mean you don't believe her?"

"How could I have emphysema? I smoked, okay but only a little, for maybe three years. Doesn't make sense. Emphysema's for the hardcore."

"You didn't believe her? You didn't believe your own doctor?"

"Oh, who cares? The cancer is back. Fucking crab. Here I thought I'd beaten it off with a stick. What am I going to do?"

Quiola sat down in the middle of the messy living room floor, then laid flat on her back, on the cool hardwood and took several deep breaths, while Amelia curled up on her belly. C.C. slid off the couch and onto the floor with them both.

"Where is it back?"

"In my lung."

"When did you find this out?"

"Today. This morning."

"And the emphysema?"

"Just before the surgery. But I still don't think –"

"I don't care what you think," said Quiola rolling onto her side, spilling the cat. "And I'll tell you one thing. You are not going to any doctor's appointment alone again. Ever. I intend to stick to your side like glue. Emphysema is a disease, not an article of faith. What would your father have said?"

"Doctors make mistakes, too."

"X-rays don't."

"Yes they do if they aren't read −"

"Enough!" Quiola got to her feet and walked out.

✦

Having planted, like so many Americans, a victory patch to support the troops during the War, the Davises continued to grow fresh peas, beans, chives, basil, corn, so when Liz took C.C.'s hand and headed into Nancy's summer garden, it was full to bursting with flowers, early vegetables and sprouts of what would soon become the late summer crop.

"You have it with you? Yes?" Liz asked. "Good. Shall we bury it next to the other one or find a new spot?"

"Next to the other one. Mom said we could pick flowers for the dinner table."

"Lovely. So, do you remember where we buried the other one?"

C.C. pointed at an apple tree that sat between the pear and cherry trees.

"Fine." Liz moved past the black-eyed susans, the peas and beans until she stood with C.C. at the foot of the apple tree. She put down her basket of gardening tools. "Pick a spot," she said, as a yellow butterfly zigzagged by. It was just after lunch, and the sun showed signs of muscle, so that after Liz had put on her gloves, knelt on one denim knee and had been digging for a while, she worked up a light bead of sweat. C.C., dressed that day in a crisp jumper, watched and fingered the piece of paper in her pocket.

"There," said Liz. "that should be deep enough. Hand it over."

C.C. withdrew the paper from her pocket, and looked at the words, then turned her blue eyes up at Liz. "It will be gone, won't it?"

"All gone. I promise you, Ted won't hurt Tuck. When a person buries a secret-secret, it's all over. The other one didn't come back, did it?"

"No." C.C. held out the piece of paper. "Ted is okay?"

"He's fine. He's just a boy, that's all. Boys are funny. They like to scare girls. They like to stir up trouble. Ted just wanted some attention, that's all. He got it and it's over." She mounded dirt on top of the secret-secret, written out on the paper, and got off her knee, brushing dirt from her jeans. "Feel better?"

"I do. I really do!"

"Told you." She shook off the spade, adjusted one glove and selected a pair of shears. "Carry the basket?"

"Okay." C.C. took the handle. "Mom said black-eyed susans, yellow daisies and the larkspur."

Liz stared out across the garden. "Really. You mother has her ideas, doesn't she?"

"Yep. Like when she cooks, too. If Daddy cooks dinner, you never know what will happen. Like when Mom went to have Tucker. Daddy made us dinner, and it was steak and onions with fried potatoes. Can you believe it?"

"But that sounds yummy! What's wrong with it?"

C.C. laughed so hard she almost dropped her basket. "Oh, Aunt Liz, of course it was yummy. Daddy's dinner is always yummy, but it's *wrong*, don't you see? Because you don't make steak with *fried* potatoes, steak goes with baked, or maybe twice-baked."

"Oh, I see. Your mother does have rules, doesn't she? And what's the plan for tonight?" She began to cut black-eyed susans, laying them on one side of the basket.

"Soft-shelled crab, coleslaw, peas, bread and butter. I like that. Do you?"

"Peas when they're fresh. Crab, always. Especially soft-shelled ones – and your Mother knows it, too."

"Yep. She said it was because of your show you're having in the City."

Liz half-smiled. "Not much of one, but your Mom is an optimist."

"What does that mean?"

Liz leaned over the larkspur, and cut a bunch. "It means she has faith in me. She thinks I'm a good painter."

"You are! I know you are!"

"Thanks, honey." Having cut the flowers Nancy wanted, Liz put the shears away and took the basket from C.C. who asked, "Want to see the crabs? Dad has them in an ice bucket in the pantry. I think they look like big bugs. Don't you?" She shaped her hands like claws. "When they wave their arms and made them go like this?" She made a clamping motion with her clawed fingers. "Big bugs from the sea. But I'm going to eat them up before they can eat me!"

✦

Parker Moore moved with slow deliberation from one hive to the next, his bee veil, a sheer cloth that he'd had his wife sew to an old hat, closed, checking that no moths had been about, wreaking havoc with his swarms. Around the turn of the century, he'd switched from his inherited, old-style hives to the Langstroth modern ones, which had, in only one season, doubled his local profit. Pleased, he'd added to his apiary until he had about a two-dozen colonies.

"Father?"

Parker turned toward the voice of his youngest daughter who stood at a distance, arms folded across her chest, her light summer dress a size too big, a hand-me-down from her sister, Anita. With her sun-darkened skin and light eyes, she was a handsome girl, *too handsome for her own good,* her father thought.

"What does your mother want?" he said impatiently.

"She says you got to talk some sense into your son."

Parker turned back to his hive. "Tell her I'm busy."

"But he's gonna enlist."

This made Parker Moore straighten up. Taking his daughter by hand, yanking his veiled hat off, he nearly dragged Lizzie across the farm, marching, at a good clip, away from his bees, past the far barn, the near barn and in through the back screened door of the house, which he slammed.

"What the hell nonsense am I hearing?" he shouted at his eldest as he made his way from the kitchen to where Parker Junior – called Park – stood, beside his mother.

143

His son stiffened, and looked his father square in the eye. "I'm going over."

Sara Moore, seated at the dinner table, wore what Liz thought of as "Mother's stone-face." Her thin-lipped mouth set in a straight line, her blue eyes hard as marble, she shook her head. "Father, your son has lost his mind."

"No," said Park. "I have not. I'm a man. My country is at war. I know my duty."

"Your duty?" said Parker. "Your duty is to this family and this farm, not to some idiot in a Southern swamp. We've got troubles enough here without you running off to fight in another man's quarrel. Let those foreigners solve their own problems."

"But it is our problem. The *Lusitania* –"

"– was in the wrong place at the wrong time. Don't dump Wilson's garbage on me, boy."

"You voted for him."

Parker became very still as the young man spoke, eye of the hurricane still, which made Sara clasp her hands. Lizzie started edging over to the kitchen. The silence did not break until Parker at last intoned, with the finality of an ax-stroke, "You have work to do. So do I."

"Father –"

"Did you hear me? Jo shouldn't have to muck out all three barns by himself."

Park said nothing. He glanced at his mother, then turned on his heel and marched past Liz, out the kitchen door.

"Wait!," the girl said and hopped out the door after her brother, caught up and jogged along beside him. "You're not going to go, are you, Park? You're not gonna leave us?"

"Just watch me. Just you wait and see." He raised his voice as they neared the barn. "Jo? You in there?"

Liz stopped dead, letting her brother hurry on. She watched his back, blinked, watched and then murmured. "He is going. He's going all right."

✦

Quiola unbuckled the noseband and throatlatch, scooped her hand under the crownpiece, and encouraged Splash to relinquish the bit. Slipping on his halter, she cross-tied him, hung up the bridle where Mike could see it, and unbuckled the girth. Splash stood quiet, watching.

"So you caved," said Megan, checking her cell for messages.

"You could call it that."

"I thought you didn't want to move."

Quiola lifted her saddle and saddle pad off Splash, set the saddle on a tree and flipped the pad upside down on top of it. Somewhere in the distance, one of the horses whinnied. Splash let go some pungent gas. Quiola wrinkled her nose.

"Thanks, buddy. Phew. Feel better?"

Megan grinned. "He does. So?"

"No, I didn't want to move. But she's going to need me. The cancer is back."

"Oh, God. I'm sorry. I thought –"

"So did I. Hoped, anyway." She clipped Splash's lead to the halter. "Does he need a bath?"

"Not really but you can give him one, if you want."

"I'd like to." She stepped into the tack room, got a carrot from her stash, and offered it to the horse, who snapped it up in his soft lips. "You should see this house, Meg. It's gorgeous."

"That's a bonus, then, isn't it?"

"Oh, yeah, sure."

Megan put a gloved hand on Quiola's shoulder. "It'll be all right."

Quiola kept her face turned to Splash, and said, "I wish. But she's lying to me. She told me don't worry, she's going to beat it. But I didn't like the tone of her voice, so I phoned her doctor. She's dying, Meg. Where she's at, people don't bounce back and she's keeping that little fact to herself."

"Maybe. Maybe it's a little bit of denial, too?"

"Oh, yeah. That too." She stared down at her own hands. "I'm not good at this."

"Hey, girl, nobody is. Listen, if you need anything, you know you can ask?"

Quiola nodded.

"You okay?"

"Yeah."

"You sure?"

"Go on, Meg. I know you have a lesson, and yes, I'll be here Monday.

"Sorry I have to run. You try to have a good weekend."

Quiola leaned against Splash's wither and took off her helmet, with a deep sigh. The horse craned its neck, nibbling at her shirt, then licking the flat of her offered palm.

"Okay," she said. "A bath. I can do that, at least."

✦

C.C. stood before the mirror, staring at her newly re-bald self. She could scarcely believe she'd been forced through another molt, hair coming out first in little tufts, then in large, extravagant clumps until she went back to a barber and had herself shaved again to save herself from looking like a mangy dog. A wracking cough came up from the bottom of her feet and pulled her into a fetal position at the sink as she gagged over a wad of greenish-clear mucous. Panting, she washed it down the sink and closed her eyes. Every morning now for the past whole month had started like this, in the bathroom like this, hacking up part of her lungs, panting, wondering if she'd ever catch her breath again. She leaned against the cold porcelain of the sink and closed her eyes, just breathing. When she opened her eyes, she sat down heavily on the terry-clothed toilet seat, a cheek in one hand, taking as much air as she could, weariness like water washing through her. After a few minutes, she got back on her feet, cleaned her face, put on her robe, slippers and tucked a brown plastic medicine bottle into a pocket. After brushing her teeth, she opened the glass door of the shower, turned the taps and adjusted the temperature. Stepping across the large master bedroom, in which she'd installed a four-poster queen, a relic from her childhood, she opened the bedroom door.

"Quiola?"

The cat appeared in the hallway, mewing.

"Good morning, Amelia. Quiola? You up?"

"Huh?" came a sleepy voice from the next room. C.C. stepped down to it and pushed open the already open door. "Do you know what time it is?"

Quiola squinting, mumbled, "What?"

"Rise and shine."

"What time is it?"

"Six."

"Middle of the night."

"Just because it's dark? Come on – you've got to help me decide which of the new things I should show." She drummed her thin fingers against the door lintel. "I can't believe it's finally happening. A solo show! Do get up – Amelia wants her breakfast."

"You mean C.C. wants a soft-boiled egg," Quiola muttered into the pillows. "Just give me five more minutes."

"Fine. I'll be in the shower."

Back in her bedroom, C.C. shut the door and locked it. Sitting down before a small desk, she took the medicine bottle out of her robe's pocket, put it on the desktop next to a stack of envelopes, which she quickly sealed, one after another, and stamped. Then she put both the bottle and the letters in a satchel and snapped it shut.

✦

Quiola pushed herself up on her elbows and looked over the wreckage of half-unpacked boxes, open suitcases, objects out of place. She'd sold most of her furniture, given to charity what she no longer wanted, paring her life down to this bedroom and C.C.'s former studio. The "shed" had become, both upstairs and down, pure studio space and since the two houses stood on adjacent lots, they'd had a gate put in the fence between them. That way, when they went to the "shed" they didn't have to bother with cars or the road because the path lead out the back screened porch of the main Carriage House, across a gentle hill and right to the shed's front door.

Frost made the grass brittle stiff, and a light dust of snow clung to the ground. Bundled in several thick layers of wool and flannel, C.C. carried a thermos of coffee. Quiola opened the gate, and they made their way under a flat milky sky to the "shed". Once inside, Quiola pulled her hat off, chucked mittens, unbuttoned and began laying the fire, while C.C. went to the kitchen for two mugs. She poured coffee without taking off a single item of clothing, and carried it from the kitchen to the fireplace, where Quiola had the blaze at a nice snap.

"Did we get everything out of the basement?" she asked.

"Yeah. God it's cold in here."

"It'll warm up in a few minutes. So. What have you decided already?"

C.C. shrugged. "Nothing. I just can't believe Kempton & Shelf want to represent me, after all these wasted years. I hope Naomi isn't too upset by my leaving her, but Kempton & Shelf! When a gallery like that calls, you jump. Must be Lizzie's doing."

Quiola fanned her palms near the growing fire. "I expect you're right – but it isn't as if you dropped into a well. You've been showing."

"Mostly not and you know it. I've had the six in Naomi's gallery shipped over to Chelsea already. Should I build the show around them?"

"It's your show."

"Yeah, I know, I know but –" a cough stopped her and held her, made her find a tissue in her pocket to spit. "Disgusting," she muttered, panting a little.

"You okay?"

She put her palm to her forehead, as if taking a temperature. "I wish it would just stop but it won't, will it? No. Let's go back to the house – I can't do this now, I can't make any decisions right now."

"Go back? When I just got the fire started? Oh, no. Wait a minute. Tell me you didn't. You didn't, did you?"

"Oh, damn it, of course I did. You know I did."

Quiola stood up. "Jesus, C.C. when I said not to."

"I can't help it."

"But I don't care. I didn't want you to do anything."

"It's nothing big. Some champagne. No cake and no candles, okay? No candles. I bought a duck. You like duck."

"But you can't taste it, can you? Why torture yourself?"

"It's not torture. I think my taste buds are coming back." She smacked her lips. "Duck sounded good to me."

RETURN OF THE CRAB

"You are incorrigible. But it's not even lunch yet. Let's first make some choices about your work, before you run amok in the kitchen."

"All right – I think I should use the Paris group – you know, the ones I finished in the late eighties? At the heart of the exhibit, and then move to more recent stuff. "

"Nothing before the 80s? Nothing from –"

"No. I'm done with that."

"But for context –"

"No. This is about the artist am I now, not the student I was."

"Fine," said Quiola, moving to the other side of the room. "Let's have a look through everything, shall we? Do you think you might find the energy to do something in the next month, to add in?"

✦

Lizzie bent her head low over the paper, trying to steady her hand. The perfect and perfectly dead bee sat beside the paper on the big wooden table, its black lace of wings stiff and flat, its hairy legs curled underneath the bright yellow and black furry body, an ordinary drone that had simply died. Trying to capture the bee precisely, she found herself annoyed at how her hand sometimes did not do what she wanted, and how sometimes when she started a sketch the proportions were wrong – the wings too small or the polished bug-eyed head too big. At the sound of the back door opening, she looked up, checked on the baby in his cradle by her feet, and then retrieved her pencil, which had rolled to the edge of the table.

"How're you coming along?" said Parker, stepping in from the kitchen. His face and ears were ruddy with cold. She shrugged as he took her sketches off the table.

"Hmm," he said, looking over the several attempts. "The wings on this one –"

"I know. I'm gonna try again."

"Good girl." Parker put the drawings back down. Crouching to the cradle, he checked on the baby, pulling the wooly blanket up to the boy's chin. Standing, he gazed out the window.

"Snow tonight," he said. "I can taste it. Where's you mother? Lizzie?"

He turned around at her silence and found her as if in a trance, her light olive eyes mossy, almost blurred, her dark cheeks blanched, and her lips had thinned as if in a terrible wind.

"What's wrong? Lizzie? Are you sick?"

She dropped her pencil, swung her legs around the bench and knelt on the floor near her brother's cradle. She touched his little hand lightly, then glanced back at her father in a panic. "It can't snow," she said. "Daddy, tell me it won't snow tonight!"

"What the devil's gotten into you? Child? Come here."

She got up off her knees and went to stand between his blue-jeaned legs, looking down at his socks.

"Look at me when I speak to you, girl."

She did as she was told.

He examined her face, but now her cheeks were rosy, her lips as plump as ever they got, her olive-green eyes, green. "I want you to get into your coat and boots," he said, "and help me and your brothers round up the horses. Better get them settled before the snow. Your sister can watch Gus. Not that he needs watching when he's dead to the world like that."

"Daddy, he needs watching. Please, let me stay with him?"

"What the hell is wrong with you? You're too old to whine at me like that. Run along, get your things and I'll fetch your sister. Gus'll be fine. Look at him. Sound asleep, big and fat and all full of milk."

"No he won't. He won't be fine."

"What the devil? Are you trying to weasel out of work? You ought be ashamed."

She stamped her foot. "Am not, Daddy. I have to watch the baby. Somebody might steal him."

Parker's big farmer's hand swung out and whacked the girl across the face. She staggered a little, and tears jumped as the side of her face burned.

"That's for foolishness," he said, sternly. "Now do as you are told."

"What foolishness?" said Anita as she came around the hallway corner into the dining room, her hands full of folded kitchen towels. "Dad?"

"Your sister is acting crazy. I can't make out what's wrong with her. Lizzie, ten minutes. In the near barn." He walked into the kitchen, shrugged himself back into his working coat and boots and stepped outside.

"What was that all about?" asked Anita.

"Gus needs watching."

"'Course he does, he's just a baby."

"I need to watch him. It's gonna snow."

Anita put the towels down on the table. "So *that's* it. Snow tonight? So early –"

"It can't snow. It just can't."

"Lizzie, what do you mean? Father said you were being foolish. Were you?"

Liz clasped her hands. "I don't know."

"You don't know?"

"Something scary will happen, in the snow that's coming tonight. And Park, too. He's going to go this winter. Just like Gus."

Anita took her sister's hands gently in her own. "Elizabeth," she said. "You are talking nonsense. Do you hear me?"

But Lizzie wasn't listening, and her still, frightened face chilled Anita who squatted down and pulled her sister's nose a little. "Pumpkin, you've just been having bad dreams. Look at Gus. He's fine! And Park is going away – he's going over there, like the song says."

"He is? I thought Daddy said no."

"He did, but your brother is a man, now and as stubborn as Daddy. Before winter's over, he'll be gone to fight the Krauts."

Lizzie blinked. "You'll watch Gus?"

"Of course I will. Mama will be done with folding the laundry soon, and we'll both be with him. Nothing bad can happen, now, can it?"

"I guess not."

Anita stood up. "You'd better go help Father."

✦

She hadn't seen Ted since they'd settled their mother's estate. But the Return of the Crab made her seek him out, one more time. Not for solace or comfort: she'd been through that portal of hope one time too many. No. She simply needed to say goodbye. She told herself that his response wouldn't matter.

It took her three days to get him, not just his assistant, on the phone and even then he wasn't responsive to her suggestion that they meet, so she ended up ambushing him, by taking a train into the City and showing up at his office at precisely the moment his assistant said he'd be in. He agreed to meet her that evening before dinner for a quick drink at a place their parents used to take them to lunch, an on-again, off-again family reunion, before Tom Davis's heart, and Nancy's memory, began to fail. It was a rather large basement space called The Bistro. She was surprised to find it still in business after thirty-odd years, then surprised again when she came through the revolving doors to a techno-retro '50's-modernist fantasy, all white and chrome and clean, minimalist design, lime and light blue. She remembered the place as darkly lit with fake-Tiffany pendants hung over mahogany tables hugged by red-leather banquettes with brass fittings.

Ted was already at the glass and chrome bar, nursing a two-olive vodka martini. She was shocked at how old he looked, but seeing her surprise reflected on his aging face, she laughed. "Cancer, Ted. You know what it can do."

"Charlie," he murmured, standing briefly to brush a kiss past her cheek.

She hopped on to the barstool next to him. Well, she tried to hop. She made a pass at hopping, and landed well enough to feel proud of her attempt. "How're the kids?"

"I have three of them," he said, morosely. "Which one do you mean?"

"All of 'em. How are they?"

He closed his eyes and swirled the olive-laden twizzle stick around the martini glass. "Anna's gone to graduate school in California; Jason gave up on drag-racing and is studying law; Theresa's about to enter high school. They're fine."

"And their mothers?"

"Getting alimony on time."

"And the wife?"

"Her name, Charlie, is Belinda. She's fine."

"Good. Now that we've gotten all the nicetics out of the way, I'd like to order tonic water and lime."

He waved the bartender over, asking, "What happened to a G & T?"

"Gone with the Crab," she said, as the young woman in black and white headed their way. "You want another round?"

"Sure."

After the order was put in, he turned his chair around a bit and said, "I thought you were through with chemo?"

"How would *you* know?"

"Belinda. She knew."

"Okay, then, how did *she* know?"

He shrugged. "But aren't you, Charlie? Done?"

"Done. Yeah. That's the word."

"So why did you suddenly get the urge to lay eyes on me? Can't be Mom, we were just up to the cemetery last week. You know the last time I saw her alive she thought, when she could think of anything at all, that we were Al and Pam Kroenen, of all people. I had to tell Belinda those two have been dead longer than I can remember."

"She wasn't well."

"Of course she wasn't well. I'm just glad she never had to hit the end-stages of Alzheimer's and forget how to swallow. Let's talk about something else, shall we?"

C.C. stared at him. How was she going to tell this man anything? Who was he, this Ted Davis, a physician with no compassion, her brother? She hadn't a clue. An image of their father diapering Tucker clicked suddenly, without warning, into view like an old-fashioned film slide. She clicked it off and took a long, cold sip of tonic.

"So?" said Ted. "Just what did you want to talk to me about? Remember I've got a dinner date in twenty minutes, uptown."

"Would you look at that," she said, wonderingly. "A whole basket of 'em."

"Yeah, hard-boiled eggs. Protein, to keep the drinking crowd afloat."

She reached up and took one, cracking the shell on the bar. "Salt and pepper? Thanks." She took a bite. "Honestly, Ted, I just came to say goodbye."

"Oh, what are you moving overseas again? Back to Paris?"

"No. But I have – plans. Nothing's settled you understand, but I wanted to be sure to tell you in person."

"Really? I don't see why. You haven't bothered to call since Dad died." He sounded bitter. She could've shot back *my phone hasn't been ringing off the hook either!* and equaled his bitterness, but what she said was, "Well, here I am, telling you," and then, having finished her egg, she pushed herself off the stool, downed her tonic in one long swig, found a twenty and, laying it on the bar, said quietly, "Goodbye, Ted. Hope you have a nice uptown dinner. I've got a train to catch."

PART IV

SWAN SONG

10. TO BE GRACIOUS, AND SEEM HAPPY

Shivering, her bare scalp itchy under an expensive wig she wore for the "event," C.C. hugged her camel-hair coat close, and leaned against the concrete front of the gallery, near the modest sign of Kempton & Shelf. Streetlight caught the few soggy flakes, but the night felt profoundly dark to her. A car rounded the corner, headlights swept the walls and asphalt like a spot might hit a stage and if she made a dash, there'd be a shriek of breaks as the car slammed – but no, the car was Moby and it rolled to a harmless stop. Sighing, she shoved herself off the wall, opened the passenger door, and got in.

"I think," said Quiola, as she turned up the heat, "the 'event' went well."

C.C. rested her forehead against the window, watching but not seeing the city in motion. "What an idiot I am." She found a Kleenex, wiped the lipstick off her mouth hard, took the lipstick tube out of her pocket and chucked it in the plastic garbage bag hung round the stick. "First time and the last time I'll ever wear the stuff. No wonder Mom called it warpaint. I felt like a POW back there."

"But it was a fine opening –"

"Now you sound like Mom – 'just be gracious, darling, and seem happy.' How many times I heard that piece of wisdom! I wonder if Liz has any idea how – how – how fucking humiliating –" she coughed, the whole chilly horror of the polite crowd she'd just left squashing her, as if in cahoots with the Crab. "I just want to go home. That fiasco was worse than being buried alive. I want to forget the whole mess."

"Buried alive? At Kempton & Shelf? I'd give my eye-teeth for a fiasco like that." She lurched the Volvo suddenly, roughly, around a pothole.

"Are you trying to kill us? Go ahead, be my guest."

A black silence icier than that winter's evening took over, but when Quiola pulled Moby up the Carriage House drive, C.C. was asleep, snoring ever so softly into her wig, which had slipped sideways to hang indelicately from the bald ridge of one ear.

✦

Sitting on a high stool at her kitchen island, Nancy Davis frowned. "Let me see…you can take the…no, wait. You can take the girl out of the kitchen but… dang…it's an old saying. I just can't remember it." She gave her daughter a mute appeal for help.

"That's all right, Mom, I can't remember it either. Never was good with sayings and jokes. Can't ever remember the punch line." She handed her mother a peeler and a potato. "Help me get them done?"

"Oh sure, sweetie. I like potatoes."

"I know you do."

"What kind are we having?"

"Mashed. I just told you."

"You did? No you didn't."

"Never mind, Mom."

"All right, darling. You'd like these peeled?"

"Yes, Mom." C.C. wiped her hands on her white chef's apron, and opened the oven. Cinnamon and clove wafted into the room. "Pie's doing nicely, "she said and turned around to find her mother peering at the peeler as if it were a device of startlingly new technological invention.

"Mom? Could you peel the potatoes?"

"I – I don't remember how to use this thingie," she said sheepishly. "Maybe we could just boil them?"

"Mom, we're having mashed –"

"Well, then, why didn't you tell me so?"

"I just –" C.C. shook her head. "Never mind."

"Honestly, if you don't tell a person –" Nancy put the peeler down on the island with a sharp rap. "Your father will be ashamed of you."

C.C. drew in her breath, then let it out gently.

Nancy got up and walked toward the living room, calling Tom's name. C. C. followed after her. The living room, dimly lit, was empty and Nancy stood in the middle of that domestic emptiness with a puzzled look on her face. "Where's your father? I just left him five seconds ago in here with the *Times*. Honest to Pete that man can vanish when he wants to! Tom!" Her voice grew sharp with irritation. "Tom!"

But instead of her husband, Quiola appeared at the archway to the hall, her shoulders wrapped in a wool shawl, her hair a nest, her sleepy face concerned.

"What's going on?" she asked.

"Charlotte!" said Nancy, slowly seating herself in the wing chair Tom used to favor. "You didn't tell me we had company! And where's your father gone?"

Quiola glanced sharply at C.C. who said, "He's gone, Mom – remember?"

"Gone? Gone where?"

"Out," said Quiola as she sat on the couch near Nancy. "He's gone out for a bit – a little walk."

"I see. I'm sorry, do I know you, dear?"

Quiola put out her hand. "Quiola Kerr – I'm a friend of C – of Charlotte's."

"Delighted!" she said, and turned to her daughter. "How nice!"

"Yes, it is. Tell you what, why don't you sit here for little while – I'll get you some tea. Quiola can help me finish dinner."

Nancy lifted her feet onto an ottoman, shifting deeper into the chair. "Would you dear? I feel a little tired just now."

Quiola took off her shawl and draped it over the older woman's knees. "There you go – I think it's a bit chilly in here, don't you?"

"Oh, I don't want to take your –"

"That's fine. I can get a sweater."

"I'll be right back with the tea, Mother."

Nancy closed her eyes. "Don't rush on my account."

Quiola followed C.C. into the kitchen, and whispered, "You're right – she's getting worse. But she seemed so – lucid last night."

C.C. filled a teakettle with water. "She can go a week normal, and then she has, I don't know, a spell like this – but she's never forgotten about Dad before – why did you tell her he'd gone out?"

"I heard her calling for him – that's what woke me. And she sounded so sure he was in the house."

C.C. shook loose leaves from a tin into a tea caddy, screwed it shut. "I wonder if she'll notice when he doesn't come back – ever. A day nurse isn't going to be enough. I'll have to look around at homes or hospice. Poor Mom. I'll have to talk to Ted."

Quiola wandered over to the kitchen island, sat on the stool where Nancy had been, picked the peeler. "He knows how she is?"

"He knows. The nurse keeps us both up to speed."

"Does he know I'm here?"

"I certainly haven't told him. It was good of you to come up from the City for the weekend, Quiola. I should've said so last night – I really appreciate it. How's the apartment working out?"

"Fine. I really love the place. And well – I've met someone."

"That didn't take long!"

"I knew you'd be upset. Let's talk about it later."

"No, no," said C.C., checking on the tea. "If you mentioned her at all, this one's serious. So? What's her name?"

"His name is Luke. Luke O'Connor and he has asked me – what's that noise?"

"It's Mom. Mom?" She went back into the living room to find Nancy crying in a hopeless, helpless way. "Mom – what's wrong?"

Nancy blinked, and rubbed one eye, then unrolled the tissue stuffed inside her sleeve and dabbed at her tears. "I'm sorry," she said, with an attempt at a deprecating laugh that failed. "I was just thinking about your brother."

"Ted? Why? I know he doesn't see you as often –"

"No, no, not Ted. I was drifting off to a nice nap when I just saw his little face as he was that morning, you know, in the kitchen in his jammies, blond curls all tousled, and his nose all red – you remember he was just getting over a cold? He looked so near that I reached out to give him my tissue, like I did that morning so he could wipe his face, and then I guess I woke up – and remembered. Oh! I don't want to remember that, Charlie. I don't want to remember *that!*"

C.C. put her arms around her mother's shoulders, and said, "It's all right, it's all right. You don't have to."

✦

The morning after C.C.'s so-called fiasco of an opening at Kempton & Shelf, schoolmaster Splash saw the devil – literally, in Quiola's mind – and shied. One minute she was posting easily down the fence line, feeling, as she shouted to Megan, "– what you mean by Splash carrying me, doing the work," and the next minute she saw a shape leap toward her, and then the sudden arch of Splash's painted neck, a roll of white in the eye and all of the power of the animal surging. She made an instinctive grab for the bucking strap, missed and for a suspended moment saw her own legs in the air as she was ejected into pure space – then hit the sand like a catapult stone. The world contracted to noise and a wracking arching weight crushing her chest; dimly she felt other people at her side, and hoof-beats vibrating the earth until Megan's voice pierced the chaos with, "Take it easy! Quiola! Do you hear me?" which somehow helped to calm her, bring her back from the moon of shock to the fact that her wrist was throbbing, her face was bloody and she couldn't seem to breathe or focus.

"Wind knocked out of her." That was a man. Not Mike – who?

"Where's Splash?" asked Meg. "Who *was* that crazy woman?"

"Mike's got him penned, but he can't get near him. Horse is full of steam – never seen him like that. That woman scared him but good."

"Fool, running at a strange animal – where did she go? What's she doing on my farm? Call the police."

"She all right?" That was Mike. He touched Quiola's wrist. "It's beginning to swell. Better wrap it –" and that's when she blacked out.

When she came to, she was in an ambulance, strapped down, wholly immobile, with a paramedic beside her. "Ah, hello. Welcome back. Your blood pressure's finally rising a bit – I got all your information from your teacher, and we're on our way to –"

"I know," said Quiola. "I know exactly where we're headed. St. Matthews."

"Okay, so where does it hurt?"

"My wrist, here, my right side —"

"You been riding long?"

Quiola tried to laugh but her ribs hurt too much. "No, not long."

And then the journey became a series of repetitive questions about pain. Her face was still plastered with blood and sand from the arena and she felt tiny grains worming their way down her boots, her neck. Everything and everyone moved very fast around her immobility until suddenly she was alone in a dim emergency room, her butt burning from a shot — "like a massive upload of aspirin" said the nurse — her face mercifully wiped clean, her arm laid on a pillow resting on her lap, like it was a fragile tiara.

Now able to breathe again, she stared at the ceiling, when the door creaked open, and, almost shyly, Megan's face peered in.

"Meg! What are you doing here?"

"Hi, honey." She sat down on the institutional metal and foam pad chair beside the door. "I followed the ambulance here in your car, with your gear and all — I wanted to make sure you were all right. What did they say?"

"I've broken my wrist. X-rays soon."

"Hurry up and wait."

"Yeah. Do you have your phone? I should call C.C."

Megan unclipped her cell from its holster. "This should be fun."

"Exactly." But the "fun" was postponed when no one answered either at the house, or on C.C.'s cell. Quiola left calm messages, trying to sound as matter of fact as possible. Handing the phone back to Megan, she asked, "Can you stay a little longer? I can't tell you how comforting it is, to have someone familiar near."

"In the hospital? Oh I know. You stay in the horse business, you are bound to end up on the inside of a cast, sooner or later. Anyway, I've canceled the rest of my day, and plan to drive you home. My husband can come fetch me, at your house, if that's all right with you?"

"Miss?" said a young technician. "Sorry — but I'm here to take you for x-rays." The young woman glanced at Megan. "It should only take a few minutes."

Meg nodded and within five minutes Quiola was wheeled away as a desperate loneliness inhaled her, and although the techs — all of them women, all of them young — were kind, the pain in her wrist sliced through medication, and she began to dry-heave so badly the red-head ran for a plastic bucket just in case. The techs kept apologizing to her, but she seemed to hear them on some kind of excruciating time delay, so that it wasn't until she was being wheeled away from the dark x-ray room with its massive machinery and whirring cha-thunk operation, that she mustered enough will to say, "It's all right."

Returned to Megan limp and throbbing, Quiola managed a weak smile.

"They beat you up back there?"

"Kind of. I can't imagine what that would've been like without pain meds."

"Make sure the doctor gives you something for tonight."

"Yeah. Say, Meg, what happened back there with Splash – is he okay?"

"Just goes to show there is no such thing as a bomb-proof horse. You know Splash – he's so calm. But that crazy-ass woman came running at him, waving, of all things, a crow-bar and as I've always told you, he still has the mojo in him." She shrugged. "He's a horse. Horses are flight animals. He flew and didn't bother to carry you out of the danger zone. He was all hot, too. We had God's good own of a time calming him, and when Bob finally did, he stood there heaving and shivering."

"Bob?"

"My old trainer – he just happened to be on the farm today. Good thing, though. He's dealt with just about every kind of horse accident that can happen. He called 911, and the police, who caught that woman. Charged her with trespass."

"Did anyone recognize her?"

"Not around here. Name's Evelyn Porter."

"Evelyn? But it can't be! She's in California."

"You know her? Quiola, that's serious. That woman had a fucking crowbar! I mean, she said she just needed some help with her car but since when –"

"Good God. I'd better talk to the police."

Meg glanced around. "Are you safe here? They just fined her, is all – maybe we ought to call the police now."

"I know Evelyn. She won't come here."

"That's good. Still oughta call the cops. Man, I could sure use a smoke."

"Why don't you? I'm sure I'll be here another hour at least. Or more."

"Left them at the barn."

"Take mine – pack's in the car. I'm going to quit anyway."

Megan gave her a quizzical look. "You are? Why?"

"It's going to sound silly –"

"Silly? It's smoking that's silly. And a bad habit, but I've never been able to quit. I'd worry more about that crazy ass woman –"

"The thing is, Meg, I never smoked before I started riding. C.C. thinks I have a death wish. But that's not it. That's not it at all, and Evelyn showing up today settles it."

"What? Why?"

"Because she's threatened to kill me before. Don't worry, I *will* call the police – my point is, I don't want to die. I don't have a death wish. But I think I've been trying, in some weird way, to reconnect with my mother – my mother's people. Tobacco was sacred to them, and so is the horse. But my mother was –" she hesitated, then chose the American name "– part Chippewa, and they were fishermen mostly, and even if they did use tobacco, they also harvested wild rice and corn and maple syrup. Beaver, deer, wolves, the elk, the deer, the moose, and dogs mattered to them, not horses. But Mom taught me really very little about her – my – heritage. She wanted me to grow up white like my father, be an American. And I did, more or less. But I guess it's gotten to me, that loss of someone she was, and of a way of being. It's been gathering inside, like rain –"

"You!" said Meg, tugging gently at Quiola's toe. "You are darn right, that is one very silly reason to start smoking. My excuse is no better, though. When I was thirteen, I just wanted to look cool."

Quiola laughed. "Go on, then, sneak out of here for a smoke! Don't worry about me. Evelyn is crazy, but she wouldn't dare come in here. I'll be fine."

✦

With the top of her borrowed, bright yellow, brand-new VW bug down, C.C. drove at a fair clip up the two-lane Route 6, snaking out across quiet empty woodland of Cape Cod to Provincetown. It was early summer, 1989, and C.C. was in high spirits, exhilarated by the fine day and the unusual prospect of a whole summer in P-town. She hummed to herself as the warm, lively air whipped her hair about her face.

The woods grew sparse as the highway dipped toward the harbor town, and the tang of the sea, now close at hand, grew sharp. She took 6 only so as far as Howland, then steered the beetle down to Bradford; she was to take possession of an old house that her friends, Pete and Mark, two writers, owned and had lent to her for the summer – they were on an anniversary trip to Florence. The house sat on the corner of Priscilla Allen and Bradford, a two-story white clapboard with hunter green shutters and trim, the front lawn wholly given over to a mass of variegated wildflowers, honeysuckle, cornflowers and Queen Anne's lace. Turning the bug onto Priscilla Allen, she bumped into the sandy driveway behind the house, and parked near the detached garage. She checked the time: ten a.m. Quiola's ferry wasn't due – but then she glanced up sharply into the rear-view to see someone sitting on the back stoop of her borrowed house, curled up inside a striped woolen blanket of yellow, red and orange. The person stirred, stretched and before C.C. had time to register anything like surprise, Quiola's dark eyes had found her own in the rear-view mirror.

"What the –" she said, nearly throwing herself out of the car.

Quiola grasped the wrought iron railing and pulled herself to her feet, yawning. She slipped the blanket off her shoulders. Dressed in a sweatshirt, blue jeans and Converse sneakers, she looked like a kid.

"Heya!" she called.

"What are you doing here so soon?"

"I couldn't wait. I had nothing to do, no one to see in Boston, and – I just didn't want to stay there – it's too full of memory. This is better. I've never been out to the Cape before. Never got around to it, when I was in college."

"How long have you been waiting?"

"I took the ferry over last night, found a nice place to eat and, you know, wash up, then I came here."

"Here? For the *night?*"

"It was mild, and the stars are good company."

"Apart from how uncomfortable concrete is, weren't you afraid?"

"Of what? Local strays?"

"You could put it that way, I guess."

Quiola followed C.C. inside the house. "You are too much! I was on private property, and this town is hardly full of mean streets. Wow, this is nice," she said, glancing around as C.C. switched on the overhead to show an old-fashioned kitchen, white with blue trim and blue rose wall-paper. The room opened, through an arch, to the living room in which dark-oak bookshelves of books dominated.

"I've only been here once before," said C.C. "Mark and Peter bought it after Peter's novel became a finalist for the PEN Faulkner Award, and he got that two book contract from FSG, remember?"

Quiola nodded. "Yes, of course I remember. I went to the congratulations party in the City. Besides, it's where I met Luke."

"That's right. But – Quiola, you must be stiff as a board from a night on a porch, and I bet you could use a bathroom?"

"Well – now that you mention it –" and so together they found the first floor bathroom, set off the front vestibule. While Quiola tidied up, C.C. went back outdoors for her luggage and Quiola's duffel, which she'd been using as a pillow.

Vagrant, thought C.C. happily, *little vagrant.* She lugged the duffel inside to Quiola, who was peering at a glass-fronted bookshelf.

"So much Faulkner," she said.

"Mark's idol. What have you got in this bag, stones?"

"No, but I stuffed a whole summer into it. Where should I put it?"

"That depends on where you want to spend the nights."

Quiola's face went still, her dark eyes became, if possible, darker. "I thought we'd already settled this, C.C. You know that just because Luke isn't here doesn't mean I'm well, available." She put the duffel back down. "I'll leave, if I must. I can turn around and go back home –"

"– to a man."

"Yes. Back home to my husband. I was dating a man when you first met me, a thousand years ago, now, don't you remember? Do we have to do this again? You know I wouldn't have agreed to come – not if we were going to have to go all through this again. I cannot be who you want me to be – I'm not who you've dreamt me, I never was. You made me up, while the real live me wasn't looking!"

"I love you," said C.C. simply. "I always have, and I always will."

"Christ."

"But it's true – you can't tell me you never loved me. I won't believe it!"

"Don't shout at me."

"I'm not shouting. I guess I just can't –"

"– believe me?" Quiola shook her head. "But you know Luke! How can you think I'd lie to him? I tell him everything. He trusts me. We trust each other."

"You lied to me once before."

"No, I didn't. I never lied – I just, well, I just left things out – for a while. I thought we'd done with this, years ago! Evelyn was a mistake, a terrible, terrible mistake, C.C., and I'd give everything, *everything*, to have not made it. But I did. How many years do I have to *beg* you to believe me?"

"Luke's not a mistake, then."

Quiola stared at her ex, her face flushing. "No. If that's what you were hoping, then I'm truly sorry. You should have told me. And I think, now, that I should leave."

"Don't go. It's all right. Let's find you a room."

"I think I should go," she repeated.

C.C. took a deep breath, and then let it out, visibly deflating herself. She perched on the arm of an armchair, and smoothed back her hair. "Please don't leave. I'm sorry. You're right, I shouldn't have, it's not fair of me. Not fair to Luke, either – he trusts me, too. So please, I'm offering my apology. It won't happen again."

"Why can't you just let me go?"

The older woman closed her eyes and laughed unhappily. "Love."

"C.C., I love you. You know that. But I'm in love with –"

"– Luke, and have been, for some time. Yes, I know it. I saw it. I do believe it, even if part of me just won't behave. But I will. I'll be an adult. I'll behave." She opened her eyes. "Let's go upstairs."

167

"I don't know – maybe it would be better if I did leave. I don't want to hurt you. I never wanted to hurt you, even when I left for Berkeley, but I was so young. I just had to – I don't know. I felt I had to break away, I had to find out who I was – not the Quiola you'd made."

"But I didn't make you up, love. I'm not that inventive."

"You know what I mean."

"Yes, sadly, I do. That's the strangest part – I know very well, but then I see you again, and my heart misbehaves me." She stood. "Come on, let's try to forget it. I promise to be a good girl. Lord knows the both of us could use a quiet working vacation, which is what this is. A quiet. Working. Vacation."

Quiola picked up her duffel, and the two women went upstairs, talking of other things, of friends and family, of Liz, of safe, shared things, deliberately cordial again. After exploring the two-story extent of their summer retreat, they walked up to Pearl Street and into Provincetown Arts Center – C.C. had been asked to teach a three-week painting workshop there. As they meandered into the pebble-stone courtyard, Quiola said,

"I don't suppose you might have mentioned my work to –"

"No. I can't do that. I told you I couldn't. That's not the way this place operates, or at least I'm not going to make it operate that way, and besides, I did finagle you some studio space."

Quiola averted her eyes quickly, nodding as they approached what looked to be a door to an office, but turned out to be an auditorium. No one was there, so they went back to the bright, sunlit yard again, this time running into a resident who located for them the main office. And all that morning, as C.C. and she were introduced, given a tour, shown the workshop rooms, the studios, the grounds, Quiola smiled, and was silently polite. No one asked her much of anything, and she assumed C.C. had merely informed the Center that she'd arrive with a friend, rather than with someone who had an MFA from Berkeley and was a Native artist to boot, although she never presumed on her lost heritage, and rarely shared it with anyone. She'd never told Evelyn, thank God. She'd never told Liz Moore, even though Liz lived in the land of her birth and of her mother's people.

Despite her silences, though, Quiola thought she was, after all, someone whom the Center might, perhaps, maybe just might be interested in, despite her lack of fame, but no, because C.C. would not speak the words for her, would not give her those professional words that might have unlocked a few doors, and neither would she speak those words for herself. She had her pride, and she would not seem a beggar.

I'll work, she thought grimly, *I'll just keep working, as Luke says – it's the process, not the outcome, I don't need to sell, to be celebrated, I just need to live and to work, and that's the chance I have this summer. I don't have to teach, I don't want to sell myself, I can just be and work.*

✦

Rose carried her infant daughter tucked close to her heart in a thick cotton sling of her own devising, snug, safe as she could make the child as she hiked out across the sheer lake rock, making her way toward what whites called the Witch Tree, Manido-Gree-Shi-Gance, spirit-little-cedar, the ancient conifer that grew tough and tenuous from the crevices of the rocks above the Lake, her thick yet spindly root-legs clenched, running bare over the rock, grasping what little earth she could find. The lake wind was up, and Rose knew Kitchigami would be howling. Already the bitter breath of winter had eased; small golden marsh flowers unfurled along the banks of rivers and streams. Moose would mate, and the air would be sharp with love.

To plan to leave Grand Portage had been easy for Rose, but actually leaving, this was where the pain began – she'd had no idea the pain would start inside like this, a shredding that tore first at her throat, tightening it, trapping her inside. If she wasn't careful to keep mending herself, she'd blow away into a thousand pieces and who would nurse Quiola, bring her strong into the world? Not her own mother, Marjorie, who hung in the past like a full moon unwilling to wane. Not Marjorie Otter, who had brought Rose here to this very spot when she'd been ten, to leave an offering to the mandigo. Not the Marjorie Otter who'd forced her daughter to fast at thirteen, who taught her primitive nonsense as knowledge. Primitive rituals,

169

magic, pagan idiocy — it all embarrassed her, at Catholic boarding school and she'd prayed to Our Virgin for release.

Yet here she was, bending to it again, taking her own girl to the spirit-little-cedar, asking for the medicine to help her do this thing, leave and become what she wanted her daughter to be when she grew — strong, alone, free of the past.

11. MEIG'S POINT

C.C. stepped into Quiola's bedroom and kissed her damp forehead. Drugged up on codeine, awkward in her plexiglass cast, Quiola didn't move. C.C. gave the cat a quick chuck under the chin, and left. She pulled a cashmere cap over her baldness, buttoned up her coat, and taking her satchel with her, went out the door, leaving the Carriage House in the quiet, chilly gray dawn. Moby started up smooth, and she backed the car out of the icy drive. The frozen neighborhood was tranquil, silent, the sky overcast as she drove toward Meig's Point, stopping once to snap open her satchel, remove a handful of stamped letters and drop them inside a postbox.

Deprived by distance of Montauk Point, she took Meig's as her consolation prize that morning. Raised beside the Sound, she'd grown up on its beaches, depended on it to be there, waiting, patient, quiet under each successive winter sky. *At least the water,* she told herself, *is still the Sound.* Pulling into the wide, empty lot, she parked; if she were home, she'd be grinding coffee beans, perhaps tasting the caviar she'd bought, attending to Amelia's little demands or stepping down to the "shed" and the smell of oil paint and linseed oil…her cell phone rang, but she let it go as she undressed in the front seat of her creaky white behemoth. Naked, hairless, her flat, knobby-scarred chest dimpling from the cold, she wriggled, clumsy about the steering wheel, back into her coat. A little breathless, she checked the time. Her cell phone rang again. This time, she answered.

"Liz."

"Ah, thank goodness. Where are you? You sound like you're in a tin can."

"I am. I'm in the car."

"At this hour?"

"Needed a ride, that's all. Is something wrong?"

171

"I just wanted to hear your voice, Charlie. We haven't spoken in a few weeks, and I'm an old woman. I could pop off at any minute. Why haven't you called?"

"I guess I haven't felt much like talking."

"I see. How is Quiola doing?"

"Ah, the damn fool broke her wrist. Fell off the horse. She's all right otherwise. But I don't know if it's hit her yet – it's her right wrist, so no work for her, unless she can train her left hand."

"Oh, my. She'll go nuts."

"I would. But she's a tough cookie. She'll get through it all right."

"And are you, Charlie? Getting through?"

"Getting through? I am. Yes. Don't worry."

"You aren't a tough cookie, you know – never were. Stubborn, but not tough."

"No," breathed C.C. "I'm glad you called. I didn't realize it, but I needed to hear your voice, too. It gives me courage. But I have to go now."

"All right. Please take care."

"I am – bye," and she folded the phone shut, setting it on top of her pile of discarded clothing. When she opened the car door, the wind sliced right through the coat, but still she felt warm. Grabbing her satchel off the car floor, locking the door, she turned into the wind and walked against it, head bent to keep the sand out of her eyes, cross the boardwalk to that little sheltered nook, half hidden but open to the sea, the same nook where Quiola had gone to recover from her drunk. For a little while she sat huddled there, watching the infinite variety of water. Then she opened her satchel for a brown pill bottle and water. Popping the top off, she cupped all the pills in her palm and downed them with swallows of water, one by one until she couldn't see straight and then, quick, she "shed" the winter coat and lunged into an awkward dash to launch her scarred, diminished body at the cold December Sound with a ferocity only a lover could muster, an ardent arrow of human fury, shot at the frozen heart of a winter sea.

✦

Quiola woke. She struggled to sit, unused to the drag of the cast on her forearm. For a minute she sat staring like a zombie, thinking, *damn drugs*. Amelia, jostled from her warm spot, jumped down from the bed and when Quiola got up, followed her into the hall, needling in and out between human legs.

"C.C? You awake?"

No answer. Yawning, Quiola went back to her room, and gingerly shrugged into a robe using her one good hand and teeth to tie the belt, then shuffled down the hall to C.C.'s bedroom and knocked. Nothing. She knocked again; opened the door. The bed was made, the room tidy, empty.

Downstairs she found a note on the kitchen counter, next to the coffee pot.

Q –

Had to run an early errand. Be careful of your hand. Coffee's scooped, water's in the pot so just turn it on. Caviar and crumbled egg. Toast. Kisses.
Love you –
C.C.

Amelia mewed, pawing at the free-hanging ends of the terrycloth robe.

"Stop it, cat," said Quiola as she turned the coffee pot on, put a slice in the toaster-oven and went to get that morning's *New York Times*, waiting for C.C. to come home, but by lunch, she knew something was wrong. She tried C.C.'s cell, left a message, called the police (who could only say to call back in twenty-four hours) called Megan and then Peter and Mark and then any friend she could think of (except Liz; no need to bother her so far away) but everyone said soothing things like maybe C.C. just wanted some time to herself, wasn't she upset about the show? Or maybe she'd gone Christmas shopping, you know, or to the library, or perhaps she had an appointment she'd forgotten. By suppertime, Quiola called Ted.

CLINTON, CT. Early this morning, a woman's body was found near the breakwater on Meig's Point, at Hammonasett beach. Wearing a woolen cap, otherwise naked and bald, the woman was badly battered and as yet unidentified. An autopsy is scheduled to be performed to determine the exact time and cause of death. Police ask anyone who might have information leading to the identity of this woman to please contact local authorities.

"We had such a nice dinner together —" Quiola said and cleared her throat. "I mean of course she was tired, but happy. The next morning, when she was gone so early like that, I believed her note, she had errands to do, you know, getting ready for the holiday —"

"Quiola, you couldn't have known," said Liz firmly.

"Maybe —"

"No. Not even guessed. I know she was fine. I spoke to her myself that morning."

"You did? She seemed okay, didn't she? I mean, the night before, we talked about normal stuff, like should she bother with a garden next spring and so on, though she kept saying to me 'what a tickle I've got in my throat' when we both knew it wasn't just a tickle. They found Moby in the parking lot, just above Meig's Point. It was all so deliberate. She'd contacted the Hemlock Society. No botch-job for her."

"She was always thorough. One last installation performance."

"Oh, Liz how can you —"

"You know I'm right. Those letters she sent that morning only proves it."

"I can't open mine. I just can't bear it. Why would she do such a thing?"

"As you said, she was deliberate. How's Ted handling it?"

"Bastard."

"You too? My, my, what has that boy done now?"

"He's contesting the will. I'm just glad Nancy and Tom aren't alive to see this."

"I wouldn't worry. I'm sure he won't get far."

"So the lawyer says. In the meantime, I'm going through her work. She was wrong to feel so badly about the show. Kempton & Shelf want more."

"Of course they do, now they do. Be wise, my dear, for Charlie's sake. Be wise and make the most of this. Remember, suicide sells."

"That's just gruesome."

"It may be gruesome," said Liz. "It's also the truth."

✦

"Just what is it with you?" C.C. asked Ted, both of them home on Montauk for the holiday season, 1956, she from Smith, he from his first year at Yale Medical school. He'd been picking at her all day about every little thing. Now as they hung bulbs and ornaments on the tree in the living room, he'd just told her she had no idea –

"...how to make a tree look balanced."

"Is that what they taught you at Amherst?"

He moved the little star she'd just hung to a higher branch. In the next room the phonograph played Nat King Cole's 'The Christmas Song', a rich, muffled soundtrack for their argument.

"God, you are conceited," she said, snatching the little star and putting it back where she'd first hung it.

He stared at her.

She put her hands on her hips.

"I learned a lot at Amherst," he said.

"Bet you did."

He shook his head, took the little star off the branch again and hung it as high as he could reach. The tree was a seven and half-footer; Ted was six foot one and C.C., a foot smaller than he.

"You bastard," she muttered.

"What kind of language is that for a young lady?" said Nancy, standing at the threshold of the room, with a tray of four cocoa mugs.

"Oh, Mother," said C.C. "Ted's being impossible."

Nancy put her tray down carefully on the coffee table. "Ted?"

"I'm trying," he said, "to make the tree look nice. Balanced."

Nancy eyed the half-dressed fir. "Balanced?"

"See? Mom doesn't care!"

"Of course the tree needs balance," said Ted. "Something around here does."

"What's that supposed to mean?" asked C.C.

"Nothing."

"Well, I think the tree looks fine," said Nancy. "Where's your father?"

"He went to fetch the Gaineses from the station."

"Bother," said Nancy, frowning.

"No kidding," said Ted.

"His cocoa will get cold," said Nancy, still frowning. "Here, you take your cups. I'll put ours back in the pot, keep it warm." She picked up the tray. "I guess I'll split mine with Liz, if she wants some."

"She won't. Too sweet, said Ted."

"Is it?" asked Nancy, looking at the remaining mugs on the tray. "I'm sorry."

"It's fine," said C.C. "Just right."

"Hmm," said Nancy as she headed back to the kitchen.

"Why'd you tell her that? This is the way she always makes it." He shook his head. "Never mind."

"Like I said – what is it with you?"

"Nothing! Nothing."

"You sure are being –"

"Look," he said, putting his mug down. A drop of hot chocolate jumped to the tabletop. "I just want a little normality around here, okay? Just a normal family, a nice normal Christmas – like 'Father Knows Best.'"

"Mom makes hot chocolate, Dad picks up aunt and uncle from the train, sissy and brother hang ornaments on the tree. How much more normal could you get?"

He glared at her. "She's not my aunt. Not yours, either."

C.C. rolled her eyes. "She might as well be, by now."

"Well, she's not. And I'm tired of her. Why can't she and Paul stay in Beatnikville and leave the rest of us alone? Crazy old woman."

"Ted!"

"What?" He picked an ornament out of the storage basket and pulled away tissue paper. "Ever since I can remember, Liz Moore has been nothing short of a lunatic."

"She's Mom's best friend."

Ted shrugged and hung the green and red bulb on a branch.

"Without Liz, I don't think Mom would have –"

"Don't, Charlie. Just don't."

"Don't? But –"

"But nothing. Mom and Dad – all of us – would have been better off if Liz Moore never set foot over the threshold. She's a menace."

C.C. sat down slowly on a flowered ottoman. "How so?"

"She as jealous as one of her damn cats. For a start."

"Jealous? Of who?"

"Dad. Tucker. You. Me. Anyone who Mom might love."

"Oh, that's ridiculous."

He shrugged again. "Tuck was her favorite."

"Lizzie's?"

"No, dumbhead, Mom's. And don't tell me you couldn't feel it. After Tucker – Mom was destroyed. I swear she couldn't even see me, like I was a ghost."

"That's why I'm saying, Liz helped –"

"Oh you would take her side, wouldn't you? Creep. But you always liked that witch and I guess people like you have to stick together, huh?"

"People like –?"

"You know. Perverts." He flushed.

C.C.'s face whitened. "That's what you think."

"That's what I know. I told you, I learned a lot at Amherst, especially about you 'girls' at Smith. As a doctor, I know it's a mental disease and all, so I feel sorry for you – but not for your so-called auntie. I figure maybe she's the reason you're the way you are, always being here, and you taking lessons from her. Maybe she converted you."

"That's crazy."

"Is it? How come you've never had a boyfriend?"

"Liz is married to Paul. Or did you forget about him?"

"He's an old drunk. Mom won't be offering him any cocoa, that's for damn sure. Bet she's got the whisky poured."

"Ted."

"What?"

177

"These people are our friends –"

"Not my friends," he said and snatched another ornament out of the basket, but the tissue tore and the ornament, bare, rolled from his grasp to break with a clean glassy pop on the hardwood floor.

✦

Alone one cold dawn, at the same hour C.C. had left the house for the last time, Quiola took a large, woolen blanket she'd found in the cedar chest of the "shed" out into the yard, poured coffee from a cafetiere and finally opened C.C.'s posthumous letter. In the envelope she found a miniature acrylic, just a sketch, suggestive; on the back, the words "Vixen – essence of Quiola" and the sketch of her own dark features had the quickness of a carnivore, a slight cunning, playful smile.

"Oh, C.C. –" she said aloud.

Dearest:

By now you will know where I've gone, what I've done. Please try not to grieve hard, or blame me. I am not, perhaps, as strong as other people. It depends on how you look at it. You were raised Catholic, and for you, what I have chosen is wrong. But this is my choice. I choose. To me it is right. Perhaps we choose to be born, as well; our parents' earthly choices merely a manifestation of our own soul's will, which would certainly throw a spanner into most life and death debates. I choose death, not because I've refused life, but because death comes. I see him hanging about with his scythe, a farmer on the way to harvest. I am ripe. It is time. Know I love you. Always.

With all my heart,

C.C.

Quiola folded the letter up and slipped it back into the envelope with the sketch. She sat for awhile doing nothing, until her coffee went cold. Then she collected her things, and walked back up to the Carriage House, only to see Mark's Toyota Corolla parked off to one side of the garage. He and Peter stood like refugees on the front stoop.

"Hey!" she called, hurrying up the slate walkway.

"Quiola," said Mark, hugging her, and handing her over to Peter. "You two," she said, stepping back. "What in the hell are you doing here?"

Peter smiled. "We're on a little road trip. Had a hankering for the City, got in the car, and I-95 just took us to your place."

"Come in, then," she said, unlocking the front door and stepping into an empty, echoing space.

"My God, Quiola, what's happened? Where's did all the furniture go?"

"Oh, I can't live here anymore. She loved this place, but it's too big for just me, and without her −" Quiola shrugged. "I gave some of the older things to Ted and Belinda, when they stopped contesting the will, then sold what I didn't need. I'm going to move back into the 'shed' as soon as I can rent this place. Want some coffee?"

"Love some," said Mark. "I can see why you prefer the 'shed'."

"Me too," said Peter. "It's cozy. I'd work better in that space than this one."

"So how's the new one going?" asked Quiola, grinding beans.

"Oh, my. Touchy subject," said Mark, throwing a quick glance at his partner.

"I'm tapped out," Peter explained. "That's how it feels. I write a line, cross it out, write another three and need to scream. It's not happening right now."

"Me too," said Quiola. "But with this −" she lifted her cast, "− at least I have an honest to god excuse until it comes off."

Peter put a gentle hand on her shoulder. "You need a break of a different sort."

Quiola kept her gaze firmly on the coffee pot. "I need to keep busy."

"That, too."

"You never told us," said Mark, "what happened with your crazy ex − the one who spooked the horse and broke that wrist?"

Quiola smiled grimly. "I took out a restraining order, and I gather she just left. Went back to the West Coast, and put a continent between us again. I think seeing me fly off Splash ended something for her. At least I hope it's over, now, and for good. It's exhausting to have your mistakes follow you around."

179

Just then, the doorbell rang.

"Um, expecting someone?" asked Peter.

"No – and don't worry, it won't be Evelyn, trust me. Just let me go see –" she left the coffee pot on and went back through the empty, echoing house to peer through the spy-hole, then open the door.

"Good morning – Miss Kerr, is it?" said a short, rumpled man with an ingratiating smile. "My name is Ben Griffin." He stuck out a rather pudgy hand.

"Yes? What can I do for you?"

"I'm a reporter for the *Clinton Gazette*. I was wondering if you could tell me a little bit about your unfortunate friend – she was a friend, is that right?" He glanced at his notebook. "Charlotte Calliope Davis? That's a mouthful, isn't it?"

"Please," said Quiola roughly, "go away." She shut the door before the man could say another word.

He rang the bell.

She locked the door.

He rang the bell again, which brought Peter out from the kitchen, worried. "What's going on?"

"There's a reporter out there. Sniffing about for dirt on C.C."

"Oh brother!" He took Quiola's good elbow and tugged her back to the kitchen, even as the doorbell rang again.

"Ghoul," muttered Quiola. "They're all ghouls. Lizzie warned me: suicide sells. But somehow I wasn't prepared for things like this."

"Let's have some coffee," said Peter, soothingly.

"What's up?" asked Mark.

"A reporter. He wants to know more about C.C. Nothing nice, let's just say."

"Oh, yuck."

"Please, talk about something else," said Quiola. "He'll go away eventually."

"Well as a matter of fact, Mark and I have a proposal for you. We'd like to take this place off your hands, in a sense – we'd like to rent it from you, and open a gallery here. A green gallery, too, something both earth and artist friendly, and a warm, inviting place for art we like, not for profit, for you and me and people like us."

"We'd call it the Charlie Davis Gallery – what do you think? You could finally mount a full show of your own, mixed media, everything. And we have some connections, we know people in the business –"

"– like you –"

"Guys!" said Quiola. "I paint. I throw pots. I've no head for business, and no real contacts."

"Oh, yes you do," Peter said, eyeing her. "Quit with the pride, girlfriend. You can call Liz Moore for us. With her in the mix, the Charlie Davis Gallery will have legs!"

Peter's idea blossomed as if organic, a thing of the earth. Liz, to Quiola's shock, was only too happy to promise the ice-blue *Wirkorgan* she had in her bedroom as the center piece for the gallery's first night opening, a gift that was a instant sensation, plastered in full color in that Sunday's *New York Times* Arts & Leisure section. The mere existence of what critics dubbed simply "The Blue" proved electrifying. But what was truly astonishing to everyone, including Quiola, was the way in which "The Blue" and the other work showing that night – C.C.'s *Planets*, and her last sequence, so painful on it's own, somehow made serene in converse the sheering cold of "The Blue" while Quiola's watercolors danced – all seemed to pulsate, throbbing with a visual music that was an orchestration of light and dark, of color that seemed almost to chime, a *vibrato* of three visions, fusing, at last and as if by design, into one.

✦

November 12, Lutsen, 1917. The night and the snow fell together, hard and brutal, without mercy or mind. Each of the Moore boys was forced to carry a lantern for safety's sake, and the string of light moved slowly once the storm had abated, and dawn crept in over the blanketed land. Hunting hounds, three of them, snuffed but did not bay. Parker pressed his old roan on through drifts, following his long-tethered dogs as thick air stabbed the lungs. The horse staggered, and he pulled up just as the sky grayed to light.

"Father!" said Park. "We've got to stop. It's no use." He kicked his own mount up beside his father, and lifted the lantern. "We're all beat and Lizzie's half-froze to death. We should go back."

"No."

"We've been at it for hours. Don't you think we would have found –"

"Don't. We're going up to the old Novitsky place. Now – or I'll beat the life out of you." He twisted around in his saddle. "All of you – on up to Novitsky's."

Johannes – Jo – the oldest after Parker, had Lizzie belted to him, in the saddle. He gathered the reins in one hand and hunched forward, trying to shield her from the wind as he nudged the horse after his father. The younger boys, Sven and Ralph, followed and the family made a ragged line of light. What might have been a short ride dragged on into a dreary morning as they fought through the snow, searching. None of them spoke as they came to the abandoned Novitsky land that Ojibwe family had given up farming for fishing a generation back. As they rode on, the dogs began to howl a trail. Parker tugged them to a halt and dismounted to check the ground – sure enough, fresh prints, half filled in but still visible. Remounting, he let the anxious dogs have their heads again, and baying out clouds of breath, they led the family to what had once been a barn, standing now doors open to the weather, the roof worn to ribs. The five lanterns converged bright as the Moores rode in and the dogs bayed at their success. Parker threw himself off the roan and ran into the shadows at the dogs, and at the man and the boy, huddled together in a half-sheltering corner of the dead barn.

Jo struggled to unhook the belt that held Liz to him, as the other boys moved in to help. One of the dogs began suddenly to howl. A horse blew and stamped.

"Is it Gus?" said Jo, letting Lizzie down and dismounting himself, the last of them.

Parker stepped out of the shadows into the lighted circle of his living sons, with the dead baby boy, stiff and blue about the lips, in his arms. Liz walked up and just took the body from him and he let her do this, let her take the baby and cradle him close, as if her warm child's breast might give Gus comfort, somehow. But then she lifted her head and howled, inhuman, pure grief, so pure the dogs took it up until Liz had exhausted her throat with pain.

Dearest Lizzie:

By now, you will have heard that I am dead. I can't recall a time when I didn't ask of you, didn't consult, didn't wonder what you would think about – whatever. For once, then, I've made up my own mind. After that fiasco at Kempton & Shelf, I didn't see the point of living. The only thing I'd been slogging on for died that night. I know how Mother must have felt, after losing Tucker. You knew, didn't you, that you held my mother's heart? She loved you – up until the total erasure of her disease, she loved you so fiercely! I doubt she could have gotten through losing Tuck without you – she always said, you were the only one who felt as she felt, the only one besides my father who knew what it meant, to lose a child so awfully in a sudden way.

But you must know this. Ted sure did, and he hated it. I knew, and didn't mind and that was something he couldn't forget, or forgive. I write this knowing you know, but having to write it out, all the same, like we used to do with secret-secrets.

Please bury this in Lutsen next spring, near some favorite tree.

Love always,

Charlie.

12. LUTSEN

Years after the night of his death-bed confession, Liz could not help but picture him as a young man, big and bearish on the thick-legged, round-bellied roan cantering down the dirt road to his farmhouse, the mud and snow frozen stiff from another night's dip below zero, one arm awkward and full of a shrieking bundle even more bundled than he against the weather. In her picture, the sky was blue and flat and cloudless and he kept his face as clear and as flat as that sky when he walked up the stairs into his wife's kitchen. He sent his oldest boy out to stable the roan, then turned to her, his wife, Sara Svetson Moore, there beside the kitchen hearth, seated on her sturdy pine hearthside chair. She met his gaze as he stood beside her, the warmth of the kitchen melting the needles of ice prickling his overcoat and boots. He had not stopped as he always did to take off boots or coat, because of the child.

Sara's mild eyes took him in, all of him down and through to the squalling mistake he carried in his arms. She put aside her knitting, and stood up.

"Give it to me, Father," she said, reaching her arms as she did into his, and under the squirming bundle. "You never could hold a child safe."

"She's to be named Elizabeth, mind. I promised."

"Promised?" and on her tongue, the word hissed while that baby girl shrieked, each inhale a wheeze, each exhale a wail.

You were named after her half-sister. You were hungry and cold and had just lost your mother, a fact that sent me, on my sturdiest horse, up the road and past the Cut, to the homestead on which I'd found her, my Paulette, a breed so bewitching and young and poor, stuck there with her grandfather and his no-good, drunken bastard of a son. Those two she lived with, one drunk, the other old and shamed, they gave you to me when she died, because I was

your father and because I was Parker Moore, a man of means in these parts,
a man who lived by the work of his own two hands. We may not have has
much, but what we had, I made.

"Lizzie," said Sara. "I will call her Lizzie," and in the warmth of her
new mother's arms, or simply from exhaustion, the baby hushed,
peering out of her bundle with olive-green eyes, eyes a color no
other Moore child had.

Shakily, Liz brushed out her thin, no-color hair and listened to the
roar and boom of a lashing Lake Superior. A storm had swept down
from Canada blasting an already frigid Lutsen with more snow. She'd
gotten up early as always, but once she dressed and went into her dark,
silent kitchen, found herself without appetite, without even a trace of
desire not even for coffee, so she took the little elevator to her studio.
The Lake sounded even fiercer up in the loft, booming hard against
the rocky shores, and the sky darkening as if toward night again.

She sat down before the neat, almost finished self-portrait, done
in the style of her *Series B*, but not of that series. On the canvas, the
figure of a slim, dark young woman, almost but not quite a girl, in
the blue-dark shadow of winter dawn trees, the glance of her eyes
inward, lidded, a swift, furry sylvan thing caught in transition, as if
she had once been wild, only becoming human as the light turned
over the land. Or maybe it worked the other way around and soon
the girl would scurry, leaving paw-prints in the snow. Liz painted
her name on the back of the canvas, then wiped clean the brush and
took her private elevator downstairs again. If anything she was even
less hungry than when she first got up. She checked her watch; Sara
would be over that afternoon, to fix lunch. Carefully and slowly
she built a fire in the massive stone hearth of her living room, just
as her father had taught her, and once it no longer needed human
prodding, she took a throw from off the back of her couch, curled
up with a novel and turned a few pages until she felt a tug and so
rested her head on the arm of the couch, where Sara soon found her,
the fire still bright, lending her dark cheeks a deceptively live heat.

NY TIMES December 20, 2003 – Elizabeth Sara Moore,
abstract painter, one of the last true modernists, died at

11:50 a.m. today at Treetops, her estate in Lutsen, Minnesota according to Beth Moore, a niece and spokeswoman for the family. The cause of death was heart failure. Liz Moore was 95. Daring, outrageous and undiscovered until she was in her declining years, Ms. Moore was nothing short of a one-woman artistic phenomenon; over the course of eight or more decades her experimental style and bold vision altered time and space, marshaled nature into culture, and presented the visual arts with a new pair of eyes. Few artists have experimented so broadly; none living today equal her power to see what others do not. In a surprise turn of events, Beth Moore revealed that her aunt was part Ojibwe, of the Grand Portage Band. Born in Lutsen Minnesota in....

✦

Treetops. It had been an obvious name for a house that, as C.C. had said, in the lovely spring of 2000, "...Lizzie's mother had built, sometime in the forties." She pulled their rental onto 61, heading for Lutsen, Minnesota. "Sara Moore hired an architect, someone she knew, and he's the one who built and designed the place to her liking." C.C. had slipped easily into the role of local informant, relaying to Quiola what she remembered Lizzie as having said, back in 1967, as the two older women had made their way up to Lutsen, for Parker Moore's funeral.

"Her mother had left her father, didn't she?"

"In practice. Not legally. They never divorced. Sara lived at Treetops until she passed away, and Parker Moore stayed on the farm, where he died. His funeral was grim – Lutheran and tense. Of course everything was wilder, back then," she said. "Took longer to get up to Lutsen. Even now, I wouldn't want to try it in winter. Don't know how Liz manages, to tell the truth. But she has family to help."

"I find it hard to believe I'm here at all," said Quiola. "Doesn't seem real. I wonder if Mother would be angry at me."

C.C. smiled, concentrating on the slick road. It wasn't raining, but the Lake mist that morning made everything damp. "I can't believe your mother never, not once, brought you here. It's so beautiful."

186

"And terrible if you are poor, lonely, bright and a girl – and pregnant. So Mom used to say. I don't doubt it. I bet high school kids up here have a that wild-horse roll to their eyes, 'get me the hell outta here.'"

C.C. laughed. "Some of them do. It's weird to see punk-mohawks and piercing in Grand Marais. I thought that all ended with the '90s."

"Nothing goes out of style anymore. I never thought I'd see bell-bottoms again. Should've saved mine, they'd be honest-to-God antiques."

Suddenly she took a sharp breath. Even though she'd seen the Lake in Duluth, even though they'd been driving alongside Superior for some time, the full expanse of it hadn't made itself felt, not physically felt, until that moment, just before Gooseberry Falls. The morning fog had thinned to mist, and the ever-changing Lake weather decided to offer up that overwhelming horizon, under a blue-pink sky.

"I told you it was beautiful," said C.C.

"Words." Quiola stared out at the bold scale of the rugged coast, unleashed from cityscape, alive in its own skin.

"They'll tell you up here as you approach the Boundary Waters that if you don't like the weather, just wait three hours. Or drive a mile. The Lake is so deep and so cold, it's like a huge refrigerator, and makes its own weather patterns. You're looking at one tenth of all the world's fresh water, by the way – Quiola?"

"Huh?"

"Never mind."

And so they drove the rest of the way in silence, while Quiola watched the Lake be her fickle self, changing color every few miles from dark to light, blue to slate gray chop, now sharply defined, now shrouded in fog, rough to calm, moldy and odiferous then fresh with pine. She jumped a little when C.C. pulled off the main road, surprised at how fast ninety minutes had passed. "We're here already?"

"You weren't driving." The car humped along Rollins Creek road. "I hope Liz remembered to get in some food. I don't know why, but she likes to empty the fridge. While we're there, listen to the way she talks about it. She's proud at how little she keeps. I don't know if it has to do with going through the Depression, or living alone all these years, but there you are, a guest, hungry, and she'll go on about how efficient she's been with the leftovers. Except you never do see even the ghost of a leftover. Not a crust." She shook her head. "Honestly, Liz hasn't a clue about hospitality. Never did."

"I'm not very good at always keeping my eye on supplies, either."

"Ha!" said C.C. "You love to cook. You always have food on hand, in case someone drops in – you are gracious. Liz, on the other hand, enjoys keeping empty space cold. Here's the driveway –"

✦

May 20, 2004. The flight from La Guardia to Minneapolis, then from Minneapolis to Duluth went by, swift and unremarkable. Quiola was grateful. Traveling light, one knapsack, one wheeled bag, and three of everything else, she had agreed to stay a week with Sara Moore at Treetops. But that seemed a lot of time, as she watched clouds, to be away from Amelia, and home. And what would it be like to be back in Lutsen, once again, but now without either C.C. or Lizzie?

For some reason, the Alamo rental car man in the Duluth airport was nearly beside himself with joy. He whistled, he hummed, he assured her the car would be just what she wanted as he waved to his fellow car-rental competitors. She began to think he was daft, so she smiled cautiously and said, "Are you always so eager to rent a car?"

"You don't understand, Miss. The sun is out!"

She glanced over her shoulder. The plate-glass windows were alight, the sky that particularly unbearable blue of spring. "Yes. Lovely."

"No. Miraculous. It's been raining for a week. More than." He wagged his finger at her. "Enjoy the sun. Supposed to start with the rain again tomorrow. Murderous weather."

"Aren't winters worse?"

"You're from Connecticut, right? You wouldn't understand – snow, that's bearable. No sunshine for going on two weeks? Murderous."

She nodded, wanting to say "I was born here. Right here, on Lake Superior." But what did it matter? She was from the East, now.

Quiola took the keys to the rented Chevy, and made her way from the airport across town to the same scenic North Shore drive that had taken her breath away five years before, and on out past old, stately lake-side Duluth mansions. Some of those graceful places were being torn down, replaced by even more enormous new homes crowded onto a patch of lakeside land, ungainly, ungenerous, for they gave no clear view of the water to a passerby.

And all the while the power and gray enormity of the Inland Sea, Lake Mother Superior, there, glinting and ruffling her blue-gray self, mumuring back to the sad gulls' cry. At a certain point on 61, when she looked ahead, the road seemed to dive into the lake – behind, the same, an optical illusion but also a dizzying sense of being nowhere and everywhere at once.

The road was mercifully peaceful at that early hour, empty of the semi-trucks that would hound a slow driver on this two-lane road. Out beyond Duluth, the lake was sheeted with fog, which here and there lifted above steel-blue impatient waters. At Gooseberry Falls, she stopped. She wasn't expected up at Treetops until the early afternoon, so she parked in the empty lot of the park, locked herself in, crawled into the back seat, and slept for about an hour. When she woke, the sun had burnt off the remaining fog, and the parking lot had filled halfway. She got up, stretched and then drove on, past several small towns, then past the road which would take her to Lizzie's house, and on past the tiny, five-store Lutsen, down past Cut-Face Creek, and into the town of Grand Marais. The sun stayed with her, but the air was still frosty when the wind blew off the Lake. She went straight for the Trading Post, bought a green-wool jacket and then headed for a restaurant she knew, a lakeside eatery called the *Angry Trout*.

She was early for the lunch crowd, and so the only customer. The wait-staff were still rolling napkins and joking. Quietly, she possessed herself of a bayside window to watch a schooner maneuver its way from harbor to bay.

"Would you like something warm, coffee maybe?" asked a waitress. "Would you like me to close the window?"

"Oh, no, it's fine. I enjoy the fresh air. And coffee would be wonderful."

The girl smiled. "Our coffee *is* wonderful. You'll see."

But Quiola remembered how perfect the coffee had been, no doubt still was. Sitting there in the window, she could hardly credit so much time had passed since she'd been in that dining room, where time and space seemed about to collapse on her, where the sun and the sky promised, cruelly, to be eternally the same, and where, if she just looked up at the right minute, a glowing, happy C.C., her curly blond-white hair tucked under a sky-blue baseball cap, all coiled energy and delight, would be coming back from the rest-room, alive and whole again.

"Shit," she muttered to herself. The North Shore's chilly embrace had softened the tough old dog chew she thought she'd become.

As she scanned the menu, an old man sat at the next table. She didn't notice him at first, and was nearly finished eating her sandwich, when the man, sunburnt an alarming mahogany, his thick hair white and grey, said, "Excuse me, don't I know you?"

Quiola smiled. "I don't believe so. I'm a visitor."

But he kept on searching her face.

Discomforted, she said, "Well, my mother grew up here –"

His gaze cleared. "That's it. You look like Marge. Marge Otter."

"Oh, yes. She was my grandmother. Did you know her?"

The man was shaking his head, his eyes now averted, but seeing, still, a face he knew. "I asked her to marry me, once. She refused."

"I'm sorry."

"I'm not! Such a stubborn one! She'll go around with me, to pow-wow, in spring, and on Memorial day for those of us who died in World War I or the War we both remember best, and she might wear a Jingle Dress to make me jealous, or tease me with maple and wild rice and even let me take her to Church, but she always said she'd married, as the Good Lord commanded and that was that. Oh, I don't blame her. I'm a fisherman. Hard business. Mind if I sit?"

"Please." Quiola was fascinated. Never at any point in her life, did she think she'd meet someone who'd known her grandmother. "Mr. –?"

"Novitsky. But you should call me David."

"My name's Quiola."

"I know, I held you, once. You weren't more than this." He placed his hands a tiny baby size apart. "Rosie left us for the city. But a city's no place for an Otter."

Quiola felt a tempo of quick anger. "She was a good mother."

His dark eyes sparked. "Unlike her own? Hmm?"

"My grandmother, I gather, was a difficult woman."

"Difficult!" He pursed his lips. "Have you come to visit her?"

"Have I come...whatever do you mean?"

He slapped his knee meditatively with a one-hand beat. "She lives up yonder."

Quiola stared at the old man, as if he'd just dropped down from another solar system. Her mind, and time, stopped and for one, upside down moment, she went hysterically blind – nothing focused. Then the old man was there, and her check, still to be paid. Trying on calm like a new garment, she opened her mouth to speak and found only the sound of silence. She tried again. "I'm sorry, Mr. Novitsky, but there must be some mistake. My grandmother died more than forty years ago." Hadn't her mother always said, *Sweetheart, you are better off. Believe me. Mother was iron. No give to her, no bend. A switchblade and a heart got cut to shreds if it came near.*

"So, then, you'll visit? I can show you the way. My, but Marge'll be surprised, don't you know."

The name, *her* name – but it had to be a mistake! And so, to make him go away, she said she had to go just then, and she gave him her cell number (she could always have it changed), and told him sure, she would meet his old friend, if he so wished, while she was staying in the area. But as soon as she got back in the rental car, she regretted it. The old man was crazy.

But what if – Quiola pulled out of the parking lot, thinking *no, it couldn't possibly be true. He's a crazy old coot.*

Rollins Road, when she found it, was still no better than it had been five years before: a dirt path, pockmarked by winter erosion. She eased off 61 and down into the muddy ruts and rumbled along slowly, mildly cursing Alamo for giving her a car with no pick-up or shocks. She found the driveway easily, memory kicking in like a movie – she knew these woods, this earth, even having only visited once.

And at the end of the dirt drive: Treetops. It, too, hadn't changed. The dark red-paint, the solid, heavy beams, an architecture of cunning and comfort, Treetops nestled on its eyrie above the lake as if it had been there since forever. Stopping, she pulled the parking brake and sat for a moment, breathing in the bracing cold. She could hear the Lake, and just barely make out its foggy horizon, a melting of one element into another. A gull mourned. She got out of the car. As she did, she could hear the creak and resonant slam of a screen door, and then from the deep shadow of the gabled entrance stepped a woman, dressed in dark green sweats and a gray pullover. She had long, straight brown hair and waited politely for her guest.

"Welcome to my home," said the young woman. "I'm Sara. It's Quiola? Have I pronounced it right?"

"Yes, thank you."

"Come on in. Mom and I have been waiting for you."

"Not too long, I hope."

"Not at all." Together they walked up the wooden porch planks to the solid front door, and back, as far as Quiola was concerned, into one of the most perfect human spaces she'd ever had the fortune to know. First, the heady perfume of the place, dominated by woodsmoke, with undertones of onion, bacon and coffee, a hint of evergreen, which wasn't surprising given that the cabin was built of knotty white pine. When she stepped into the house, she stepped into the past; she knew these odors, of food and fresh air, of wool blankets and a hint of cedar from closets and chests – Treetops.

Beth Moore stood near the fireplace, still straight as a fishing rod, with the bend and grace of one as well. She put out her hand.

"I'm so glad you could come. Aunt Elizabeth spoke of you, and of the Davis family, quite often."

"All good, I hope," said Quiola, falling back on one of her mother's phrases.

"Oh, hardly that. My aunt wasn't made of sugar and light, now, was she? No. She spent her last hours here, thank god. Not someone you want to try to force into hospital, or a nursing home. It would be to your everlasting regret."

"Mom –"

"What? We both know she was a witch."

Quiola started, but Beth merely warmed her back at the fire as Lake Superior's muted thunder filled the silence for a moment or two, until Sara shrugged and said to her guest, "Let's get you settled. We can rake Gran over the coals later."

Treetops had a guestroom perched in the eaves over the kitchen; it could only be reached by going back outdoors, and up a heavy-beamed, switchback staircase where once a handyman had lived, to help maintain the place.

"It's a bit inconvenient," said Sara as she helped Quiola lug her things up the staircase and inside. The room was, like the rest of the house, redolent of wood-smoke and paneled with pine. "But the other guestroom, inside, is all torn up. We had a leak, and the room is a mess. I'm sorry about this – you'll have to come inside to use the bathroom. Or if you don't mind," she added, sliding open a closet door, "there's a chamber-pot."

Quiola stared in mild disbelief at the heavy ceramic pot with its discreet cover.

"Will you mind?"

She did, but she said, "No."

"Well, then, I'll leave and let you get unpacked. Mother's a bit old-fashioned and we will serve a tea in about an hour. Please join us." And with a shy smile she left.

Alone, a buzzing thing started to zip around inside Quiola. She hung her spares in the closet, laid out her flannel on the single bed, and so on, coming last to her watercolors and traveling sketch-book and all the while the buzzing thing kept at her until she realized it was exultation, a confused high, like fizz off the top of a champagne bottle: she was being uncorked. She sat down on the bed with a thump, landing like a hot air balloon with a whoosh, and surveyed her nest – the place was cozy, the wall to wall indoor outdoor, oatmeal in color and both soft and durable, made her want to take her shoes off. And the child-like writing desk beside one of the two windows seemed to beckon, sit here, post a letter, sketch a little, stay with me.

Beth Moore's afternoon tea was not an elaborate affair – Earl Grey with a plate of flat, ginger cookies. Dinner was equally sensible: broiled walleye, which Sara had caught. Conversation was direct and simple: Quiola's trip, the weather, and the house, and some politics – feeling out new territory. But once the two younger women finished clearing the table, and Beth had laid another fire, Quiola sat down in a chair and asked,

"Do you have any idea why Liz wanted me to visit Treetops? I mean, I would've liked to attend the funeral –"

"I know," said Beth. "But that's not what she wanted. Hated funerals. I did my best *not* to have one. Do you mind if I smoke?"

"Not at all," but she didn't expect a pipe.

After sucking at its thin, graceful stem, getting the shag to catch, Beth said, "My aunt was very particular. I didn't argue with her. She left instructions. Detailed, exacting and a bit mystifying. But she'd lived a long time and kept her secrets, secret."

"Not all of them," said Sara.

"Really?" her mother countered, smiling. "Such as?"

"She liked to tell me stories about her childhood. You know she did. So I don't think she kept every secret she ever knew."

"All right, then. But she didn't always confide in me."

"No because you thought her a bit odd."

"Well? Wasn't she?"

Sara turned to Quiola. "Gran wanted you and I to get to know each other. I'm not sure why, but she said we should meet, after she'd passed."

Beth rolled her eyes. "Games."

"Just Gran's way. She told me to invite you up here, and that I should tell you –" She stopped herself.

"Go on," said Beth. "Tell her what?"

"Mom, please. I just remembered I'm supposed to tell the story out by the Cauldron, near the farm where they found him. Where they found Gus."

Beth Moore took another pull on her pipe. "You're supposed to tell her about Gus? I see. As I said, she was always an oddball. My father loved his kid sister, but she did get wearisome. Quiola, you seem to be in for a hiking expedition."

"I'm just supposed to tell the story out in the open, on the river."

"How much fun! A hike up the Temperance for an old, sad story!" Beth set her pipe down on the mantle. "Aunt Liz also wanted me to give you this –" she took a small white carving off the mantle, along with a notebook. "Honest to Pete, why you had to truck all the way up here for these things I don't know when UPS would've been more efficient."

The carving was about two inches tall, an inquisitive otter upright on his tail, as if about to give an address. Quiola smiled. "It's lovely." "It's made of ivory walrus tusk," said Sara, "by a native artist, from Alaska. Gran found it in a local gallery. If you look inside the notebook you'll find some information about the artist and his work." Quiola opened the large yellowing notebook, or rather a sketchbook of Liz's, one from the early 1960s, to find the card about the otter. "But this is too generous," she said. "One of Liz's notebooks must be worth a pretty penny."

"It's what she wanted. I have to say, Sara always understood Aunt Liz better than anyone, and I must confess I'm not one for art. I simply don't understand it. Well, except as a picture to warm up a wall – I like that one, over there, for example, her last. But most of Liz's work doesn't warm up anything."

"No, that's not how I'd describe it. Most of it." Quiola walked over to the small canvas of a girl turning wild or a wild thing, turning girl.

"Oh, Mom. You just don't give it a chance."

"Waste of my time. I just don't get it. That one at least tells a story I know, or at least it seems to."

"*Series B*," said Quiola, "told stories."

"*Series B*?" said Beth. "Something she did, I gather – like I said, I wouldn't know. But it's getting late, and I should be off. I'll see you both tomorrow, for breakfast?"

"Sure, Mom, that's fine. Quiola, would you like to go upstairs now? Pardon me for being so forward, but you look tired. I know traveling always takes me down a peg."

Quiola smiled gratefully. "I am tired. Very."

But she woke in the dead middle of the night, out of a dream where she seemed to be searching for a lost animal, not Amelia but something dearly beloved and despairingly lost; and woke into a thunderstorm that shook the eaves of her nest. Lightning illumined the blinds in the window as if someone had turned on an arc. Percussion rumbled up the mountains and back down. She watched the play of light and sound, dozing, now dreaming of a bear which looked more like a wolf or a dogbear, and it followed her quiet and dangerous; when next she woke, the thin light of morning paled her room. At five, she sat up, got out of bed. She could still hear a terrific wind as she pulled on a robe and ruffled her hair into something better than it was. She had to pee, and she didn't want to use the chamber-pot, so, quiet as she could manage, she cracked open the door to her room, to go downstairs. Not even a breath of a breeze blew. Yet the sound, terrific, boomed on.

It was the Lake.

The Lake was throwing herself about like a despairing lover in a tawdry romance, anguished, wave after pounding wave; Quiola could feel the power of water shake the earth as she padded across the wooden plank porch, and quietly opened the kitchen door, thinking that way in less intrusive than the front door. Inside the pantry and laundry room, darkness and silence, the concrete floor cold, and the air earthy, mingled with fabric softener and fruit. She moved quickly past cabinets, stove, and hearth to the bathroom and back, hoping she had not disturbed her host.

Once again in her bed, she let herself think for a moment that her grandmother might still be alive, and that David Novitsky had not been a crank. It seemed as fantastically improbable as Sacagawea's reunion with her brother in the company of Lewis and Clark, a story she carried around with her, like the creased old post-card she kept in her wallet of *Indian Symbols And Their Meanings*. The Snake Woman, or Boat Pusher, or whatever name she knew herself by, burdened with a mixed blood boy, ignored until useful, had fortitude. The idea she might also have had kinship ties never seemed to have occurred to either Lewis or Clark until she stood before her brother, a man now and responsible for his people – or so it seemed to Quiola, who'd once read the journals as if she were a detective, looking for clues to this long dead Indian woman.

Soon, she could hear someone moving about in the kitchen below, and the sound allowed her to rise, stretch, pull on the robe again and go back downstairs. The aroma of coffee embraced her as soon as she opened the kitchen door.

"Good morning," said Sara. "Did you sleep through the storm?"

"I slept fine. Coffee smells great."

"Mom will be over soon. What would you like for breakfast?" But Quiola wouldn't let herself be treated, and so the two women made the meal together, silent until the eggs set. Then, Quiola said, "Do you know David Novitsky?"

"I know the family. His youngest sister went to high school with Mom. Why?"

"I met him yesterday. I got here early so I drove into Grand Marais for lunch. He introduced himself because I reminded him of – someone."

Beth knocked, then she stepped into the pantry. "Good morning."

"Mom. Quiola met Mr. Novitsky yesterday."

"Really? From what I hear in town, he keeps to himself, mostly. Where did you meet him?"

"He came over to my table and said – you see, I – I was actually born here, in Grant Portage, but my mother left and never came back. Anyhow, David Novitsky said I reminded him of my grandmother. Marjorie Otter. Do you know if –"

"Wow," said Sara. "Mom –"

"Yes, I know. I see. I told you she was a witch!"

"Beth? Sara?" said Quiola. "What do you know? What have I said?"

"Family," said Sara. "We're family – second cousins or something. No wonder Gran – no wonder – I can't believe she never said anything to me – or to you."

"But I don't understand –"

"Maybe," said Beth, "Aunt Liz thought it best to protect your mother's wishes, Quiola. And Marjorie's as well. Rose Otter left, as you said, and never returned. If you ask, Marjorie will say that she has no children."

"Ask? She's really alive, then?"

"Why of course – I mean – oh dear –"

Quiola had started deep breathing: in, out. "I'll be okay," she said. "It's just – I just can't – Mom told me Marjorie Otter was dead. I had no reason to doubt –"

"Sit," said Beth, pulling back a kitchen chair. "Now, please. You look like you're about to faint."

Quiola sat. "All these years, all my life, I thought she was dead!"

"Mom –"

Beth crouched next to Quiola, to be able to look her eye to eye. "Quiola, listen to me. Your mother made a choice, didn't she? Not you. You were a baby. If Rose Otter closed that door, and left her own mother in the past, I guess she had her reasons. It may be best to leave the matter alone. Do you hear me?"

Quiola started. "I'm sorry. What did you just say?"

"That maybe it might be best to leave this thing alone. Leave it in the past."

✦

"Here's the cauldron," shouted Sarah, gazing down into the rush and roar of a place on the Temperance River people called the Devil's Kettle. Quiola gazed too, dizzied by the water's furious revolving ride until Sara turned away and walked a little distance, and sat on a boulder. Quiola followed, leaning against a slender white birch, her arms folded across her chest. "So, Sara, what happened to Liz's brother?"

"Gran found the cradle empty, as she'd feared. A Novitsky, a white Novitksy, had stolen the baby, and he did it, we think, for revenge. He'd lost his half-sister, then that sister's baby girl, to Parker Moore, and he was a drunk, anyway, a no good, my father used to say. They tracked the man and found him, but both he and the baby were dead."

"Oh, God, that's awful. You know, I lost a child I loved, once. Not my child, but I loved him, all the same. And C.C. lost her own baby brother, in a fire, a long time ago. All of us – I wonder just how much Liz knew?"

"She knew this much: she was Marjorie Otter's kin. My grandmother, Paulette, she was the younger sister and they were the daughters of Elizabeth Novitsky, who was part-white, and Ralph Otter, a full blood, as they used to say. Grandpa Sven was about sixteen years older than Gramma when they married, but that wasn't unusual, not in the forties. Still isn't, really. Of course Parker Moore never forgave his son, Sven – Grandpa – for marrying, I mean actually and legally marrying, what my great-great grandfather would have called a half-breed, even if Parker Moore was willing to share his bed with one. Or rape her. No one really knows what went on between

Parker and that other Novitsky girl, Elizabeth's sister, except that Gran was the result, so I guess it's a lost history, now."

Quiola closed her eyes. "I can't quite believe this."

"Me neither."

"So – tell me, what is she like? Marjorie Otter?"

"She's ancient, of course!" said Sara lightly. "And you want to know the truth? The more time we spend together, the more she reminds me of you. Or you remind me of her. Whichever. She's intense. Quiet. But she has something in her I envy – a certain joy, a way of being with others and the world oh, I can't explain it, but I can feel it, whenever I'm with her. Do you think – would you like to meet her?"

Quiola shrugged, and silence pooled between the two women inside the roaring of the cauldron, until Sara said, "Otters are full of it, that same joy, you know, they're impish, inquisitive. Silly, even. Perhaps Marjorie has been taken over by her name. Does that make sense? Or does it sound – I don't know, like magical thinking?"

"Magic?" Quiola laughed. "My mother would have said power, not magic. And it makes sense, too." She brushed her palm across that spot just above the heart, where her flesh bore the sleek, undulating silhouette of a river otter at play.